Terrifying Tales & Sinister Sightings

SPIRITS OF HASTINGS

*Collection of Ghost Stories
from Hastings, East Sussex, United Kingdom*

COGHURST PRESS

Copyright © 2022 The Untruth Seekers All rights reserved

The characters and events portrayed in this book are fictitious. Any similarity to real persons, living or dead, is coincidental and not intended by the author.

No part of this book may be reproduced, or stored in a retrieval system, or transmitted in any form or by any means, electronic, mechanical, photocopying, recording, or otherwise, without express written permission of the publisher.

ISBN-13: 9798423768393

Cover design by: Molly Morrison
Printed in the United Kingdom

ALSO FROM
THE UNTRUTH SEEKERS

Fearsome beasts, terrifying giants, and plucky fairies are just a few of the creatures populating the folklore of Sussex, the historic county on England's southeast coast.

Starting with the modern celebration of the Jack-in-the-Green festival, this collection of stories traces the roots of nearly 2,000 years of Sussex's tall tales, mythology, and folklore.

If you have stumbled upon this weathered seaside town, we invite you to join us on a self-guided walking tour of Hastings' and Saint Leonard's most ghastly sites.

The haunted trail map will take you through an incomprehensible maze of narrow twittens, eclectic collection of weathered and wayward architecture, and rust-streaked ships lining the pebble beach.

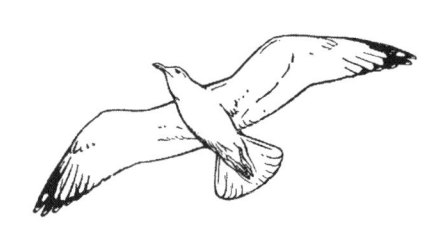

Some say a soul is tangled somewhere

in the flesh and sinews of the body ...

Introduction

Greetings, good reader. It must delight you to know that you are holding in your hands a curated collection of very accurate and excellently researched tales from the fishing town of Hastings, East Sussex.

Most of us know this town for its incomprehensible maze of narrow twittens, eclectic collection of weathered and wayward architecture, and rust-streaked ships lining the pebble beach. You may have also encountered the ruthless aggressors of the region, which terrorise the young and old alike, snatching ice creams from hands and chips from mouths. These sky demons require no introduction.

You may have guessed that sinister tales lie beneath the cracked asphalt, squawking seagulls, and tired, blinking lights of the seafront arcades. Hints lurk in this wind-swept town, just a curl of mist, a yawning shadow, an errant word carried on a breeze, a strange smell. It passes quickly—only registered as a flicker of movement or the rise of hair on the back of your neck. You might shake it off, asking yourself, 'What business do I have with spirits?'

But the truth is, you were right. The spirits of Hastings are not, in fact, *your* business.

They are officially and unequivocally *our* business. You see, we are the Untruth Seekers, who are tasked with the solemn duty to collect all the facts, alternative facts, and alternatives to the alternative facts across the rainy Great British Isles. I'm sure you've seen us in threadbare raincoats, briefcase in hand as we scuttle from one curious case to the next. Or perhaps you've seen us hunched over a cup of tea, staring blankly into the ceramic as if contemplating the darkest of thoughts. And all things being equal, we probably are. You may assume that this dark disposition is because our job deals with otherworldly apparitions, howling spirits, and skeletons that claw from moss-covered graves.

But you would be very much mistaken.

No, there is nothing more fearsome in this world than to be ignored. Worse, to be forgotten entirely. And, dear reader, I'm afraid to report precisely what happened to many of Hastings' stories. As these whispers of the past grow fainter, they have been neglected by the modern world. Facts, people say, should be facts. The alive should be alive, and the dead should quite properly remain dead. And indeed, it is a compelling argument, isn't it?

However, from time to time, when the mist rolls in from the sea or you look at a grainy photograph of people who have long ago abandoned this world, you would quite like to believe otherwise. It might be nice, you think, for the line between the real and unreal to bleed like ink on wet paper. Would it be so bad to leave an imprint of yourself on this world like a greasy fingerprint on a windowpane, innocently inconspicuous but visible when the light hits it at just the right angle?

The Untruth Seekers have seen quite a lot of greasy windows. Hastings, it might interest you to know, is as greasy as the splash guard on the warming tray at the *Old Town Fryer*. A great many stories and souls have accumulated in this place, which has hosted human settlements for at least 2,000 years.

So, dear reader, please enjoy this book of tales. May they transport you to a different era, entertain you, and perhaps, send a shiver dancing down your spine. If they seem true, please accept our most sincere apologies. While many of our stories contain a seed of truth, it is never our intention to provide any sort of historical knowledge whatsoever.

About the Untruth Seekers

The Untruth Seekers provide accurate and excellently researched historical accounts of local stories across the British Isles. We plant the seeds of history in our fertile imaginations, allowing them to grow into neatly packaged tales that are simpler, more digestible, and a good deal tastier than the truth.

Our resulting body of work is stories that terrify and entertain all audiences. Well, ages twelve and up. Children under twelve most certainly have better things to do than fill their minds with this tosh.

All our hair-raising tales of spirits and sinister goings-on are linked to particular places. They make an excellent self-guided walking tour for the daring, enthusiastic, and physically fit. By visiting these places, you may be lucky enough to glimpse an apparition slipping through the veil. Or perhaps you will return home with only blisters on your feet and a few Instagram photos (which you can tag us in, @UntruthSeekers).

A NIGHT AT THE STAG INN

Story One

Rain pounded against the windows of the Stag Inn, running down the panes in rivulets. Steve Wilson was collecting glasses from the last group of customers, who had pulled the hoods of their plastic raincoats up before they opened the door and exited the pub. Water and wind crashed in as the group stepped onto All Saints Street, and the door slammed against the wall before someone wrestled it closed. The pub fell silent except for the staticky warbling of the Eagles' recent song from the battery-powered radio.

Thunder rumbled, drowning out the last notes of 'Hotel California' as Steve, now alone, brought the glasses behind the bar and dropped them into a soapy bucket. The lights flickered and went out. Thick, impenetrable darkness descended. Fortunately, Steve had never been the sort to scare easily, and his only reaction to the sudden power cut was a groan of irritation. He had hoped to clean the glasses, restock the bar, and return home to watch a bit of television before bed. Apparently, that was too much to ask for.

'*Up ahead in the distance, I saw a shimmering light; My head grew heavy, and my sight grew dim; I had to stop for the night,*' came Glenn Frey's voice from the dark void that surrounded Steve. Dust stuck to his fingertips as he ran his hands across the shelves to where the manager kept a torch. Since they had run cables down to the cellar below the inn, they had not needed the torch much, but he was glad they had kept it. When Steve flicked it on, the beam was only a pale circle.

Static cracked as Glenn Frey continued. '*So I called up the Captain, "Please bring me my wine"; He said, "We haven't had that spirit here since nineteen sixty-nine …" And still those voices are calling from far away …*' The radio crackled. '*Wake you up in the middle of the night …*' It sounded like he was singing from the end of a long tunnel. '*Just to hear them say …*'

The roar of static swallowed the following line. Steve flashed the beam over to where the radio sat on the shelf above the bar. He rubbed his thumb over the AM/FM dial but only found more static. Stuck at work during a power cut without music to get him through. Just his luck.

Upstairs, something banged. The faint beam of Steve's torch bobbed as he jolted. The inn only had one guest, but when Steve was starting his shift, the manager had told him the guest had gone to Eastbourne. Steve had assumed they had gotten trapped in the storm and decided to wait it out there, but maybe they had slipped in without him noticing.

Steve flicked off the radio, grabbed the spare set of keys, and climbed up the stairs to the guest rooms. Inky shadows lurked in the corners of the dark hallway that stretched out before him. He stepped towards the door of the only occupied room and knocked.

The banging sound returned with enough force to cause the door to rattle on its hinges. Whatever was happening in that room, the guest probably wouldn't be getting their deposit back.

'I'm coming in,' he shouted at the door as he fumbled through the keyring to find the right one. 'Do you hear me?' He shoved the key into the lock, and there was the scrape of metal as the lock mechanism slid open.

Steve shoved the door open and stepped into the room. A burst of cold air slammed into him. He gasped, his mind slowly registering that the window was propped open. A wardrobe stood beside the window, and the door flapped open and closed with each gust of wind.

He raced across the room and tugged the window down. It slid into place, and the room suddenly fell silent.

'Idiots,' Steve muttered as he stepped back. The carpet slurped under his trainers, thoroughly soaked. The wallpaper around the window was waterlogged and already bulging. He pressed on it as if he could smooth it back into place but froze when he heard something thump in the pub below. A knot formed in his stomach. He had locked the door after the last group of customers left, had he not? The knot tightened.

Footsteps sounded on the stairs, moving fast. Steve whipped around to face the bedroom door. Had the guest remembered they had left the window open and come rushing back? The footsteps stopped in front of the door, followed by knocking.

'You're too late,' Steve called. The torch in his hand blinked and went out. Darkness fell. 'You've already lost your deposit, and we might charge you damages besides!'

The pounding accelerated, shaking the door in its frame. The wrought iron knob twisted from side to side. 'Help me!' came a gruff, panicked voice from the other side of the door. '*Mijn God!* Dey're coming!'

Fear crashed over Steve, and he desperately pressed on the torch's button, crusted with disuse. When the light didn't return, he banged the cheap plastic against the heel of his hand. 'Who's chasing you?' he cried.

'Help me!' The words were thick with a foreign accent that Steve didn't recognise.

Suddenly, a beam of light burst from the torch. Emboldened, Steve lunged for the handle. The door swung open with a creak, revealing an empty hallway. Steve's circle of light scanned the hallway, stopping at patches of discolouration on the carpet. He strode down the hall, descending to the pub to find only chairs, tables, and the brick fireplace in the bar below. The pub was empty, but the wet patches continued from the stairs to the bar.

The radio clicked on. '*You can check out any time you like,*' crooned Glenn Frey. '*But you can never leave!*'

Stiff with fear, Steve knelt beside the trail of wet patches, lowering his nose to the floor. He would quit this job and never look back if it were blood. But when he sniffed, only the briny scent of seawater filled his nose.

Breathing a sigh of relief, Steve pushed himself to his feet and followed the trail of wet patches around the bar. The door to the cellar hung open. He approached the threshold, pointing the beam of light at the stairs. The damp patches continued, looking as if footsteps had emerged from the cellar below. But the trail only went one direction, and when Steve arrived at the bottom of the stairs, he only found the pub's stock of kegs, bottles, and crates.

To this day, Steve remains certain that someone was with him in the Stag Inn that rainy night. However, it wasn't until he went to Amsterdam that he heard the accent again. Steve is now certain the voice belonged to a Dutchman. But who or why he was in the cellar of the Stag Inn, Steve could never guess.

LAVENDER HOUSE

Story Two

Passing Saint Clement's Church and continuing up Croft Road, one would find a row of daub and wattle houses built sometime in the Tudor era (1485-1603). During that time, they would have been the homes of wealthy merchants. With Queen Elizabeth I on the throne in 1558, craftsmanship was developing quickly, and demand for luxury items was on the rise.

In Hastings, the Wycliffe family was well-known for their fine jewellery. Business was booming as their craftsmanship became more widely known across East Sussex and even London. The family's two daughters, Marian and Cecily, managed the jewellery shop on what is now the High Street.

The elder sister, Marian, had always been the more fashionable of the two, and she spent long hours admiring the sparkling gemstones. Often, Marian was so enamoured with the jewellery that she neglected the customers.

Fortunately, her younger sister, Cecily, was there to pick up the slack. Cecily didn't care much for things that sparkled, and she tended to her flowers when she wasn't dealing with customers. Her favourite was the lavender she had planted in window boxes and the family's garden behind their house.

Cecily had always loved how lavender whispered of the exotic mountainous areas of the Mediterranean. It had travelled so far, yet it remained strong and firmly rooted in her rain-soaked English garden.

Beyond that, Cecily always sensed there was something extraordinary about the plant. The flowers seemed to droop when sales at the jewellery shop were slow but straightened like soldiers being called to attention when a promising customer approached. She'd even heard rumours that local witches used the plant for serenity, devotion, and warding their houses.

Marian, however, never spared more than a passing glance for the lavender. She couldn't understand why Cecily would pay more attention to the silly purple flowers than the glittering gemstones set into intricate gold and silver settings.

As word of the Wycliffe's success grew, it wasn't long until suitors came calling. Marian became enamoured by a well-spoken young man from Lewes who wore a handsome coat, doublet, and hose. Cecily didn't dare tell her sister, but she didn't much care for him. Worse, the lavender in the window boxes at the shop wilted every time he called on Marian.

When the shop next received a delivery from Lewes, Cecily was waiting. Feigning a casual interest, she asked the coach's driver about Marian's gentleman caller. The driver rubbed his chin thoughtfully before informing her that, in fact, he thought that man already had a wife. Yes, he remembered a wedding at the previous May Day festival between a young man of that description and a rather homely young woman.

Cecily rushed home to report her findings to her sister, who slammed her bedroom door in Cecily's face.

'You're always trying to destroy my happiness!' Marian shouted through the wood.

Cecily seethed with anger at her sister's wilful ignorance, which could very well destroy the family's good fortune, but as usual, she returned to the quiet calmness of her garden. Surrounded by her favourite plant's floral and somewhat evergreen woodiness, she came upon a solution.

When the young man from Lewes next arrived at the shop, he found bunches of lavender hanging from the doorway and windows. He stepped over the threshold, and his face scrunched up. The man sniffed, trying to fight the growing sensation.

Finally, he released a mighty sneeze that some say startled the seagulls away from Hastings for a whole week. If you are familiar with the persistence of Hastings seagulls, you will recognise the magnitude of this achievement.

Sniffling and blowing his nose, he retreated to the street. Cecily hid a chuckle behind her hand as Marian stormed out after him.

Marian took his sleeve, leading him towards the family house on Croft Road. 'It's high time you meet my parents, anyway,' she told him.

However, Cecily had hung more lavender bunches from the doors and windows of the family house. And perhaps it was the presence of lavender, or maybe the young man from Lewes had fallen unwell at the idea of meeting Marian's parents, but he was soon clutching his stomach and racing out of the house. The next day, he returned to Lewes, and the Wycliffe sisters never heard from him again.

A queue of new suitors arrived shortly after. One by one, they left the shop sneezing and coughing until none were left. Finally, Marian had all but given up on finding a suitor when a young man from Kent arrived. Cecily didn't need to do much research to discover he was a rake with a gambling debt that followed him from town to town like a shadow. As usual, she hung bunches of lavender around the shop and house before bed.

The following morning, Cecily awoke to find only limp bits of string hanging from the windows and doors. Crumpled lavender bunches were piled in the garden, and the Kentish man sat at the breakfast table with a grinning Marian and their parents.

Cecily tried again to ward him off with lavender, but Marian always found it and tossed it out. The Kentish man clung to the Wycliffe family like a leech, and it wasn't long before he married Marian. Cecily was still unmarried when their parents died and couldn't inherit the Wycliffe family business. Instead, it passed to Marian and her husband.

The Kentish man quickly gambled away his good fortune. Frustrated by his bad behaviour and worse business sense, Cecily left and moved to a country house. Even Marian was driven to despair when they were forced to sell the shop and the family home. Fortunately, they received a generous anonymous offer, which they quickly accepted.

The day Marian and the Kentish man moved out, they turned to find the new owner approaching. She stopped in front of the house, lowering her hood to reveal none other than Cecily Wycliffe, who had found success by selling her prized lavender.

Cecily lived in the Wycliffe house until she died peacefully in the mid-seventeenth century. All these centuries later, it has been reported that her spirit still lingers in the building, now known as Lavender House. The fresh, woodsy scent of lavender marks her presence. For the pure of heart, it will bring a calm sense of joy, and those with ill intentions … beware.

THE MERMAID'S
KISS

Story Three

In January 1749, a grey sky loomed overhead as the three-masted East Indiaman slid away from the dock in Amsterdam. Captain Johannes, dressed in a red coat with gold brocade, stood at the ship's helm, named *Amsterdam* after the city where it was built. Johannes breathed deeply, inhaling the scent of freshly cut wood and the pungent odour of tar, the unique smell of a ship embarking on its maiden voyage.

On the deck below the bridge, the crew scrambled to secure the rigging of the billowing white sails above. Passengers leaned against the bulwark, waving frantically at the spectators on the rapidly retreating dock. The *Amsterdam* was heavily armed and carried trunks of supplies and silver to the colony, but the representative of the East India Company had barely glanced at the ledger.

Instead, his entire focus seemed to be on an item the size of a small melon that was wrapped in canvas and locked in a safe in the captain's cabin. According to the ship's logs, there were 330 souls aboard, all eager to arrive in Java, the far-flung outpost of the Dutch East India Company. Some were expecting to make their fortunes, others wished to reunite with family, but it was just another delivery job for Johannes and the crew.

A gust of wind swept past him, rustling his beard and nearly knocking the tricorn hat off his head. He clamped it down with one hand while he adjusted the gleaming helm. The *Amsterdam* cut effortlessly through the choppy water as it left the bay and set course to the southwest, heading through the English Channel on a journey that would take them around Africa to Asia. Despite its impressive size, the *Amsterdam* would be little more than a speck on a seemingly endless expanse of water.

Johannes had always loved how the sea stretched into the distance and the way it seemed to blend seamlessly into the sky. However, he did not like the way storms tossed vessels around like toy boats in a bathtub, but it seemed he would not have a choice. Dense, black clouds had gathered in the distance. The wind kicked up, and soon the gloom bore down upon them.

Sheets of rain battered the crew as they furled the sails. Wind barrelled against the vessel, nearly launching Johannes from the bridge. He tied a rope around his waist and turned back to the helm.

Clinging to the handles, Johannes guided the *Amsterdam* over waves that grew to the size of hills. The ship rose on the heaving swells, falling just as quickly. A wave crashed against the starboard side, the spray as tall as the *Amsterdam's* masts.

A crew member screamed, but Johannes gritted his teeth, turning the helm to guide the ship's prow to cut through an oncoming wave. The vessel tipped prow-first into the trough. A foam-crested wave swept across the deck. It would keep afloat as long as the ship cut forward through the waves.

Another crew member shouted. The rumble of thunder and roaring of the wind swallowed the sound. Through the curtain of pounding rain, Johannes saw someone point toward the port side. Johannes's gaze followed the gesture to see the swell of a wave. Hand over hand, he cranked the helm, trying to position the ship to brace against the tide.

He was too slow. A wall of water crashed into him. His hands emptied, his stomach hollowed as the world vanished, and the weight of the cold, ruthless sea dragged him down. He churned through the water with no sense of direction while saltwater burned his nose and pressed into his lungs.

And then, a face appeared through the gloom. Thick, greenish hair framed the flash of iridescent skin, almost like the scales of a fish. Two big round eyes peered back at him, wide with curiosity.

If Johannes had even the slightest bit of air left in his lungs, he would've gasped. As it was, he waited, suspended by water, as the creature darted forward. A necklace of glowing sea coral, decorated with shells and pearls, hung around her neck, holding the darkness back. The creature's neck and shoulders pushed through the greyish water, and finally, the upper body of a woman. But not exactly a woman. Scales covered the mermaid's arms as she reached for him.

Her long, webbed fingers cupped his face. She surged forward, pressing her lips against his. Air pushed into his lungs, relieving the crushing burning.

The mermaid withdrew, her hair floating around her face like tangled seaweed. Still, she looked at him with those unfathomable wide eyes.

Something tugged at his gut. He fumbled to investigate the tightness around his torso, finding the rope he had tied earlier. He was dragged through the water, going from dark grey to greenish grey. Beams of light sliced the dark water, and then he burst through the surface of the sea. Suddenly, everything was clear and bright. Seagulls squawked overhead, flapping white wings against the pale blue sky.

A voice rang across rippling waves. 'Captain!'

'Is he alive?' someone asked.

'Can't be,' came another voice. 'Impossible!'

'It's been hours,' another person added. 'All we've got is a corpse tied to a rope.'

Johannes coughed, the salty dryness of the seawater tearing at his already dry throat. He waved both arms over his head. 'I'm alive!' he shouted.

The crew burst into a flurry of activity, and the rope around his waist tightened again. They dragged him to the ship. Johannes flopped over the bulwark and landed on the deck with a squelch.

Crew and passengers crowded around him, pelting him with questions about how he had survived in the sea for so long. The gale had carried on for hours, they told him, tearing off the ship's rudder. A mist had descended on the vessel, as thick as a curtain. They had been floating aimlessly in the current since, unable to go forward or back. But the Captain's survival must be a miracle.

The explanation of the mermaid pressed at Johannes's lips, but before he could utter a word, one of the crewmembers broke into a fit of coughs.

Another man patted him on the back. 'Should we get a physician?'

The coughing crewmember shook his head and pushed him away. 'No, it only started after the storm. Must've swallowed too much seawater.'

'Or maybe it was the mist,' another sailor added. 'They say that an unnatural fog like that can blur the line between this world and the others. Strange things can happen, who knows what kinds of monsters could appear—'

Johannes cut him off. 'That's enough.' If he tried to explain what he had seen underwater, he would seem just as mad. Sailors were a superstitious lot, and the mist and coughing would be enough to keep them yammering away without mentioning a mermaid. Johannes climbed to his feet, and the concerned faces swam around him. He grabbed onto the bulwark to steady himself. 'Let's see about that rudder. Once we fix that, we'll be on our way.'

But the *Amsterdam* would never be on its way. The gale had ripped off the rudder entirely, and there was nothing to replace it. Perhaps they could have tried to find another solution or maybe sent a dinghy to shore for help, but later that day, the sailor's cough didn't improve.

Worse, he wasn't the only one who had it. A chorus of wracking coughs rose from the crew and passengers of the *Amsterdam*. They spat out globs of sticky phlegm, and by morning, they found the first corpse.

A cabin boy, no older than ten years, was brought to the deck. His eyes were sunken, and his lips were white, but most disturbing was the greenish sheen of his skin. By afternoon, the dead cabin boy was joined by two more corpses: an elderly passenger and a crew member who had a reputation for drinking too much.

'Don't worry, it's only the weakest who are dying off,' Johannes heard a crew member mutter to another.

'Canaries in the coal mine, though, innit?' replied the other between fits of coughs. 'They've signalled our doom.'

When the first sight of land appeared between the bluish greys of the sea and sky, people scrambled for the dinghy. Fights broke out, and shouts filled the air, punctuated by gunshots.

Even Johannes was too terrified by the contagious coughs to wait any longer. Before night fell, he jumped overboard with the others still fit enough to swim to shore.

The survivors of the *Amsterdam* didn't know it at the time, but they were arriving on the English seaside in a place called Bulverhythe. Here, many of them found new lives. The *Amsterdam* reached her final resting place on the sands opposite the 20th-century railway sheds, which can still be seen when the tide is out.

MICHAEL AND THE DRAGON

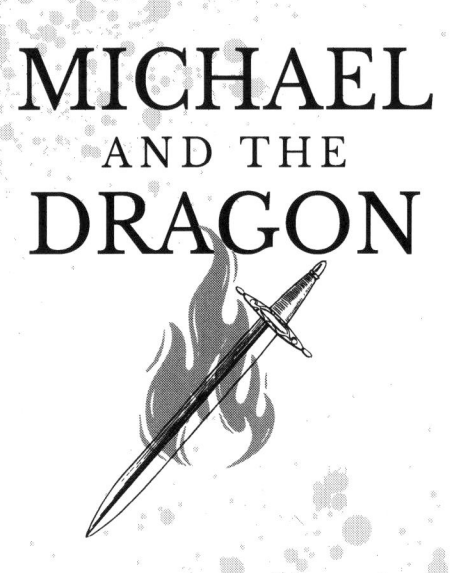

Story Four

In 410 A.D., the Romans retreated from England, taking their intellectualism, laws, and order with them. For the next several hundred years, the darkness of uncertainty and lawlessness swept over the thick woodland of the country. Frequent raids on the coast chased away most hope for peace, calm and the advancement of human knowledge and technology.

Struggling to maintain a settlement in this unstable environment was Haesta, the chieftain whose people, the Haestingas (the ending 'ingas' means 'followers' in Old English), established a cluster of wooden houses with steep thatched roofs on the headland at White Rock. In one of the smoky longhouses, a young lad named Michael was trying to shoo a stubborn ox through the door.

It was a cold, foggy morning and the ox seemed more than content to stay inside where Michael's mother was cooking over the fire in the middle of the one-room house.

Michael stomped outside to pick some grass and brought it in, waving it in front of the ox's nose.

'Don't you want some of this sweet grass?' Michael said. 'Come and get it!'

The lazy ox snorted and shook his head, looking away and flicking his tail.

'Lazy old thing,' Michael muttered and went around to the ox's backside, leaning against the animal. His feet slipped on the packed dirt floor as he pushed, but the only result was a long, bored-sounding moo.

'Hurry up and get that ox out,' his mother called from across the house. 'He needs to eat something.'

It wasn't Michael's problem that the creature was too lazy to eat, but no one argued with his mum and lived to tell the tale. He pushed the ox again, finding the animal's backside to be sturdier than any wall.

A clicking sound came from outside the house. Suddenly, the ox was gone, and nothing was holding up Michael. He landed on his hands and knees. When he looked up, he saw Avery, one of the local girls, smirking at him. She wore a roughly woven dress, and twin blonde plaits framed her face. As he watched, Avery clicked her tongue against the roof of her mouth, and the ox trod towards her outstretched hand.

Michael was impressed, but he could hardly say that to a girl, especially not a smug one like Avery. Everyone in the village praised her ability to handle animals. Everyone always went on about how patient and skilled she was, but they never said anything nice about Michael.

'I *nearly* convinced him to go out,' Michael grumbled.

'Sure.' Avery stroked the ox's thick neck, who seemed perfectly content to follow her to a patch of damp grass. 'Have you heard about Old Eamon's flock?'

Still feeling defensive about the ease of Avery's interaction with the ox, Michael crossed his arms over his chest. 'Eamon has twenty-nine sheep. Everyone knows that.'

'Twenty-two now,' Avery said with a frown. 'You really didn't hear about the attack last night?'

There had been more frequent attacks on the village's flocks lately. People assumed there were wolves in the woods that crept out under cover of darkness, but this was the first time someone had lost so many sheep in a single night.

'Eamon is meeting with the chieftain at the Great Hall now, and there might be some more news.' Avery started in the direction of the Great Hall.

Michael cast one last glance at the ox, now happily munching away, and raced to follow Avery down the path to the cluster of longhouses that comprised the village. The Great Hall stood tall amongst the thatched roofs. Several villagers had gathered outside the door, and as Avery and Michael approached, the door swung open.

A red-faced Eamon stormed out. 'If you won't do anything about it, then I will!' He turned to the cluster of villagers. 'I'll give my biggest, finest horse to whoever captures the wolf that killed my sheep!'

A murmur rippled through the crowd. Even Michael's hope rose at the sound of the reward. His mother would stop nagging him if he returned home with a horse. Beside him, Avery was the only one whose expression didn't light up at the sound of the reward. She frowned at Eamon with her blue eyes narrowed.

Questions rose from the crowd as the chieftain pushed out through the door after Eamon. He tried to quiet the murmurs, but Michael had heard enough. Eamon's homestead was on the edge of the village, perched on the cliffs that overlooked the sea. If the flock had been out to pasture, they would've been on the grassy slope nearby, which was edged by tightly packed trees. Michael had learned to follow tracks and set snares. If he started soon, he would have a good chance of catching the wolf before it struck again.

The only problem was that footsteps were following him. When he glanced over his shoulder, he groaned. 'Why can't you leave me alone?'

'You're planning to catch the wolf, aren't you?' Avery asked.

It seemed silly to respond to such a dumb question. Michael picked up his pace.

Avery walked faster. 'I don't want to hurt the wolf.'

'Then go away,' Michael said.

'Listen, I just want to help you.'

'Really? You want to win Eamon's horse without helping me kill the wolf? No thanks.'

'No, I don't want to help you kill the wolf. I want to save it.'

Michael spun around. 'And do what with it?'

Avery shrugged. For once, she didn't seem smug. 'I don't know. Take it somewhere else, I guess. I can help with the traps. It will go faster if there are two of us.'

Michael wanted nothing more than to ignore her and continue, but once other people started to hunt, his snares would be nothing compared to their spears, axes, swords, and bows. Arguing with Avery would only waste time.

'Fine. But keep out of the way.' Michael led the way to Eamon's homestead. Chickens scampered towards the house, and the bleating of sheep came from a wooden pen behind it. They circled it and headed towards the nearby forest.

Michael and Avery set a few traps made of rope loops that would tighten when the wolf passed over them, hanging the creature by its ankle. It wouldn't be comfortable, but it would keep the wolf alive until Avery figured out what to do with it.

Satisfied, they sat down in a coppice to wait. As night fell, the flicker of torches passed between the trees, followed by the voices of other hunters entering the forest. Frustration needled Michael as stars speckled the night sky but still, there was no sign of the wolf. Avery slumped against Michael, her eyelids closed and breathing steady.

Then, a low, rumbling growl came from somewhere in the underbrush. Michael sat up. Avery rolled off his shoulder, jolting awake.

'I'm not sleeping!' Avery mumbled.

Michael held a finger to her lips, and something rustled from the direction where he'd heard the sound. Avery must have heard it, too, because she rose to her knees, her eyes scanning the darkness.

Leaves rustled as something brushed past them. Michael rolled to a crouch, reaching for the knife on his belt. Something crunched in the leaves, creeping closer—another footstep, followed by a snort. A puff of warm air that smelled like burnished copper swept towards him.

Michael slid the knife from its sheath. Branches snapped, and whatever it was, retreated.

'It's leaving,' Avery hissed.

Michael's mind emptied of any rational thought as he dove after it. He crashed through bushes, branches tugging at his clothes and scraping skin. Perhaps it was the promise of the reward, or maybe he secretly wanted to impress the impossibly smug Avery, but he scrambled after the sound. It grunted as it crashed through the underbrush ahead.

Michael's heartbeat pounded in his ears as trees and bushes, little more than inky black shadows, flicked past. His lungs heaved, sweat pricked his skin, but still, he pursued the creature.

It withdrew to a rocky outcropping, and Michael skidded to a stop. Someone tumbled from the bushes, nearly slamming into him.

'Avery!' he cried.

She shushed him. 'Look, there's a cave.'

'Wha—' He stopped when an orangish glow cut against the darkness, illuminating the jagged edges of a cave. Avery was right. But what kind of wolf invited fire into its cave?

Avery headed towards it.

'Wait, Avery, that's no wolf—'

'Idiot,' she muttered as she picked across the chalk cliffside.

Michael dropped his voice as he scuttled after her. 'But what if—' She waved him away. 'Listen, Avery, it could be dangerous!'

Avery whipped around with a finger pressed to her lips. A deep wheezing sound filled the night air, blowing out and in like a blacksmith's bellows. Light flared with each gust, and the orange glow from the cave silhouetted her as she crept closer.

She stopped at the mouth of her cave. Her hand shot up, pressing against her lips for a long moment.

Behind them, a whistle rang shrilly through the night. A dog barked.

'Michael!' Avery called from inside the cave.

His leather shoes slipped over a boulder as he raced after her, his fingers closing around the hilt of his knife as he yanked it out. He stumbled into the cave with the blade raised, and he slashed at a monstrous creature before realising it was only a shadow cast across the wall. Spinning around, he searched for a target.

Avery knelt on the other side of the cave beside a glistening red lump. At her feet, a long head with yellow cat eyes breathed out a burst of flame that shot across the floor. It flickered out, and there was a gasping sound, followed by another burst of fire.

'It's a dragon!' Michael dove for the creature, ready to attack it like the heroes in the stories. Slaying a dragon was even better than killing a wolf.

Avery shot to her feet and knocked him away. The knife tumbled from his grip, and he dropped to his knees, scrambling after it. Hands tightened on the back of his shirt and jerked him back.

'Don't you dare!' Avery's voice echoed in the cave. 'It's a dragon!'

'Exactly!' Michael tried to twist away, but she held firm. 'It's a dragon, and I think it's sick!'

'All the better for slaying!' Michael reached again for the knife, but it was too far, and Avery was stronger than she looked. 'Don't tell me you want to save dragons as well as wolves.' Anger made his words come hot and fast. He didn't try to temper his annoyance. Surely, Avery wouldn't be this delusional.

She hesitated. 'Well, why not?'

Michael glanced back at the creature. Sharp teeth were visible under its lips, and it was twice his height. Even a madwoman wouldn't want this creature to live. 'What about the sheep?'

'It's a dragon, Michael.' The wonder—admiration, even—was impossible to ignore, but before Michael could talk sense into her, voices came from the mouth of the cave. They were gruff and impatient, the voices of real hunters.

Avery looked at him, her blue eyes wide with fear.

'Just play along,' Michael whispered as he pushed past her. He picked up the knife and turned towards the dragon, raising it above his head. 'Die, you monster!'

Avery screamed, and the dragon's long, snake-like neck snapped up. It let out an ear-splitting screech. Michael dove for the beast, swinging the knife just over its head and driving it into the rock behind it.

The dragon shrieked and wiggled back.

'Play along!' Michael hissed at it, but the dragon writhed, throwing Michael to the stone floor. He landed on his hip, and pain shot up. At least Avery's screams and the dragon's reaction were making the scene believable.

The dragon paused, tilting its head as if finally understanding. Those big yellow eyes blinked once, then twice. And the big red lump toppled sideways, its small front arms clutching at an invisible wound on its chest. The dragon kicked its legs up, tail wagging like a dog's. It let out another screech, this one louder but somehow more dramatic than the previous sounds.

'What in Woden's name?' one of the hunters said.

The dragon flopped onto its back, tongue lolling from its mouth.

'It is slain!' Michael cried, raising his knife victoriously.

The hunters gaped at him.

'We should hurry to tell Eamon that his flock is safe!' Michael announced, but they were frozen in place. No one's eyes moved from the dragon sprawled on the cave floor. 'All the sheep of Haestingas are safe!'

Still, no sign that anyone had heard him. He approached, waving them away from the cave. If they inspected the creature, it wouldn't take long for them to realise the dragon was anything but dead.

'Dragon's bodies catch fire when they die, so we need to go unless you want to suffer a similar fate as this monstrous creature!' Michael pushed one out of the cave. He was fairly sure that it was phoenixes that died in a burst of fire, but hopefully, the hunters wouldn't know the difference.

Across the cave, the dragon breathed, and fire bloomed from its scaled lips.

'You see?!' Michael shouted.

The hunters retreated from the cave, scrambling down the boulders in the darkness.

'Was that really—'

'How is it—'

'How did you—'

'A sneak attack,' Michael explained as they retreated from the cave, which was now alight with dancing orange flames. Smoke poured out into the night air. He hoped Avery wasn't too hot, but he knew she would never forgive him if he gave up on the charade now.

The hunters started back towards the village with nervousness clear on their faces. Questions poured out.

'How did you escape unscathed?' one asked.

'It singed my eyebrows, see?' Michael gestured to his face, glad it was too dark to see clearly.

'But you only had a knife!'

'Of course, I had a knife. How else would I get past the razor-sharp jaws and claws? I snuck up on it and struck before it even had a chance!' The story was becoming increasingly absurd, but he kept talking to distract them as they returned to the village. 'I stabbed it seventeen times!'

The hunters didn't dare argue as they went to the Great Hall. Animal-lard torches flickered, golden light spilling out into the bluish night as the chieftain opened the door.

Michael didn't need to say anything as a hunter rushed to tell the story. If they doubted him, no one showed any sign of it.

After a long moment of listening, the chieftain waved his hand to silence them. 'But how can we be sure that Michael slayed the beast?'

Everyone turned to Michael. Words caught on his lips. He didn't have any proof, did he?

'Maybe we should go back to the cave to check,' someone suggested.

'No!' Michael blurted before he'd thought of a reason why. 'That's… not a good idea.'

The chieftain turned to Michael. Doubts swirled in his eyes. 'And why not?'

'Because… dragons… the corpse lit on fire, didn't it?'

'At least we can collect the ashes.' The chieftain gestured for several hunters to go.

Michael's hands clenched into fists. Maybe Avery and the dragon would be gone by now, but what would the hunters do when they found an empty cave? What if the dragon really was ill?

'Wait!' Avery appeared in the doorway. Her blonde hair had worked free from her plaits, and dirt streaked her cheeks.

Everyone turned to look at her. Murmurs broke out.

Avery staggered forward. 'Michael dropped something.' She held something gleaming and red in her hands. Light flashed across the surface, and Michael recognised the colour and sheen of the dragon's scale. But it was not a normal scale. Michael was no expert, but it looked like an egg.

Michael cleared his throat. 'Oh, yes. That's mine.'

From that day onwards, Michael was known as the dragon slayer. The story was passed down over the years, and like the way the wind and tide shaped Hasting's coast, the story eroded and shifted until it barely resembled the original. The dragon became almost demon-like, and Michael went from a dragon slayer to a saint.

A stone church was built on the cliff overlooking the sea, and it became the most well-known church in the Anglo-Saxon village of Haestingas, which later became Hastings. Saint Michael's Church stood until the 15th century before finally crumbling. For all appearances, the hallowed grounds are currently an ordinary asphalt street known as Saint Michael's Place.

A dragon's egg is said to possess magical powers, though we may never know which ones and to what extent. The Normans stole Michael's egg at the Battle of Hastings. After they brought it back to the European continent, the records became increasingly patchy.

The Untruth Seekers' investigation uncovered that it passed from hand to hand in France, had a brief stay in Germany, and ended up in the Netherlands. The mysterious whereabouts, we believe, come from the fact that tragedy seemed to follow the egg. It's unclear why exactly, but most of humanity's attempts to control nature have had predictably disastrous results. Beyond that, all speculation about the dragon's egg falls into pure fantasy.

Despite the ceaseless march of time and layers of truth and untruths, the church's 12th-century seal marks the story—or a version of it—as it depicts Michael waving his weapon over a dramatically flailing dragon, giving the performance of a lifetime.

THE
DUTCH CAPTAIN

Story Five

When Johannes, the Dutch captain, washed up on the shore of Bulverhythe, he'd already lost his ship to a ruthless gale and most of his crew to disease. The local English folks weren't particularly friendly, and they spoke in rough, fishermen's accents that had not been a part of Johannes's English lessons back in the Netherlands. Worse, the locals were suspicious of the Dutch survivors who seemed to carry such foul luck with them.

Johannes, and what remained of his crew, convened at the Bo-Peep pub on the edge of Saint-Leonards-on-Sea. When they emptied their water-logged pockets, they had enough for a couple of nights' board and a few pints. They sipped at the yeasty dark brown ales as they discussed their plans.

'We need to go back to Amsterdam,' one said.

'But how?' another asked.

'There are plenty of ships in Hastings,' someone suggested.

'We don't have any money to pay for passage. No one will take us across the Channel out of the goodness of their hearts.'

Johannes tapped his fingers on the table as his crew argued. It was true; they were marooned in this strange, savage land. As the captain of the *Amsterdam*, he had even more to dread than the rest of them. How could he explain to his employers that the *Amsterdam* had sunk and taken all the weapons and supplies down with it? And what of that strange package in the safe in his cabin? The East India Company had been so insistent that he deliver it safely, but in just a short time, he had lost that too. He would never find work as a captain again, that was for sure. If he were allowed to step foot on another ship, he would be lucky to get a job swabbing the deck.

Johannes slowly sipped his ale, his mind churning. No, surely, there had to be a better option.

'We can find work here, then,' a crew member suggested. 'All we need to do is earn some money, and we'll be back in the Netherlands by the end of the year.'

'By the end of the year? Do you expect us to drink this warm piss water' —another crew member held up his ale— 'for a whole year?'

'Besides, how can we find work when we don't speak English?' another grumbled.

'English? Is that what they're speaking? Doesn't sound like English to me.'

'It doesn't matter. We know how to sail, and this is a seaside town. How much talking does finding a fishing job require?'

It was likely the best option, but Johannes's limbs filled with dread at the thought of spending a year scraping fish guts off the deck of a rickety fishing boat. After all, he had been the captain of the three-masted *Amsterdam* and employed by the East India Company. No, there had to be something better. Perhaps he could dredge out some of the silver and guns that had been intended for Java. But then again, the remains of the ship had washed to shore a few days ago, so the English men had probably already cleared out anything of value that hadn't ended up on the seafloor.

Or better yet, what about the mysterious packet in the safe that he'd been given to transport? He was the only one who knew it was in the captain's cabin. Even if the English scavengers had already picked over the remains of the ship, they might not recognise its value.

A crew member's voice jarred him from his thoughts. 'What do you think, Captain?'

'We'll look for fishing boats tomorrow,' Johannes said in an authoritative, captain-like tone.

A burst of conversation followed, but Johannes wasn't listening. He had finished planning his route to the wrecked *Amsterdam* before finishing his ale. The crew was still bickering when he retired to his room, and he waited until the voices faded and the lamps were extinguished before creeping out.

Gusts of icy January wind swept past him as he followed the road from Saint Leonards to Bulverhythe, which was little more than a cluster of thatched-roof stone cottages huddled against the wind. Beyond the village, silvery moonlight illuminated the coast. The broken boards and crooked masts of the *Amsterdam* rose from the sands like the bones of a great skeleton.

Pebbles crunched under Johannes's boots as he approached, and then the stones gave way to wet sand. Water splashed around his ankles, then his knees, and finally rose to his waist. He knew the ship inside and out. Even in its current state, he quickly found the prow and worked his way back towards what had once been his cabin.

Waves gurgled against the side of the smashed hull, and something knocked hollowly against the wood. The hair on the back of Johannes's neck rose. When he splashed towards the cabin door, he found an empty barrel bobbing in the water. He pushed it away from the cabin wall, and the knocking stopped. He pinched his nose and dropped below the surface of the water. A wave of cold swept over him, passing through his red jacket, skin, muscles, and permeating the very core of his bones.

In the pitch-black water, he spread his arms and grasped for anything solid. His fingers found an iron bed frame. Then, a ledger, with its pages now turned to mush. He stretched further, finally finding the smooth, cold surface of the safe.

Johannes's lungs pinched as his fingers fumbled across the metal of the safe and found the nob of the lock. He twisted the lock forward, backward, and forward again. The latch snapped open. He removed the soaked canvas-wrapped packet before pushing off.

His head burst through the surface of the water, and he gulped in a lungful of air. In the pale moonlight, he saw something slip out of the water a few metres away. It wasn't uncommon to see seals in the English Channel, but a shiver danced down his spine regardless. This was no seal. Moonlight gilded the face, and shadows pooled in its features, but even so, he instantly recognised the mermaid who had saved his life after the gale.

She raised a webbed finger to point at the packet tucked under his arm. Her stiff, rubbery lips moved, but the sound wasn't recognisable as a word. 'Cur—' she said, forcing the sound out. 'Cuuuur—'

Sailors often warned of merfolk, and perhaps it was all idle superstitions, but hadn't the crew and passengers aboard the *Amsterdam* fallen ill after she kissed him? And now the creature had returned, this time to steal the only thing of value left. Johannes tightened his grip on the packet and lunged for the shore.

The mermaid cut through the water after him. Her cold, slippery fingers tugged at his arm, reaching for the packet. He kicked her away, but the water seemed to suck him back as he scrambled across the sand.

When he felt pebbles under his hands and knees, he risked a glance back at the water. Lazy foam-tipped waves lapped at the sand, but the mermaid was gone.

Johannes knew he couldn't return to the Bo-Peep, where the crew might notice his wet clothes and wonder why he had returned to the *Amsterdam*.

He carried it all the way to Hastings and crossed the Bourne River, but he was too exhausted and cold to continue. The Stag Inn was closed, but when Johannes banged on the door, a bleary-eyed barkeep let him into one of the rooms.

Johannes had stripped off his wet red jacket with gold brocade. It wasn't until he had piled on blankets with the packet tucked beside him in the bed that his ragged breathing calmed, and his pulse slowed.

Somewhere in the splashing of his scramble back to shore, he had heard the mermaid's voice again. He couldn't be sure, but he could have sworn that the mermaid had wheezed a single word.

'Cursed.'

THE HAWKHURST GANG

Story Six

In the late seventeenth and early eighteenth century, the Sussex economy had been humming along. Wool and mining had gainfully employed most people, but then the winds of industry shifted to other regions, taking most ordinary folks' wealth with it. What remained, however, was the trade of goods arriving on the southern coast and making their way north to London. And like moths drawn to the flame, so too are the impoverished drawn to the flow of wealth.

In the village of Hawkhurst, the instinct to avoid taxes and, even better, smuggle stolen goods was so strong that it developed into something much more sinister. Starting in 1735, the Hawkhurst Gang controlled much of the illicit trade of tea, brandy, rum, and coffee from France and the Channel Islands.

They had well-established routes from Deal to Poole in Dorset. As it was often remarked, 'Hawkhurst ruled the Weald'. And they did so with a reign of unrivalled ruthlessness, meeting in pubs to plan their various endeavours—from piracy and smuggling to violent confrontations with the customs authorities.

By the mid-eighteenth century, the prosperity of the port towns was almost entirely dependent on smuggling. Everyone wanted in on the illicit trade, and then the Hawkhurst Gang grew to an unwieldy size. The coast guard and customs officials were circling closer, eager to find any weakness to exploit.

It was a seemingly ordinary night in 1748 when customs officials armed with rifles closed in on the Royal Oak in Hawkhurst. The gang members were enjoying a few pints of ale and Thomas Kemp, a young recruit, was entertaining them with a song.

Thomas had a pleasant, cheerful demeanour and he was not at all the sort of lad one would associate with a notorious smuggling gang. But truth be told, he wasn't particularly talented or hardworking. He'd tried his hand at business, but he hated ledgers and calculating figures. He'd considered joining the priesthood, but he was so undisciplined that the church kicked him out after only two weeks. He preferred to spend his time drinking, singing, and gambling—interests that made him unsuitable for most industries.

However, Thomas did alright in the Hawkhurst Gang. All he needed to do was wave a rifle around to impress his boss, William Gray. Then they would end up at a pub to enjoy the evening's entertainment and for Thomas, that was enough. Alas, for Thomas, it was short-lived.

The customs officials burst through the door of the pub. Ale splashed as pint glasses crashed to the floor. Screams echoed against the wood-beamed ceiling as gang members scattered. Some ran for the back door, only to find they were surrounded by officers. Others whipped out their rifles and suddenly, ear-splitting bangs tore through the pub.

Thomas dove under the table, sliding under cover just as a bullet slammed into the floorboards behind him. He scrambled for his rifle, but he had been so busy singing that he forgot to load it earlier. By the time he found gunpowder and bullets, the customs officials were leading out gang members at rifle point.

'Hands up, you bloody wastrel,' an officer snarled as he knelt to point his rifle at Thomas.

Thomas lowered his own rifle to the floor and slid out from under the table, raising his hands as requested. Several bodies with large, red patches blooming through their jackets and trousers were sprawled over chairs and on the floor. Thomas's vision blurred as he staggered out of the pub. He wouldn't consider the bloodthirsty gang members friends, but it was quite another thing to wish his colleagues dead.

Outside, away from the acrid stench of gunpowder and iron tang of blood, the March air was cool and fresh. Officers lined up Thomas and six other surviving gang members, including his boss, William Gray. They were carted off to

Newgate prison in London, but Thomas barely registered passing through the commanding gate, or the building's grand façade as he was brought inside. He remembered the clang of iron against stone, the damp air that stank of sewage, and the despair churning in his gut.

Thomas had every reason to give up hope in Newgate prison, but iron bars would prove insufficient against the notorious Hawkhurst Gang. While the prisoners queued up to receive their daily allotment of gruel, William Gray whispered in Thomas's ear. 'Tonight is the night. We'll meet by the gate where they bring in the supplies.'

Finally, Thomas had something to hope for. That night, he laid awake in his cot while a guard passed. He heard a grunt and the *thwack* of something cracking against a skull. When he shot to his feet and pressed his face against the iron bars, he saw William Gray standing over the guard's body. William Gray took the guard's keyring and passed it to the other gang members. The key turned in the lock of Thomas's cell and the door swung open.

Thomas crept down the hallway with the other members of the Hawkhurst Gang to the supply gate. Someone muttered something about bribing the guards, and when they tested the gate, they found it unlocked. However, a light appeared in the prison window behind them. The guard's body and their empty cells had been discovered. A shrill whistle cut through the night air.

William Gray threw the gate open, and the gang members spilled out of the prison, racing down the street.

'Split up!' William Gray shouted.

Two gang members tore down an alley to the left, three turned right, and then Thomas and William Gray were alone. They sprinted down the street, the sound of whistles and shouting nipping at their heels. Thomas ran. His ragged panting and pounding heart drowned out everything but the desperate desire to escape. And then, something happened.

Thomas tripped. Pain shot from his shoulders as he slammed onto the ground, rolling to a stop.

William Gray stepped closer, looking down at him. 'Get up, you idiot!'

Thomas tried to push himself up, but his body was stiff with fear. The whistles pierced the air behind them, growing louder.

'Stay there, then. When they stop to arrest you, it will give me time to escape.' William Gray's voice was cold and merciless. He was ready to leave Thomas to a miserable existence at Newgate prison if it slightly increased his odds of escape. Thomas had always suspected he didn't mean anything to William Gray, but the confirmation made something harden in his chest. His hand shot out, gripping William Gray's ankle.

'What are you… Let go!' William Gray's heel dug into his wrist, but Thomas held firm. He yanked and William Gray crashed to the ground, landing hard on his back. 'You mangey cur!' he howled.

Thomas scrambled to his feet. His stomach hollowed as he looked down at his boss writhing on the cobblestones. It felt like a bucket of ice water had dropped on him. Somehow, his feet moved backwards, and as if in a trance, he turned. Then he was running again. It felt he ran for a million years, but at the same time, the moment streaked by in a flash of dull grey buildings and fog.

The next day, Thomas saw a newspaper announcing that the other six members of the Hawkhurst Gang had been arrested. Now, only Thomas remained free. He travelled lightly and called in favours owed as he made his way south to the coast. By then, Thomas had changed. It might have been seeing the bodies of the fallen, the soulless prison, or the ruthlessness of leaving William Gray on the street.

Whatever it was, the carefree young man who had been arrested at the Royal Oak had been replaced by someone harder and more ambitious. After all, William Gray was no longer the leader of the Hawkhurst Gang. And that was a gap that Thomas was well-placed to fill.

It was January 1749 when Thomas found himself on Hastings' High Street. The flickering flames of the streetlamps weren't enough to push back the darkness, and at the end of the street, he saw an orange square of light.

It seemed to float in the inky darkness, but Thomas knew it was the small window of the smuggler's cottage. A candle in the window was a signal to smugglers that the customs officials weren't out tonight. Reassured, Thomas passed through Waterloo Passage to the soggy bank of the Bourne River, which was in the process of being paved over. He tried not to look down at the greenish, sewage-laced water of the river as he crossed a rickety bridge that swayed precariously with every step.

The stony face of All Saints Church loomed overhead as he turned down the narrow street lined with slumped buildings. Some were the daub and wattle structures of a bygone era, but the Stag Inn was modern brick with rectangular windows and doors built symmetrically. Thomas stepped up the inn's stairs. Inside, the pub was dark except for a few embers glowing in the hearth. The barkeep sat in a chair beside it, his head lolled back and his mouth hanging open. A low, rumbling snore rose from him.

Thomas poured himself an ale and circled back to the sleeping barkeep. 'Interesting security,' he announced.

The barkeep startled awake. His bleary eyes took a moment to find Thomas's face in the darkness, but his expression melted into a sheepish smile when he did. 'Ah, Mister Kemp,' he said. 'Fancy seeing you here. I thought… Well, everyone was saying that you'd been arrested.'

'It was short-lived.' Thomas took a long drink of his ale.

'Excellent.' When Thomas only stared at him, the barkeep rushed to clarify. 'Not excellent that you were arrested in the first place, of course. Excellent that you escaped. Yes, very excellent indeed.'

Thomas ignored the barkeep's floundering. No one dared cross the Hawkhurst Gang, least of all the barkeeps of the pubs where the gang met to hatch plans and store their contraband. Businesses like the Stag Inn prospered only because of the Hawkhurst Gang's illicit trade, and they had seen just how brutal the gang could be. As the last member of the Hawkhurst Gang, Thomas could ensure it was a profitable arrangement, as long as the barkeep held up his end of the bargain. 'I need some supplies from the cellar.'

'Yes, of course, I can see why you'd need that, but you see...'

Annoyance welled in Thomas's chest. He'd expected the usual respect that people had for the Hawkhurst Gang, especially because now it rightly belonged to him. But something was wrong, and he felt like he was being backed into a corner. In Hastings, the Bo-Peep and the Anchor Inn were also aligned with the Hawkhurst Gang, but they didn't have cellars full of contraband and weapons. Only the Stag Inn did, and Thomas hadn't come all this way to leave empty-handed. 'I hope you're not saying what I think you're saying.'

'Well, Mister Kemp, we thought you, William Gray, and the rest of your lot were... Surely, you can understand why I'd begun to have doubts...'

Anger crashed over Thomas. He shot to his feet. 'Show me.'

The barkeep rose slowly, his hands outstretched. 'Some things are left, of course, but you have to remember that I was here alone.'

'I said, show me.' Thomas glared at him and, as if to fill the silence, the barkeep kept rambling.

'No word from your lot for weeks, and the customs officials were always sniffing around.' The barkeep edged towards the door that led to the cellar. 'If they'd found things in my pub, I would've been on the hook for them. Can hardly count on all of you while you're locked up, can I?'

'What about the others?' The Hawkhurst Gang had no shortage of members. They spent the evenings leaning over pints, pistols on their laps, ready for any custom officials foolhardy enough to attempt a raid.

The barkeep shrugged as he lit a lamp. 'After the arrest, and with the customs officials closing in... Well, not too many familiar faces around here lately.' The cellar door creaked when he pushed it open. 'Do you want to see what all is still down there, Mister Kemp?'

Thomas took the lamp from the barkeep and stepped down into the darkness. The amber light pushed back the inky shadows, and the musty scent of dark, damp underground places rose to meet him. The swollen stair boards thumped hollowly under his boots. Thomas arrived at the bottom of the stairs and surveyed the space.

Thick, roughly hewn posts held up the pub above while cobwebs dripped from the wooden joists. Barrels lined one wall, and crates with brew companies' names were stacked against the other, but there was no sign of the tea, coffee, or spirits that the Hawkhurst Gang had smuggled. Gone too were the pistols and muskets that they had stockpiled here.

Above him, the door creaked and slammed closed.

Thomas turned and started up the stairs, arriving at the top only to hear an iron bolt slide into place. He banged both fists against the wood.

'When I get out, I'll rip you to shreds, you scabby sea bass! Do you hear me, you filthy bilge rat!' Thomas continued to scream all manners of curses that only the worst sort of pirates and smugglers would know, but still, the door remained unmoved. Undoubtedly, the barkeep had handed over all the contraband to the customs officials and scared away any remaining Hawkhurst Gang members.

A few years ago, it would have been unimaginable that the Hawkhurst Gang wouldn't have held southeast England in its clutches for eternity. The Hawkhurst Gang was everywhere, and everyone had a stake in it.

But now, that grip was loosening. Just as fast and sudden as the Hawkhurst Gang's influence had developed, it was now receding. And in that peculiar way of this sort of event, it's hard to say exactly what triggered the change. Had the gang grown too big and lost control? Or had it been a mistake to try to form an association of thieves, thugs, and ne'er-do-wells in the first place? Were people tired of the violence, or had the gang gotten so successful that it went soft?

Whatever the reason, the area slipped through the Hawkhurst Gang's fingers like grains of sand through a closed fist. But for the first time in his life, Thomas had a purpose. He refused to give up without a fight.

THE
PAINTED LADY

Story Seven

Marie Brassey's paintbrush streaked across the canvas, leaving a trail of stark black against the white background. She had sketched out her mother's face, hair, and shoulders this morning, and now, she was filling in the outline.

A grainy black and white photograph of her mother sat beside her easel, her expression serious and thoughtful as she gazed at the camera lens. The woman in the image was one of the few cherished mementoes of her mother, Anna Brassey, who had died of malaria on the voyage from India to Australia in 1887.

Marie had been only twelve at the time, and she only had a vague recollection of a confident but inquisitive woman bent over a notebook on the deck of the *Sunbeam*. The specifics of the memory had faded in the four years that had passed since then. Desperate to cling to the memory, Marie read her mother's book, *A Voyage in the Sunbeam*. She could hear her mother's voice in those pages, speaking to her like an old friend.

Footsteps sounded in the hallway outside the art studio. Marie jumped, smudging paint as her eldest sister, Mabelle, charged into the room. Mabelle's skirts swished, and shoes clacked over the floorboards as she went to the balcony overlooking Claremont Street and threw open the door.

'Come quickly; the students are arriving!' Mabelle squealed to Marie's other sisters, Muriel and Constance, who followed. At twenty-five, twenty-two, and nineteen, Marie's three sisters were of the marriageable age but still hadn't found suitors. However, the students who attended their father's school, the Brassey Institute, were all male, around the right age, and from well-to-do backgrounds. Mabelle, Muriel, and

Constance elbowed each other out of the way as they jostled for the best spot on the balcony overlooking the incoming class of arts and sciences students.

'Oh, look at that one! He's so tall!' Mabelle announced.

'What about that one?' Muriel interjected. 'I've always liked blonds.'

'Blonds?' Constance scoffed. 'Tall, dark, and handsome, please.'

Inside, Marie rolled her eyes as she added shadows to her mother's hair and dress. She couldn't remember the shade of her mother's hair anymore, and the photograph was no help. She wondered what her mother would say about her daughters swooning over boys like a troop of lusty baboons. Surely, an adventurer and accomplished writer like Anna Brassey would have more interesting things on her mind. It would be a nice change, Marie thought, to talk to someone who shared her interests.

'Girls?' came a voice from the doorway.

Once again, Marie jolted, nearly smearing her painting. She turned to see her father in the doorway. Beside him stood Vanessa, a young woman about the same age as Mabelle. Vanessa's blonde hair was swept up into a loose bun, and her corset was tightened and padded to give her the most enviable hourglass figure. At least, that's what Marie's sisters always whispered when Vanessa left the room. Even though the words were a compliment, the tone never was. And they had plenty of other things to say about Vanessa, including suspicions about her intentions.

Their father was a widower, so he was free to court whomever he pleased, but Vanessa was so young and voluptuous that it was difficult to see them as a real couple. Especially because Anna Brassey had been an older, more practical woman, and she certainly did not have any of Vanessa's glamour. On the other hand, Vanessa never seemed to have anything witty or insightful to say. Indeed, it seemed rather peculiar that Marie's father would marry Anna, have many adventures and five children with her, and then choose a woman who was her complete opposite in every way.

'That's a lovely painting,' Marie's father said as he stepped into the room. As usual, he wore a waistcoat and a smoking jacket. The golden chain of a pocket watch hung across his stomach, and in one hand, he carried a top hat. He was every inch a gentleman, as would be expected from someone born to a railway magnate, an Oxford man, and the founder of the Brassey Institute. He was destined for a successful career in politics, everyone said.

But to Marie, Thomas Brassey was only ever her father. She flushed with pride at the compliment, but before she could respond, her sisters swarmed her father with questions about the new students and if there would be any parties where they could mingle with them.

Only Vanessa was left with Marie, and her blue eyes trailed over the painting. 'What a peculiar little man,' Vanessa said. 'Surely, you could paint him in a more flattering way?'

The flush of warm pride drained away, replaced by a cold, empty feeling. 'That's my mother,' Marie replied flatly.

Vanessa made a show of looking around the room. 'Where?'

'The painting is of my mother,' Marie said through gritted teeth.

'Ah, well, you did the best you could.' Vanessa shrugged as her gaze shifted to the photograph of Anna Brassey. 'There's not much to work with, is there?'

Marie twisted the paintbrush between her hands as if trying to wring its neck. Whatever retort she might have made was cut off by her father's voice.

'Alright, girls, there's no need to bombard me like this,' he announced. 'I'll ask your older brother to arrange a welcome party for all the new students. How about that?'

'Will there be dancing and music?' Mabelle asked.

'How about food?' Muriel added. 'And drinks?'

'We'll need new dresses too,' Constance said, and the other two nodded in agreement.

Their father let out a long sigh, which was enough time for the three sisters to clasp their hands together and chorus, 'Please!'

'Alright, alright,' their father conceded, which was met with squeals. 'The party will be tomorrow. But after this, you need to leave the boys to study, understood?'

The sisters were too busy making plans to listen to another word. Their father turned back to Vanessa, who slinked to his side and snaked her hand around his arm. She leaned up to whisper something to him, her eyelashes fluttering.

Marie glared at Vanessa, but Vanessa's gaze merely lingered on her for a moment before her lips pressed into a smirk. A ripple of annoyance swept over Marie, but she choked it down. After all, Vanessa had not *technically* done anything wrong.

Besides, since the Brassey sisters were rushing to prepare for the party, Marie quickly forgot Vanessa. Her sisters wanted elaborate dresses with all the bustles and frills that the prosperous era of Queen Victoria required, and their hair was curled with hot irons and pulled up into intricate updos. Mabelle even cornered Marie and added some rouge to her cheeks and lips. And then, in a flurry of chiffon and floral perfumes, the four sisters left their house on Trinity Street and headed towards the Brassey Institute.

In the rosy hues of dusk, the glamorous Venetian Gothic façade of the Brassey Institute was as elegant as ever. Golden light spilt from the expansive windows, and the striking silhouettes of gentlemen in tailored smoking jackets had already gathered in the reading room. Marie's sisters squealed with delight, clutching each other's hands as they clacked across the cobblestones towards the party.

Their father and older brother were waiting at the door when the girls arrived, dampening their high spirits with disapproving frowns.

'You must promise me that you will behave tonight,' their father told them.

A current of voices and music tinkled out from the large front room behind him, and all four sisters peered around him, trying to glimpse the party within. Mabelle, Muriel, and Constance were undoubtedly looking for the tallest, most handsome young men, but Marie was not.

Marie scanned the dark array of smoking jackets, her gaze falling on a pile of blonde curls that gleamed in the centre of the room. As always, Vanessa's hair and cosmetics were perfect, and her gown flattered every curve. The students' gazes lingered on her even though it was obvious they were too shy to approach her.

'—be ready to leave at nine o'clock,' concluded her father, and her sisters groaned in unison.

They pushed past him, rushing into the party. Marie trailed behind them, her gaze still on Vanessa.

Most of the students circled Vanessa without daring to get close, but finally one approached her. The crowd's voices and music were too loud to hear clearly, but the young man seemed to ask her a question, and Vanessa nodded. He slipped back into the crowd and returned with a drink. It was an innocent enough exchange, but when he passed the glass to her, they lingered over it. For a brief but telling moment, their eyes met.

It was not proof of anything, of course, but Marie's stomach clenched. She looked over at her father, speaking to a group of students and did not seem to notice. Marrying Thomas Brassey would be quite a favourable arrangement for Vanessa. It was no wonder she could ignore the age gap and enter a loveless marriage that promised her wealth and comfort. But it was entirely another thing to trade longing glances with students while Marie's family was in the same room.

The next hour ticked by in a swirl of dancing, music, and laughter, but Marie could not enjoy any of it. That same student kept finding excuses to return to Vanessa's side, and the longer Marie watched, the surer she became that she could end this farce of a courtship between her father and Vanessa this very night.

That feeling only heightened when Vanessa, waving a lace fan Marie's father had bought for her, slipped outside for air. The student followed, and Marie crept after him.

The air outside was cool and crisp as the bluish light of twilight settled into the darkness of night. Gaslight flames flickered from wrought iron streetlamps, casting an amber glow over the stones of Trinity Church, the shop windows lining

Claremont Street, and the uneven cobblestones. Vanessa and the student had disappeared. However, voices came from the direction of the printworks next to the institute.

Marie followed the sounds to the alley. Her nerves hummed as she edged out from beside the building, scanning the inky shadows for Vanessa. Marie expected to find her in a compromising position with the young man, but when her eyes adjusted to the darkness, all she saw was Vanessa leaning against the brick wall with her arms crossed over her chest. The young man paced back and forth in front of her.

'I don't understand why it's taking so long, Vanessa. I thought you'd have secured a wedding date by now.'

Vanessa sighed and leaned her head back against the wall, gazing up at the narrow strip of sky visible between the two buildings. 'I know, that's also what I thought. I figured Thomas would be desperate for a new woman since he has been a widower for four years.'

The young man rubbed his forehead. 'How long have you been courting, anyway?'

'An eternity, it feels like.'

'Be serious.' He sighed. 'How much more time do you think you'll need?'

'How should I know? Thomas hasn't even proposed.'

'Then, we should try something else. How much money does Thomas keep in the institute?'

Vanessa shrugged. 'A fair amount, but he would notice it's missing before we could make it down the street. And we could forget about escaping Hastings.'

'There's no choice but to remove him from the equation.'

'He's distracted by his hoard of children now. Maybe I could sneak up and fill my pockets.'

'It's not enough. We need to carry out a trunk at least, and for that, Thomas can't be around.'

Vanessa's voice dropped. For the first time, she didn't sound indifferent or bored. She sounded worried. 'What are you suggesting, Emerson?'

'We need to remove him from the equation,' Emerson repeated. There was an edge to his words that made Marie's pulse race. She wished she had merely caught Vanessa in the embrace of another man.

'Clarify,' Vanessa hissed.

'Take this.' Emerson withdrew a silver necklace from his pocket. What looked like a silver locket swung from the chain like a pendulum. 'It contains arsenic.'

Marie's hands tightened around two handfuls of her skirt, her heart pounding. A wave of fear and panic swept over her, and her head swam until she felt like she was hallucinating. No one could casually speak about murder, could they?

Emerson continued. 'Pour it into his drink tonight, and it will seem like he had a heart attack. We'll be long gone by the time anyone suspects anything.'

Vanessa didn't reach for it. 'I... Maybe we should give him more time?'

Emerson took her hand and pressed the locket into her palm. 'We don't have time.'

Vanessa finally accepted it with a sigh. With the locket swinging from her fingers, she pushed past Emerson. Her shoes clicked on the cobblestones towards Marie, whose muscles were frozen with fear. She convinced her feet to stumble back, but when she searched Claremont Street, there was nowhere to hide.

The bright lights and music from the party spilt out into the street, and Marie took off towards them. Just as a breathless scream pushed past her lips, a hand closed on the bustle of her dress. Fabric ripped as she tumbled forward, pain spiking up her knees and the palms of her hands as she slammed down to the street.

'Filthy little eavesdropper!' Vanessa huffed. Emerson's footsteps pounded behind her, approaching.

Marie rolled away, ripping the fabric out of Vanessa's hands. She scrambled to her feet, but Emerson stepped in front of her when she started towards the institute. He lunged for her. Her heart slammed against her ribcage as she considered her odds of slipping past him and reaching the institute. They seemed slim, and no one would hear her screams with the noise inside. She needed another option.

Marie whipped around, her feet finding purchase on the street's stones. She launched forward, racing towards the narrow stairs that led to Cambridge Road above. The gaslight lamp flickered above her, casting an array of dark, erratic shadows.

Her shoes clattered up the stairs as pounding footsteps and laboured breathing followed just a few steps behind her. She could feel Vanessa and Emerson's dark presence pressing on her back, tugging on her like a swirling black vortex, threatening to swallow her whole. Her lungs pinched with exhaustion, and her legs felt too heavy, too slow, but all she could think about was the top step. Her focus narrowed until all she saw was the gap between the two buildings that led to Cambridge Street.

Only a flight of stairs stood between her and her goal, then the distance narrowed. There were only three stairs … two stairs … one stair … but something hooked around her ankle. For the second time that night, Marie crashed to the ground, fear clanging through her head like the sound of a brass gong. She looked back.

Emerson gripped her ankle with both hands. In the uneven lamplight, his eyes seemed to be pools of obsidian. Vanessa swooped past him, leaping on Marie and grabbing the front of her dress with both hands. 'You stupid girl!' she cried.

Marie bucked and twisted, but Vanessa pushed her down until she felt the cold, unyielding stones beneath her. There was nowhere to go.

'She will ruin everything,' Emerson snarled as he wrestled Marie's other leg into his grip.

Vanessa glared down at Marie, her eyes glinting. The same inky black shadows that pooled in Emerson's face now also distorted Vanessa's face, but it was more disturbing because Marie had seen Vanessa's face so many times. Usually, she was exceptionally beautiful but normal. Now Vanessa was neither of those things. Something was terrifying in the way she leered down at Marie. It was as if the blackness in her soul was welling up and spewing out through those once-glamourous features.

Emerson pinned down both of Marie's legs, and her stomach twisted. She was trapped. 'We need to do something about her.'

Marie's chest ached where Vanessa was pressing so hard. She withdrew the silver locket with her other hand and raised it to her teeth, biting it and twisting off the top. A scream bubbled up, but Marie was so breathless from the run and Vanessa's weight that she only whimpered.

'Only a few drops will take care of this situation once and for all.' Vanessa held the locket over Marie's face. A viscous liquid slid out, dripping towards Marie.

She pressed her lips together. Something wet splattered on her cheek and slid across her skin.

'Don't be difficult,' Vanessa hissed, shifting her hand from the front of Marie's dress to her nose and pinching.

Marie's already ragged breath was cut off. The weight of airlessness burned her lungs, but she forced herself to ignore it. The locket and the drop of arsenic loomed above her.

Marie thought about her sisters, brother, and father, who would soon notice she wasn't at the party. She could imagine them leaving the institute, still flushed from the dancing and laughter. She could hear their voices echoing down the street, impatient but cheerful. But all that would come crashing down when they saw her crumpled body on the stairs. Screams would fill the narrow Claremont Street, a gut-wrenching marker of girls who had lost their baby sister.

Marie could not let that happen. Her head pounded; her whole body hurt. Her chest ached, begging for air. She needed a breath. It was a desperate, chest-crushing ache. But arsenic glistened on the rim of the locket and opening her lips would kill her.

The locket tipped forward. The drip of arsenic bulged.

Something whooshed past them. It felt like a sharp breeze or the flap of a bird's wings. Emerson yelped and ducked. As soon as he released Marie's ankle to cover his head with his hands, he was yanked backwards.

Emerson tumbled down the stairs, something cracked, and his shout of surprise deepened into a scream of agony. He landed with a heavy thud on the street at the bottom of the stairs.

Above Marie, Vanessa shrieked. Unlike Emerson, she clung to Marie even when the rush of icy cold air came again. This time, Marie glimpsed something black pass in front of the flickering lamp, but it was a shapeless form, menacing in its indefinability. But whatever it was, it was better than swallowing arsenic. Marie reached for Vanessa's hand and dug her fingernails into the soft skin of her wrist.

'You little cretin!' Vanessa wailed, dropping the silver locket and diving on Marie with both hands.

Marie threw up her leg, slamming her knee into Vanessa's gut. Vanessa teetered back. The swoosh of black swept past her, and Marie's gut churned with the knowledge that it was not enough. Marie raised her leg again, kicking Vanessa with all her strength.

Vanessa's hands slipped away from Marie's dress. Her blue eyes rounded with fear and her mouth formed a perfect 'O' as she tipped back and fell. She bumped, scraped, and slid all the way down the staircase, crashing down on top of Emerson, who howled with anger and pain. They untangled themselves from each other, snarling curses and insults, but Marie was no longer listening.

Her focus was on the woman just beyond the circle of lamplight. Standing in a black dress with a stern expression was the unmistakable figure of her mother, Anna Brassey. All those years missing her and all those wishes that her mother had returned from that last voyage came crashing down.

Marie scrambled to her feet, stumbling down the stairs towards her. 'Mother!'

But as Marie approached, Anna retreated. She slipped out of the lamplight and shadows swallowed her.

'Mother?'

Marie arrived at the place where her mother had been standing. But the street was empty. Heavy disappointment rushed to fill the gap where hope had been just moments before.

Vanessa and Emerson raced past her, still arguing. Their footsteps faded as they disappeared into the night, drowned out by the swell of music and laughter that came from the opening of the institute's door.

'Marie?' Mabelle called. 'What on earth are you doing out here?'

'Come back in,' added Muriel.

Constance waved for her to join them. 'There's still time for one more dance!'

Marie nodded numbly. Her sisters rushed out to help her repair the bustle of her dress, regaling her with stories of the boys while scoffing about what Marie could've possibly thought she was doing out here.

But for the first time, Marie didn't find her sisters annoying. She even found herself quite enjoying the last song of the evening, and she nearly giggled when everyone discovered that Vanessa was missing.

The next day, Marie returned to the painting of her mother. On the canvas where she had carefully rendered her mother's likeliness, there was only an empty background. Marie sat for a few minutes in front of the blank image. But when she raised her hand to paint, it felt too stiff and heavy.

In the end, Marie decided to paint a scene from her mother's descriptions of her voyage on the *Sunbeam*. A strong spirit like her mother would always look for a new adventure, and it was nice to know that no matter how far she voyaged, Anna Brassey would always find her way back home.

THE CAPTAIN'S FATE

Story Eight

Captain Johannes awoke with a start in his bed at the Stag Inn. He'd been dreaming of a strange red lizard, fire, and thick mists that clung to rugged chalk cliffs. Voices came from the pub below. With the treasure from the sunken *Amsterdam* beside him in the bed, he had no interest in investigating who had arrived at such an ungodly hour.

Johannes lay quietly, listening to the argument in the pub below. The slam of a door was followed by frantic pounding.

'When I get out, I'll rip you to shreds, you scabby sea bass!' came muffled curses nasty enough to curdle the air. 'Do you hear me, you filthy bilge rat!'

Johannes rolled over and pulled the pillow over his head. Trouble was the last thing he needed now.

The following morning, Johannes unwrapped the packet. When he pulled back the canvas, he found a smooth red item, almost like coloured glass, about the size of his hand. It was nice enough but hardly seemed worth all the fuss that the East India Company had made about it. Regardless, he was glad he had it. If the East India Company thought it was valuable, maybe he would be able to find someone in Hastings who would see its worth.

Johannes rewrapped the strange red glass-like item and tucked it under his arm. He descended from his rented room to find the windows open. Horses clattered past, and neighbours called while the barkeep wiped the bar.

'Good morning, sleep well?' the barkeep asked without looking up.

'Well enough, but I heard someone cursing and pounding on a door last night.'

The barkeep froze mid-swipe. 'Must've been one of the drunks. Folks in Hastings tend to get rowdy, you know.'

Johannes rubbed his temples, wondering if he'd imagined the sounds just like he'd probably hallucinated the mermaid. He needed to leave this accursed place if he wanted to keep his sanity and life. The fact that his crew was only a few miles away and they'd probably discovered him missing by now didn't help. He needed money to get back to the Netherlands sooner rather than later.

Outside, All Saints Street was bustling with pedestrians and carts. Seagulls swooped across the sky, settling with a flurry of wings and squawks on the mossy roofs of the street. Johannes headed straight towards the sea, which was little more than a stretch of rippling grey under a dreary sky. A salt-laced wind rattled past as he arrived at the net shops that stood like sentinels on the coast. The tall black huts crowded on the narrow strip of land between the shore and the cliffside. Beyond them, weathered ships lounged on the pebble beach.

Johannes only needed one of these ships to take him out to sea. But which one? A group of grizzled sailors in oil-slicked garb lingered around a pub with a faded sign that swayed in the wind, reading *The Jolly Fisherman*. When one saw Johannes inspecting them, he nudged the others, and they all turned to look. Their faces were set with the serious, unfriendly expressions of people who had braved leagues of empty seas and stared down storms as terrifying as the one that had claimed the *Amsterdam*.

However, Johannes was no landlubber himself. He rolled his shoulders back as he approached them. 'Anyone headed to the continent?' As soon as he spoke, he heard his thick Dutch accent.

They must have heard it too, and there was no mistaking their reaction. Their scowls deepened as they exchanged glances.

'What're you doing so far from home?' one asked.

Another squinted at him. 'Were you washed ashore with the *Amsterdam* in Bulverhythe?'

'Rumour is that the East Indiaman was carrying valuable cargo,' one said. 'But the captain took it and disappeared.'

'I also heard that the *Amsterdam* was diseased. The crew jumped ship to save themselves, but who's to say they're not all infected?'

'Diseased? I heard worse. They say something from deep beneath the waves cursed the ship.'

The sailors leaned closer, and Johannes shrank back. These men didn't seem likely to give him passage out of the kindness of their hearts, and it seemed more likely that they would discover he was carrying something valuable and try to take it.

As if reading his mind, one of the fishermen eyed the bundle under Johannes's arm. 'Say, what do you make of all the talk of something valuable?'

'Why else would a man abandon his crew in a strange land?' another said.

The biggest man in the group lunged, his big, meaty hands reaching for Johannes's throat. Johannes staggered back just enough, and all the man grabbed were two handfuls of the gold brocade on his red jacket. Johannes fell back. Fabric ripped, and suddenly he was plummeting to the ground. He landed heavily on his back, knocking the breath from his lungs. The man reached for him, but Johannes rolled away.

He pushed himself to his feet and took off running up All Saints Street. His lungs pinched, and all he heard was the rush of his breath in his ears as he raced past the *Cinque Ports Arms*. He risked a glance back and didn't see the fishermen following, so when he arrived at the Stag Inn, he leapt up the stairs and slipped inside.

The barkeep hadn't moved from behind the bar, and he looked up in surprise at Johannes's panting and sweat-soaked face. He opened his mouth, but before a single word could escape, Johannes surged forward, banging both fists on the bar. 'If anyone follows me, tell them I'm not here.'

'Why would I do that?'

'They're chasing me. They think…' Probably best not to say what they thought. Now that Johannes had the valuable red glass thing, he couldn't trust anyone. 'They're mad.'

The man's eyes narrowed. 'I mean, what is keeping my mouth shut worth to you?'

Johannes's stomach hollowed in that strange way that one felt when they missed a stair in the dark. He didn't know what he expected from a haven for pirates and smugglers in this savage country but paying off a man to keep him out of the clutches of fishermen hardly seemed fair. Perhaps it was the strain of a shipwreck, strange things in the sea, or simply the lack of sleep and frustration…

But something in Johannes snapped. He snatched a bottle off the bar and swung it down, cracking it against the wood. Liquid splattered to the floor, and the acrid scent of rum blossomed in the air. The neck of the bottle with its jagged edges remained in Johannes's hand. He whipped around, stabbing it straight into the barkeep's neck.

Johannes's vision went hazy. All he registered was a breath, sticky with blood and pain, and then the thud of the man crumpling to the floor. Something gurgled, and the pub fell silent.

Johannes spun to the door, ready to lock it, but he was only halfway across the room when he heard familiar voices.

'Where is he?' came the rough voice of one of the fishermen.

'Come out, come out wherever you are,' chorused another.

Johannes staggered back. It wouldn't take them long to look in the Stag Inn and discover the body. Was there no other way out? Perhaps not, but there was a cellar and a desperate man within. Johannes didn't have any money, but he did have leverage. He pounded on the cellar door. 'Are you down there? I'll free you if you help me.'

No answer. Johannes took a deep breath and tried again, louder. 'Do you want to be freed? This is your last chance, or I'll leave and—'

'Open this door!' came a muffled voice.

'I need to flee Hastings,' Johannes said. 'Can you help me do that?'

'Go down the street and find a boat. It's not that hard.'

'You don't understand. Men are surrounding the pub as we speak.' Johannes glanced out the window. Some fishermen were peeking in the windows of the houses opposite, while others stopped carts and searched them. A face appeared in the Stag Inn's window, and Johannes ducked. The bar hid him for now, but he heard boots against the hardwood floor.

'Then you'll need to escape by tunnel,' the voice said. 'But it's been closed off with a great many nails. You don't happen to have a hammer, do you?'

Johannes glanced at the shelves under the bar. A hammer laid between the bottles and glasses that crowded the shelves. Lowering himself to his hands and knees, Johannes crept forward.

A shadow passed across the floor as someone entered the pub. 'Where's the barkeep?' one of the fishermen asked.

'Strangely quiet, isn't it?' another muttered.

'Hello?' called a third.

Johannes flinched at the sound of at least three voices, but it was nothing compared to the way his heart raced when he saw the slowly growing pool of viscous red liquid around the barkeep's motionless body. Johannes leaned over him, his fingers reaching for the hammer's handle. His breath came in shallow, rapid bursts as he slid it closer. The sound seemed to echo in the dead quiet behind the bar.

Fortunately, and unfortunately—more fishermen had arrived. They filled the pub with noise that covered Johannes's uneven panting.

'Folks spotted his red jacket and said he ran this way,' one said.

'Where do you reckon he's going? How far can he go?'

'He's in our country now. That German will be easy to find, don't worry.'

Johannes would have been annoyed that they called him German in any other circumstance. *Mijn God*, he thought, the sunken ship was even called the *Amsterdam*. But as it was, his entire being focused entirely on sliding the hammer closer.

Just when he nearly had it, a glass tipped sideways. It wobbled. He caught his breath, staring at it with all his focus—as if he could push it back onto the shelf with willpower alone.

The glass tipped forward, tumbling once before crashing to the floor. Shattered glass burst across the floorboards as the resounding crash echoed through the pub.

'He's here!' someone shouted.

'Behind the bar!' another added.

Johannes snatched the hammer off the shelf and scrambled to the cellar door. He pulled open the iron latch and threw himself into the dark space below. Gravity pulled him down too fast to register anything except an abrupt fall, the soft body of the prisoner and his curses as they landed with a thud at the bottom of the stairs. Voices came from the door at the top of the stairs.

'They're coming!' Johannes hissed into the dark. The item had rolled away during his fall.

'What about the hammer?' Hands fumbled, and Johannes felt the hammer slip out from his grip. Somewhere in the black abyss, he heard the scrape of metal against wood followed by the screech of an old nail sliding out from a swollen board.

At the top of the staircase, a silhouette stepped into the rectangle of light. More broad-shouldered men joined the first. Footsteps pounded down the stairs, and shouts filled the dark, cavernous cellar as the fishermen closed in around him.

In the dark cellar, punches were thrown, and a pistol fired. The last thing Johannes saw was the water-stained boards of the pub above, and the final sound to fill his ears was the pounding of his own heart. Then, only the black emptiness of nothing at all.

No one can say for sure what happened that day, but even when the fishermen brought down a lamp to search for the valuable item, they found only a few scattered boards on the floor in front of the mouth of one of the tunnels built by smugglers like the Hawkhurst Gang. Thomas Kemp, now in possession of the mysterious red item, raced down the tunnel that went all the way to Rock-A-Nore. He emerged from the dark passageway near the tall black net huts and disappeared into the bustling fishing activity on the coast.

As for poor Captain Johannes, his corpse was carried out of the cellar a short time later. It is said that Johannes was called back to the sea to pay his debt to the creature that saved his life after the shipwreck.

But occasionally, guests at the Stag Inn sighted a bearded man wearing a red jacket trimmed with gold brocade, now waterlogged and dripping with seaweed. They say that the Dutch captain is returning to search for the mysterious item that cost him his life.

LITTLE
MOLLY HAWKINS

Story Nine

The Bourne River cut through Hastings Old Town's centre until it was paved over in 1749. In the early eighteenth century, upscale buildings were to the west of the river. Shoppers in their best clothes would stroll the prim cobblestoned streets and admire the shops' displays of jewellery, textiles, teas, and spices.

Little Molly Hawkins lived on the east bank of the river, however. Here, slumped fishing shacks with thatched roofs lined muddy roads. Molly's father spent long hours at sea, where he caught Hastings' infamous mackerel. However, the pay was not enough to sustain his wife and four children. To make ends meet, her mother worked as a seamstress until two years before she died giving birth to Molly's younger sister, Emily.

After that, all Molly knew was a leaky roof and meagre meals, mainly consisting of leftover mackerel that were too old or bony to sell. Still, Molly never stopped daydreaming. Her favourite thing was crossing the bridge over the Bourne River and passing through the Waterloo Passage that leads to the High Street. She often wandered the street of the west side, marvelling at the well-dressed passers-byers and glossy carriages. She peered into the shop windows, admiring the delightfully exotic products and imagining herself wealthy enough to buy them one day. Most people didn't mind the young girl because she smiled easily and walked with a skip in her step despite her ragged appearance.

One evening, Molly returned home to find that her father's catch had been swept out to sea. Her father and two older brothers went to bed without a word, but Emily's eyes welled up with tears.

'Don't worry; Father will catch more fish tomorrow.' Molly squeezed her sister's shoulders, pretending not to notice how rail-thin Emily was. The sisters fell asleep and spent the next day trying not to think about how hungry they were, but it was too much to bear by evening. They waited eagerly by the door when their father returned.

But autumn had brought an unexpected cold spell and perilous waters. The Hawkins children were disappointed to find he was once again empty-handed.

Tears gathered in Emily's eyes as Molly tucked her into bed. She didn't have any food, but she did have a story about a seamstress who lived on Swan Terrace. The seamstress was working frantically to stitch an elaborate gown for a customer but fell asleep before she could finish. When the seamstress woke up the following day, she was amazed to find the gown finished. No one was around, but she swore she glimpsed the flicker of fairy wings disappearing out the window. Emily nodded off while Molly laid awake under her threadbare blanket, wishing for a helpful fairy of her own.

No glimmer of fairy wings appeared the next morning, and Molly's empty stomach was almost impossible to ignore. However, there was no better distraction than the wealthy west side, just a short walk away. As usual, the delights of the High Street filled Molly's senses with a symphony of rich colours and scents as she passed the vendors. Then, she saw something that made her gasp with surprise.

A basket of gleaming red apples sat on the corner of a vendor's table. Molly could almost taste the crisp, refreshing sweetness of the first bite. And would her family not love to have a taste too?

When the vendor turned to help a customer, Molly didn't think. She snatched the basket and raced down the street, stuffing apples into the pockets of her frayed apron as she went.

Behind her, the vendor's voice rang out. 'Thief! Stop!'

Like a pair of apparitions, two constables in dark blue uniforms with rows of shiny buttons stepped out in front of her. One lunged for Molly, and she barely dodged his outstretched hand. The other swung his baton, narrowly missing Molly as she darted past him.

Her bare feet flew across the cobblestones, and the sound of her ragged breath filled her ears, but all she could think about was Emily's grin when she bit into an apple.

A shrill whistle cut through the air. Heavy boots pounded after her. Molly's chest was tight, but once she crossed the bridge into her neighbourhood on the east side, she could squeeze into a hiding place and wait for the constables to give up.

Molly turned down Waterloo Passage and sprinted up the stairs to the Bourne River bridge. She could almost feel the crunch of the apple between her teeth.

But then her foot slid across the thin layer of ice that coated the wooden planks, and she careened to the side. She swiped her other foot, desperate for purchase, but it was too late. Her foot slipped across the ice. The world tilted, and suddenly, the churning water of the Bourne was hurtling towards her.

She slammed through the river's surface. Ice-cold water swallowed her, holding her in a vice-grip as it dragged her down.

The constables arrived at the bank of the river a moment later. They saw Molly's head bobbing above the water and her small arms thrashing. The water was only chest-deep for an adult, but when one constable stepped forward to help her, the other held out his hand.

'What are you doing?' The first constable tried to push past the other. 'We can still save her!'

The other constable held firm. 'It was the girl's fault for stealing.'

'Yes, but she's only a child, we should—'

'Do you want all the other rabble from that side of the river to think they can get away with thievery?'

The other constable slowly shook his head. He looked back at Molly, still flailing in the water. A few moments later, she dipped below the water and disappeared.

Meeting such a tragic end would make most people bitter and jaded, but little Molly Hawkins was incorrigible even after death. According to reports, no one feels her as a negative presence. In fact, even today, the occasional apple has been found in Waterloo Passage beside the First In Last Out pub. Many believe that Molly is trying to return the apples she stole.

THE CHOPBACK GANG

Story Ten

When Thomas Kemp emerged from the tunnel, the pebbled coast of Rock-A-Nore bustled with fishermen hauling nets to the huts and fishmongers hawking the daily catch. His arms ached from clutching the item he'd stolen from the Dutchman in the Stag Inn's cellar. For something the size of his foot, it was strangely heavy. The cellar and tunnel had been too dark to see anything, and all he knew was that it was hard, smooth, and wrapped in canvas.

Whatever it was, Thomas didn't dare unwrap it with so many tattered sailors and fishermen around. Especially when the ones who'd been chasing the Dutchman would probably follow him through the tunnel.

Thomas tucked the item under his jacket as he headed towards George Street. Carts laden with bags of flour, sugar, and crates of fresh vegetables clattered past while shoppers wove around them, pausing to admire window displays before disappearing into shops. They were busy with their own tasks and distracted by greeting friends and acquaintances to notice as Thomas strode past. After escaping from Newgate prison, he had the goal of reaching Hastings to reunite with remaining members of the Hawkhurst Gang, but now that he had discovered he was the last one, he was directionless.

Worse, he was hungry and penniless. When he arrived at the market squeezed between a shop and the Anchor Inn, he was almost dizzy with the desire for the stacks of fruit and vegetables on display. Customers stepped around Thomas, and the only ones who seemed to notice his presence gave him disapproving glances before going about their business.

A voice broke through the flurry of activity. 'Step back and wait your turn!'

Heads turned as an elderly woman twisted a young lad's ear. The boy's face turned as bright red as the vendor's apples, and he backed away without a word. Having made her point, the woman adjusted her scarf demurely before turning back to the vendor. 'How much for those lovely pears?'

Some customers chuckled while others shook their heads. 'Mrs Watson sure goes out of her way to make people miserable,' one grumbled.

'That's why her only child left for Brighton,' another replied. 'Doubt she will come back anytime soon.'

Thomas watched Mrs Watson fill her basket with juicy green pears. He turned to the gossiping customers. 'And what about her husband? Is he still at the house?'

'Old Mr Watson?' The man shook his head. 'Nah, he was able to escape his wife in the best way possible.'

'Is he also in Brighton?' Thomas asked.

'Even better, he's dead!' He chuckled at his own joke while Thomas's gaze returned to Mrs Watson. With her basket full of pears, she headed towards George Street. Her steps were slow and unsteady, relying heavily on her cane.

Thomas trailed after her. He could probably snatch the basket from her, but such a bold move would attract too much attention on the crowded street. Still, his nerves hummed with impatience as Mrs Watson hobbled away. He desperately wanted those pears, but if Mrs Watson lived alone, there could be more to gain from her than simply fruit.

She turned down Market Passage onto West Street, continuing to a crooked two-story building with weathered wooden cladding, number 19. Perhaps Mrs Watson hadn't been able to manage the upkeep in her old age. She went inside while Thomas shifted from foot to foot. As soon as she closed the door, he finally approached.

Thomas raised the brass knocker and tapped it. A moment later, Mrs Watson appeared.

'Yes?' She was only as tall as Thomas's shoulder and peered up at him through thick-lensed spectacles. Her white hair was pulled back into a tight bun. 'What do you want?'

Thomas considered rushing in and tackling her, but he discarded the idea when a cart clattered down West Street behind him. It would be too easy for someone to notice.

'You dropped something at the market.' Thomas reached into his pocket and found an old handkerchief. He held it out to her. 'I thought you might need it.'

Mrs Watson wrinkled her nose. 'Never seen that dastardly thing in my life. Now, stop wasting my time and go away.' She went to slam the door shut, but Thomas stuck out his boot. The door bounced against it.

'I said, go—'

Thomas shoved in, knocking Mrs Watson back. He scrambled to shut the door so no one outside would see. Just as the door clicked into place, Mrs Watson's cane came down with a *thwap* on his head. Pain spiked across his skull. He whipped around, yanking it out of her hands. Suddenly off balance, Mrs Watson crashed backwards. She fell hard against the wall, landing with a sickeningly wet thud. Her body went limp as she slid down to the floor, blood streaking the wall behind her.

Silence filled the room for a long moment. Before Newgate prison, Thomas would have felt wretched. In fact, he would have never imagined following Mrs Watson home at all. But as it was, all he felt was a cold, dead emptiness. His gaze wandered to the basket of pears.

He bit into one as he searched Mrs Watson's belongings for valuables. She had a few pence in her purse, and her cutlery was real silver, but otherwise, this wouldn't keep him alive for long. And worse, her only weapons were kitchen knives. Again, hot frustration rose in Thomas's chest. He had come so far, only to once again find nothing of value. It hardly seemed right.

Thomas circled the house once more, kicking over furniture and tearing all the clothes out of the wardrobe. A piece of paper, covered with blotchy black ink, fluttered to the floor in front of him. He kicked it, but nothing was satisfying about kicking paper, and it only brought a fresh wave of frustration. Determined to crumple it, he snatched it off the floor. Words were printed across it.

PRAYER CARD
ISSUED BY THE SAINT CLEMENT'S PARISH CHURCH

Thomas had no interest in the prayer card, but 'Saint Clement' was familiar. Smugglers often used the nearby caves to hide contraband. What if something was left? Reinvigorated by the pears and hope, Thomas collected a kitchen knife and left number 19 West Street. As the door closed, the last thing he saw between the crack was Mrs Watson's leather shoes, which would never take another step.

Thomas was far beyond caring, however. His thoughts were only on the caves and what he might be able to find within. Even if it needed to be rebuilt, the Hawkhurst Gang was rightfully his, and thoughts filled his head of what he could do with it. He had always admired, as well as being slightly intimidated by, William Gray. And now, it was Thomas's turn to be the boss.

Outside, the pinks and oranges of dusk streaked the horizon. Seagulls, silhouetted by the fading light, swooped across the sky, landing amongst the chimneys on George Street's sharply pitched roofs. He turned on Hill Street, then Cobourg Place, and found a path that led up the heavily wooded West Hill. A canopy of branches reached overhead, and Thomas could only see scraps of the sky. By now, the sun dipped below the horizon, and the rosy array of colours shifted to indigo. Stars, like pinpricks of light through a black curtain, poked through.

Despite the bustling town below, the West Hill was still and quiet. Townspeople didn't risk leaving the cobblestoned streets because it was well-known that smuggling gangs controlled the surrounding areas. It wasn't safe to venture out, especially at night. But Thomas was the last member of the Hawkhurst Gang, and as such, the caves dug out from the hill belonged to him. He crept further down the path until the thickets edged in, and the trail disappeared. There was nothing but the chirp of crickets and whirr of insect wings.

Thomas listened harder, straining his ears. There was the faint murmur of voices floating between the trees. He started towards it, glimpsing flickering orange light through the leaves.

In front of the cliffside, two men sat on overturned crates beside a gaping hole in the rock. Two rifles were propped against the rock wall nearby. A game of dice rested on a rock between them, along with a bottle of brandy that made Thomas's mouth water. One man scooped up the dice, shook them, and scattered them over the rock. They both leaned closer to look.

'Double sixes!' one man announced. Thomas searched his memory for the men. He had no recollection of them, which meant they were probably from a rival gang that had moved in after the raid at the Royal Oak in Hawkhurst. Annoyance pinched at him. These cheating opportunists had no right to the resources the Hawkhurst Gang had worked so hard to secure. He wouldn't let them get away with it.

Thomas used the distraction to approach. Branches rustled as he slipped past, stopping a few paces away.

One of the men glanced up from the game. 'What was that?' He scanned the woods, but the darkness must have hidden Thomas because the man's gaze didn't stop on him.

'Trying to distract me from your losses, are you?' the other said.

'I don't care about the game.' The man stood and lifted one of the rifles, settling it against his shoulder.

'Sounds like something a sore loser might say.'

The man with the rifle waved a hand to shush him. 'I'll check it out.' He marched towards the woods, heading straight for Thomas, who barely had the chance to dive behind an alder tree before the man passed.

Thomas reached under his jacket, his fingers finding the hard surface of the mysterious item he had stolen from the Dutchman at the Stag Inn. He still hadn't inspected it, but there was no time now. Thomas pushed it aside and found the knife handle. Closing his fingers around it, he leapt out from behind the tree, slashing and stabbing. Surrounded by a thick layer of darkness, he only felt the splash of a hot, viscous liquid on his hands. His ears filled with pained grunts, followed by a long wheeze and then… silence.

He fell to the forest floor, feeling soft earth between hard roots and rocks as he ran his hands over the ground, searching for the rifle. The metal and polished wood were unmistakable. He lifted it to his shoulder.

The other man must have heard the unusual sounds because he, too, had abandoned the dice game. He pointed the rifle at the darkness surrounding his island of lamplight, not realising it put him in a vulnerable position. Thomas had never shot a man before, but after everything he had been through, he raised the rifle and stared down the barrel at the man. An easy target. He would have the Hawkhurst Gang back and restore it to its former glory. His heart raced with anticipation as he slid his finger over the trigger. Finally, his life would change.

All he needed to do was squeeze the trigger.

But he never did. A thump came from behind him, sounding an awful lot like an axe sinking into a tree trunk. It wasn't until a fiery, white-hot pain ricocheted through Thomas's body that he realised it wasn't a tree but his own back that had been chopped. Agony this abrupt and all-consuming had a terrible way of cleaving one's awareness from their body. As if in a dream, Thomas stumbled forward, falling to his knees, and collapsing. Something hard pressed into his shoulder, rolling him over. The last thing he saw was the haggard faces of a ruthless rival gang looming over him.

These were the men of the Chopback Gang, and it's probably easy to guess how they got this name. Fortunately for them, they neglected to search Thomas, and they never found the mysterious stolen item he carried. They dragged Thomas to one of the caves and tossed him in so his bloating corpse would scare off anyone else who dared to come up to Saint Clement's caves. His body, now little more than a skeleton, never left this cave. The whereabouts of his spirit remain unknown.

However, the Chopback Gang had many more victims, including a poor soul who had the profound misfortune of losing his life and his head. The details of the man's confrontation with the Chopback Gang remain unknown, but his ghostly apparition is occasionally witnessed searching for his head in the wooded area around Saint

Clement's caves on the West Hill. Perhaps when he finds it, he will finally be laid to rest.

As for Mrs Watson, her spirit never left 19 West Street. Even today, her sour disposition has not improved. Reports of twisted ears and the occasional *thwap* of a ghostly cane have plagued the property, but she has never been reported as a sinister presence. Still, if her rather strict approach to discipline bothers you, we recommend leaving out fruit or sweets to get on her good side. In death as in life, Mrs Watson has a sweet tooth.

THE OLD
POST OFFICE

Story Eleven

These days, if one were to stroll up Hastings High Street, they would pass the Goods Depot. In the front window, an innocuous red box is the last remnant of the building's former life as a post office. Before the current occupants moved in, the building had been derelict since the 1960s.

Various theories exist about why the building fell out of use, but what is known for certain is that the trouble started with a meticulous carpenter and coffin-maker, John Farrow, who lived there in the mid-nineteenth century. He had two sons: Samuel, the younger, and Tim, the elder.

Despite having very little in common, the brothers tolerated each other. The quiet and studious Samuel handled the accounts, while the extroverted and affable Tim dealt with customers. People knew the respectable Farrow family, but no one thought too much about them.

That was why no one noticed when Samuel became curious about the tunnels that ran under the Old Town. Most of the underground passageways were closed, but Samuel had always been fascinated by the system that had once connected the old pubs that helped smugglers evade customs officials.

Samuel hated the way cobwebs stuck to his skin or the squelch of foul-smelling sludge under his feet, but he could count on Tim to go deep into what remained of the tunnels. His brother wasn't interested in the historical significance, but he always did love a good dare. They explored most of the tunnels in the Old Town, but the night they ventured into Saint Clement's caves on the West Hill, Tim had started to get restless.

'There's never anything down here,' Tim complained as he raised his lamp. Light spilled over the cracked bricks and exposed stone of the tunnel walls, sending shadows scattering. Cobwebs stretched across the tunnel, as thick as wool. Their footsteps unsettled the brackish water pooled at the bottom of the tunnel, and the musty scent of rot and decay filled the cool, damp air.

'That's not the point,' Samuel replied.

His brother kicked a rock, and it landed with a plop somewhere in the darkness. 'Then, what's the point?'

The truth was, Samuel saw these explorations as more of an academic matter than a treasure hunt. The caves were crumbling and, if they weren't already filled or closed off, they would soon flood or collapse. It was hard to say precisely why he was so keen on exploring these passageways, but when he stood on the West Hill, he could feel their secrets beneath the ground, pulsing under the grassy lawn. But it was insane to believe that, surely. At more rational moments, Samuel suspected his curiosity was fuelled by the fact that the smuggling history of the town was receding.

It would go gradually, Samuel predicted, like the slipping away of the tide, and only when it was well and truly gone would anyone appreciate that it might have been interesting to know what was down there. After all, most of the artefacts in museums were usually just ordinary things. A pottery shard, a rusted key, a threadbare tapestry—all these things probably meant very little to their owners, who used them in their day-to-day lives and tossed them away when they ceased to be useful. Samuel somewhat fancied himself as an explorer and documenter. The type of person who remembered what others forgot.

'Did you hear me?' Tim's voice jarred Samuel back to the present.

'Sorry, I—'

Tim sighed impatiently. 'Mary will be working at the Hastings Arms tonight. Why don't we leave this, go back home'—he lifted his shoes to examine the mud caked on the soles— 'get cleaned up, and head over for a pint?'

'I think we should finish here first.' Like a hum radiating from the darkness, Samuel could feel the pulse of buried secrets calling to him.

'Finish what?' Tim grumbled.

'If you reach the end of the tunnel, I'll cover all your chores so you can go to the Hastings Arms.'

'All my chores? Even cleaning the loo?'

'Everything,' Samuel said firmly. 'The place will be so spotless that Father will be singing your praises.'

Tim snorted. 'I don't want to end up at the Hastings Arms smelling of this tunnel, though. Mary barely spares me a glance as it is.'

The pulse continued, as strong and clear as a drumbeat. 'I'll clean your shoes and trousers.'

Tim let out a long sigh and pushed past Samuel, raising the lamp. With each step, black residue swirled in the greenish water, rising from the edges of his foot to the ankles. 'You'd better scrub *and* polish these shoes,' Tim muttered as he swept a cobweb aside like a curtain.

Samuel trailed after him. The fear of things that crawl and bite kept him from taking the lead, but the invisible thread of the pulsing beat pulled him forward. He peered around Tim as the glow of the lamp pushed the darkness back.

Shadows retreated, revealing a wall of rough, uneven stones held together by crumbling mortar. With his arm outstretched, Tim stepped closer to the wall. The pounding sound filled the tunnel.

'Can you hear that?' Samuel choked out.

'Hear what?' Tim kicked at a pile of debris. Something came loose with a squelch and rolled away, coming to a stop at Samuel's feet.

Hollow eye sockets cut into a yellowing skull stared up at him. The pounding beat slammed to a stop, and silence settled heavily on him. Was this what he had been called to find? A tightness in his chest told him there was something more.

Samuel lifted his gaze to Tim, expecting to find the same breathless fear and anticipation in his brother's expression. But instead, Tim grinned.

'That's more like it!' He lowered the lamp to search the debris. 'Now, *this* is a story for my mates at the Hastings Arms.'

Samuel's mouth was dry, and his throat was too tight. 'Is there…' He forced words past his lips. '… anything else?'

'Look, a femur!' Tim held up a bone. It was a humerus, not a femur, but it was hardly the time for a lesson on osteology. 'And ribs. I think the whole skeleton is here!'

'Is that all?'

'What do you mean 'is that all'? This is the best thing we've found so far. Are you expecting a whole cemetery?'

Samuel still didn't know what he hoped to find, but anticipation rippled across his entire body. There was something here besides the skeleton, something important.

He stepped closer to where Tim had discovered the bones, repulsed yet compelled. A viscous, soggy substance was glued to black clumps of unidentifiable debris. Samuel told himself that it was only leaves and moss, even though the knowledge that at least some had to be decayed clothes and flesh tugged at the back of his mind.

When Samuel leaned closer and turned over a layer of sludge, the reek of rot rose. He pinched his nostrils closed with one hand, but when he took another gasping breath, he gulped a putrid taste of decay. Something was there; he was sure of it. And he was too close to stop now.

Samuel peeled back a wet layer. Something smooth and red poked through the sludge. The lamplight flashed across it, sparkling like a gemstone in the gloom. Suddenly, the tension that had been humming through Samuel's body disappeared.

Tim's voice came from over his shoulder. 'What's that?'

'A stone, I think.'

'Some kind of stone, innit?' Wonder edged Tim's voice.

Samuel's nerves flared when Tim reached to push back the rest of the sludge, revealing a gleaming red stone about the size of Samuel's hand. Samuel wanted to snap at Tim not to touch it. Instead, he forced himself to say something more neutral. 'We should be careful with it.'

'No kidding.' Tim leaned closer to inspect it. 'Blimey, what a find. I reckon it's valuable, right? A ruby, maybe?'

Samuel didn't know what it was, but for some reason, he thought it was more valuable than a gemstone. He pried it from the mound of sludge, the surface as smooth as glass. Raising it to the light, the red item seemed to flicker like it contained a flame. Tim reached for it, but Samuel jerked it away. 'It's not a ruby.'

'No need to get testy.' Shadows pooled in Tim's face. His lips were drawn into an uncharacteristic frown. 'We're brothers, and we both found it, so we'll share the benefit, right?'

'Of course,' Samuel rushed to say. Even to his own ears, the words sounded somewhat hollow. 'We should go up so I can examine it.'

Tim cast him another narrow-eyed expression as he led the way out. The only sound was the splashing of water as they left the cave and then the soft thud of their shoes against the wet stone staircase that ran down the hill towards town. Samuel took a deep breath, filling his lungs with crisp, sea-laced air.

'Whose skeleton was that, do you reckon?' Tim asked as they turned onto Croft Road where townspeople were going about their business. A few curious gazes trailed over their mud-soaked clothes, and hands drifted up to plug noses. 'A poor old chap who got lost wandering these tunnels?'

The red item pulsed silently in Samuel's hand, but he forced himself to focus on Tim's question. 'He could've been one of the smugglers who used these tunnels in the mid-eighteenth century. Whoever he was, he's long dead.'

Tim stopped suddenly, turning to face him. 'Well, let's see it, then.' Again, he reached for the item.

Samuel stepped back, holding it behind his back. 'I need to conduct a scientific investigation.'

'Why can't I see it now?' Tim's already uncharacteristically serious expression darkened. 'You're not planning on keeping it for yourself, are you?'

'No, I already told you—'

'Then let me see it.' Tim lunged for him.

Samuel threw up a hand, intending only to defend himself, but something soft and squishy cracked. Something warm and wet rained down.

Samuel's heart dropped into his stomach. He looked up at Tim, whose expression had crumpled into anger as blood poured down his nose. Clutching the red item, Samuel spun, making a run for the Sinnock Square passageway.

A hand closed on the back of his shirt, yanking him to a stop.

Nasally and laced with fury, Tim's voice hissed into his ear. 'Let me see it!'

'I found it.' Samuel tried to twist away, but Tim's grip held firm. 'It was my idea!'

'You wouldn't have made it down the stairs without me, you cowardly bastard.'

'You're just too dumb to understand the fear of consequences,' Samuel shot back.

'Give it to me!' Tim pulled Samuel back with one hand, scrambling for the item with the other. 'GIVE IT HERE!'

Hot, angry words bubbled from Samuel's chest. 'No, you selfish oaf, you'll spoil it with your stupidity.'

The collar of his shirt twisted, and Tim threw a punch, which landed with a thud against Samuel's ribs. Pain flared, only further fuelling the rage thundering through his veins.

'Everyone knows you're the stupid, irresponsible brother, even ask Father—' Samuel's words were cut short as Tim yanked him back. His feet slipped over the cobblestones as he was dragged down Sinnock Square, heading back to the Farrow family's shop on the High Street.

They seemed unaware of the other pedestrians who paused to watch. There was an anger about Tim, a sort of violence that no one had ever seen before—and it was mirrored in Samuel.

Everyone ventured speculations about what had come between the brothers, whispering in disapproving tones about the vindictiveness they had witnessed. It seemed odd, didn't it? But then again, brothers were often competitive, were they not? No one was properly worried until several days had passed without any sign of Samuel. Then rumours started to fly.

Tim was still around, traipsing from pub to pub, but there was something strange about him. He stopped meeting with friends, and he sat at the bar, slumped over an empty pint glass, his gaze unfocused.

The authorities were informed, of course, and though they searched the Farrow shop and flat above, they found only that Samuel's belongings were gone. He had run off, Tim claimed.

Of course, it was unusual for a reserved young man like Samuel to suddenly be so impulsive, but he was a strange lad, was he not? And did anyone really know him? Most people thought he'd finally had enough of Tim and ran off. But a sense of unease settled over the property like a fog. Nothing tangibly wrong, just a dark feeling. John Farrow passed away a few years later, and then Tim sold the building and moved to the countryside.

It was a post office and then a general store, but a few years later, the shop was put up for sale again. A few potential buyers poked around, but no one put in an offer. For some reason, most people felt uncomfortable there. Fewer and fewer came until finally, it was boarded up in the 1930s.

Thirty years later, an entrepreneurial young woman decided to buy the derelict property and renovate it. In the flurry of stripping cracked plaster and pulling up warped floorboards, she found several coffins left from the Farrow's family business. They were in various stages of completion with the lids unattached—except for one.

Even without knowing the story of the Farrow family, the young woman suspected something was wrong. A chill filled the room when she wrenched off the lid with a crowbar, and she was saddened but somehow unsurprised to find the decayed remains of a corpse inside.

Given the sagging grey flesh and lack of photographs from the mid-eighteenth century, it was impossible to identify the body's previous occupant. However, based on an assessment of the rotting clothes, age, and gender, many people believe that Samuel never made it out of the family home.

Upon discovering the corpse, the uneasy feeling that lingered over the property faded. Those who are prone to believing in this sort of thing claim that Samuel's last wish was simply to be found, and now that he has, he can finally be laid to rest.

The item the Farrow brothers found deep in the Saint Clement's caves, if it ever existed at all, has never been seen or heard of again.

THE FIRE
AT
SAINT CLEMENT'S CHURCH

Story Twelve

Dorothy 'Dot' Fuller was a witch. Everyone said it, some more publicly than others. But it was true. Her grandmother had taught her about the calming, protective properties of lavender. Her mother was equally spiritually inclined and taught her how to hang Hag Stones, pebbles with a doughnut-like hole through the middle, on her bed frame to ensure only the good dreams reached her.

As the granddaughter and daughter of witches, it was only natural that Dot had a similar preoccupation with things that could be felt rather than known. And what better time for it than the 1920s? Europe was enthralled by the mysticism of the occult, which was a welcome respite from the cold, soulless efficiency of the Industrial Revolution.

And Dot was no amateur; she had attended seances and learnt to use an Ouija board. She even had an elaborate deck of Tarot cards in the modern Art Deco style. However, it was one thing to dabble in the occult with her friends, who only ever asked questions about the young men they fancied or whether their parents would allow them to drive the family's new motorcar. It was entirely another to seriously consider a venture into the dark world of black magic. But an irresistible opportunity presented itself with the arrival of a strange bald man with wide bulging eyes, Aleister Crowley. He seemed wholly average and unassuming in most respects, but his strange eyes swirled with a hypnotic intensity.

Dot's mother had met Aleister Crowley at one of the clandestine meetings she attended during a full moon and warned Dot to stay away from him. There was something dangerously ambitious about his form of occultism, she said. Witchcraft was more akin to spirituality, and the power came from being one with the natural world, but Aleister Crowley wanted more than that. What exactly, she never specified. Unfortunately, there was nothing more appealing for a teenager like Dot than doing precisely what her mother had told her not to do.

Dot discovered that Aleister Crowley was staying in the flat above the Anchor Inn. For several days, she hung around George Street, pretending to peer into shop windows as she glanced up at the curtained windows above the pub. Occasionally, Dot saw Aleister Crowley dressed in a dark overcoat, returning from an errand with a newspaper or loaf of bread tucked under his arm. Every time she tried to approach him, he shuffled away before she could think of something to say.

Her curiosity grew until one night, it bubbled over. It was impossible to say why exactly she chose that night to slip out of bed, crawl out her window, and return to the Anchor Inn on George Street. She later described it as a compulsion—a feeling of dread wrapped in the incorrigible desire to glimpse something few living souls had dared to imagine, much less witness.

When Dot arrived at the Anchor Inn, lamp light filtered through the lace curtain in one of the windows. A shadow passed in front of the curtain, illuminating Aleister Crowley's unmistakably slumped, lumpy silhouette for a moment. Then the light flicked out, and the window went dark.

Dot's stomach tightened with a strange mix of disappointment but relief. Perhaps she could return to her bed and wake up tomorrow with only the vague, dream-like memory of this misguided venture. Before she could creep down the street, she heard a door creak. As the door to the Anchor Inn inched open, Dot darted into a dark twitten and pressed her back against the brick wall. Footsteps sounded from the pub, coming to a stop in the middle of the street.

She sucked in a breath, her heart racing. Had she moved quickly enough?

A moment later, the footsteps started again. This time, they headed towards the High Street.

Dot peeled herself away from the wall and tiptoed after the sound. As she slipped onto the street after him, she saw Aleister Crowley's somewhat round figure, now wrapped in a flowing black robe. Her hair stuck to the sweat that had beaded on her forehead, and her nerves buzzed, but that need to know propelled her to follow as Aleister Crowley continued down the High Street. He turned down Swan Terrace that ran between the Swan Inn and Saint Clement's Church.

The murmur of voices came from the other side of the church, and Aleister Crowley walked towards them with steady steps. Dot darted after him, keeping to the inky shadows that pooled in doorways or under the outstretched branches of trees. He rounded Saint Clement's Church on Croft Road, and Dot continued to creep after him. The flickering orange light of fire pressed back the darkness and illuminated crooked headstones emerging from a sea of long grass in the cemetery. Gnarled branches of trees framed a scene of robed figures gathered around a fire.

One voice untangled itself from the shapeless murmur as Aleister Crowley approached. Dot ducked behind a bush, peering at the cloaked figures between the branches.

'Welcome, High Priest Crowley,' someone said. 'We are ready to begin.'

Dot's heart pounded as her mind raced with possibilities. Would they summon spirits of the dead or use their mysterious powers to bring a horrendous curse on someone? She'd heard that Aleister Crowley, despite being English, had visited countless places from India to China, and Algeria to France, searching for new knowledge into the spiritual world. He had amassed a small but intensely devout following. What kind of dark secrets had he uncovered?

The cloaked figures circled the fire, congregating around one who held something about the size of a coconut between two hands. It was covered by a cloth, but another lifted it to reveal the smooth, glossy surface of what looked like a piece of glass. Firelight flashed across the item, and it glowed red.

'Excellent,' Aleister Crowley murmured. His voice echoed in the silence of the hushed crowd. 'Let us begin.'

The cloaked figures shifted as the one with the ball of red glass raised it above his head. Again, it caught the light, seeming to absorb it like an orb. A long moment of silence stretched over the cemetery, and then someone began to chant, 'Awake and breathe; free yourself.'

The other voices rose to join it. 'Awake and breathe. Free yourself.'

The cloaked figure lowered the glowing glass ball into the fire. 'Awake and breathe,' filled the air. 'Free yourself.' The flames leapt higher when the glass ball entered the fire, thrashing. Sparks flew.

A scream pressed at Dot's lips, but she clamped both hands over her mouth to keep it from bursting out. The firelight bathed the cloistered cemetery and narrow street in an orange light that seemed to wipe away all sense of modern life. This street was hundreds of years old, thousands of feet had walked on these cobblestones, and countless stories had played out in the buildings. It was a maze of experiences and lives, layered like strokes of a paintbrush. Most of the time, one could only see the veneer of the topcoat, but the truth was that these stories still bubbled under the surface.

Dot felt the rush of time racing past, giving new lives a brief but wonderful moment to thrive as if on the crest of a wave. Then, just as suddenly, the ruthless current of time dragged them down, burying them beneath the weight of another era that would undoubtedly come and go with the same burst of impatience.

The fire grew until it was almost as tall as the buildings that surrounded the cemetery. Smoke billowed up in a thick cloud as dense as cotton. Surely, they would be able to see this blaze all the way in France.

As if awakening from a spell, the awareness of how foolish this was washed over Dot. She should have listened to her mother and not meddled with anything more than her grandmother's folk tales, lavender, and Hag Stones. A wall of warmth pressed against her as she staggered back a few steps, but she felt a twig under her foot as she did.

Suddenly, the roar of the fire stopped. Darkness swept over the cemetery like a curtain. Dot's heart dropped as the twig under her foot snapped with an unmistakable crack.

'What was that?' came a low voice.

'It came from over there!' said another.

Dot's mind emptied of everything except the cold, hard press of fear. She whirled around and started to run, but an ear-splitting screech stopped her in her tracks. Every muscle taut, she rotated back towards the cemetery. Amongst the swirling grey tendrils of smoke, Dot glimpsed wings beating and a flash of red scales. The screech came again, echoing down Croft Road as the creature gained height. It swooped overhead, and for a moment, Dot saw the great body of what looked like a winged lizard cut against the star-speckled night sky. Wings pumping, it headed towards the East Hill and disappeared over the rooftops of the Old Town.

Dot started after it, but with her eyes on the sky, she didn't notice the loose cobblestone until it was too late. Everything blurred and went black. An indeterminate time later, light flooded her eyes. She struggled to sit up. A group of people surrounded her, including the police officer whose torch was burning her eyes.

'Did you see it?' Dot blurted.

'Everyone in town saw the fire, you silly girl! Why didn't you call for help?' Dot thought she recognised the voice as belonging to one of the shopkeepers on the High Street.

'No, I mean—did you see it? It flew...' She raised a hand to shield her eyes as she orientated herself. It had flown towards the East Hill, had it not? 'Over there!'

The crowd exchanged murmurs, and the officer kneeling beside her asked, 'Did you start the fire? It's better to tell the truth now rather than for us to figure it out on our own.'

She shook her head. Who cared about the fire when a creature was flying across the town? And not just any creature. Her heart pounded at the thought of it. A dragon. 'Someone else must've seen it!' Dot leapt to her feet. 'I can't be the only one!'

'Careful,' the officer told her. 'You seem to have hit your head.'

'Maybe we should take her to the hospital,' someone said.

Other voices muttered their agreement.

'You don't understand!' Dot tried to push through the crowd, but someone caught her arm. 'We'll lose it if we don't—'

A familiar voice cut through the crowd's objections. 'Dorothy Jane Fuller! What on earth do you think you're doing?'

Dot froze. Her mother was not to be toyed with, especially not when she used Dot's full name.

'You'd better have a good excuse for being out so late.' Her mother's voice was tight with disapproval. 'And you'd better not have had anything to do with that fire.'

'It wasn't me! I followed Aleister Crowley here, and there were people in cloaks and then—'

Her mother's eyebrows rose so high that Dot worried they would disappear into her hairline. 'Dorothy Jane Fuller, you did not sneak out to follow Aleister Crowley.'

A stone formed in the pit of Dot's stomach, which only worsened when the officer told her that no one had seen Aleister Crowley or anyone, cloaked or otherwise, in the area. Fortunately, the scorched side of the building adjacent to the cemetery indicated the fire had been caused by a lightning strike, so at least she wasn't blamed for that. Dot's mother took her to the hospital, and a nurse found a bruise on her head where she had fallen. Perhaps the lightning strike had scared her, and she'd tripped. That would explain the strange hallucinations.

But Dot wasn't convinced. She returned to the Anchor Inn the next day to confront Aleister Crowley about what she had seen. The innkeeper was confused. No one by the name of Aleister Crowley had ever stayed there, and there was certainly no one in the room now.

Dot insisted on checking the room where she'd seen the light the night before but found only a neatly made bed and untouched room, ready for the next guest. Since then, she would often explore the East Hill in case the dragon remained, but she never found any sign of the creature.

She spent years compiling evidence about the mysterious event she had seen that night, stretching all the way back to before the Battle of Hastings in 1066. There are too many gaps in the story to say for sure, but if Dot's account is correct, the dragon's egg was passed from hand to hand for more than 1,000 years. Perhaps it was the dragon's impatience to hatch, but the egg brought bad luck to anyone who possessed it.

However, the streak of back luck seemed to have dissipated after it hatched. But where the dragon went, if it was not simply a hallucination, remains unknown. The dragon has joined Hastings' many sinister stories of lingering spirits and legends of mysterious mists and creatures at sea as the sort of tale that will raise sceptical eyebrows and usher in an abrupt, decisive change of conversation topics. Few people were willing to listen to Dot's theories, and even fewer believed them. It would have been enough to drive anyone to madness.

Fortunately, the Untruth Seekers invited Dorothy Fuller to join us. You see, madness is not only allowed but is a strict prerequisite. The results of Dorothy's tireless research about Hastings have now been released to the world and is, in fact, the document you currently have in your hands. If these stories seem too far-fetched to be true, then we would kindly remind you that truth is indeed stranger than fiction.

Afterword

Are you still with us, dear reader? If so, we would like to express our most sincere gratitude for making it through this maze of tales.

We would be unspeakably grateful for a review if you enjoyed the stories. If you cannot find anything redeeming about this collection, we will also be happy with a negative review. Nothing is worse than being ignored, forgotten, and left to sink silently to the bottom of Amazon's rankings.

On the other hand, if these stories have whetted your appetite for ghost stories, we have also created a haunted trail map for a self-guided tour across Hastings.

You can find the haunted trail map at:
http://www.untruthseekers.co.uk

Please also consider following us on our Instagram account:
@UntruthSeekers

Here, we will share more secrets of this seaside town, including supernatural stories from readers like you!

Printed in Great Britain
by Amazon

The Lighthouses of Wales

Tony Denton and Nicholas Leach

▲ The lighthouse at the end of Holyhead Breakwater.

◄◄ (Front cover) The Skerries lighthouse off Anglesey.

◄ (Frontispiece) Bardsey lighthouse.

Published by
Foxglove Publishing Ltd
Foxglove House
Shute Hill
Lichfield
Staffs WS13 8DB
England
Tel 01543 673594
nicholas.leach@foxglovepublishing.com
www.foxglovepublishing.com

2nd edition © Nicholas Leach and Tony Denton 2011

The rights of Tony Denton and Nicholas Leach to be identified as the Authors of this work have been asserted in accordance with the Copyrights, Designs and Patents Act 1988.
All rights reserved. No part of this book may be reprinted or reproduced or utilised in any form or by any electronic, mechanical or other means, now known or hereafter invented, including photocopying and recording, or in any information storage or retrieval system, without permission in writing from the publishers.

British Library Cataloguing in Publication Data. A catalogue record for this book is available from the British Library.

ISBN 9780956456052

Layout and design by Nicholas Leach
Printed by Jellyfish Solutions Ltd, Swanmore, Hampshire

Contents

Welsh Lighthouse History 4

Guide to Welsh Lighthouses 11
Redcliffe 12, Charston Rock 13, The Shoots 14, Gold Cliff 16, East Usk 17, West Usk 18, Monkstone 20, Flatholm 22, Barry Dock 25, Nash Point 26, Porthcawl 30, Swansea 32, Mumbles 33, Whitford Point 36, Burry Port 38, Saundersfoot 39, Caldey Island 40, Milford Haven 42, St Ann's Head 46, Skokholm 50, Smalls 52, South Bishop 56, Strumble Head 58, Fishguard 62, New Quay 64, Aberystwyth 65, St Tudwal's 66, Bardsey 68, Llanddwyn Island 70, South Stack 72, Holyhead Admiralty Pier 76, Holyhead Breakwater 78, The Skerries 80, Port Amlwch 84, Point Lynas 86, Trwyn Du 88, Great Orme 90, Point of Ayr 92

Glossary 94

Appendix 95
Bibliography, Websites, Acknowledgements

Index 96

Welsh Lighthouse History

1717
First rock lighthouse in Wales at Skerries

1737
First island lighthouse in Wales on Flatholm

1776
First pile lighthouse built on Smalls Rock

1794
Last coal-fuelled open fired lighthouse in Britain at Mumbles

1821
Bardsey Lighthouse the tallest square tower in British Isles was built

1839
The oldest unaltered lantern still in use in a lighthouse in England and Wales erected at South Bishop

1866
The only wave swept cast Iron tower left in Britain was erected at Whitford Point

1874
A fog-light incline at South Stack to raise and lower fog signal

1916
Last lighthouse built with traditional materials completed at Skokholm

1993
Glassfibre lantern fitted at Monkstone

1995
St Tudwal's lighthouse last in Wales to be electrified

1998
Nash Point becomes last lighthouse in Wales to be demanned

This book provides a comprehensive round-the-coast guide to the lighthouses and harbour lights on the coast of Wales, from south to north, starting with the lights in the Bristol Channel and going north and then west, ending at the Dee estuary. The Welsh lighthouses form a distinct and compact group which includes some notable architectural towers of historical significance.

While the Corporation of Trinity House is responsible for most of these lights, including all the major ones, many significant small harbour lights are also in operation, and details of these have been included. This introduction provides a general overview of lighthouse development and organisation in England and Wales, focusing on the need for lights to mark the Welsh coast, and looking at how Trinity House has developed into the service it is today.

The first lights

Trading by sea has been a principal activity of all civilisations, yet moving goods and cargoes by water involves facing difficulties and dangers such as storms and bad weather, avoiding reefs, headlands, sandbanks and cliffs, and making safe passage into ports and harbours. The need for aids to navigation is therefore as old as trading by sea itself and, today, modern lighthouses operated by Trinity House are supplemented by a plethora of small, locally-operated lights of varying sizes and range, mainly around ports, harbours and estuaries, to aid the safety of vessels.

The earliest aids to navigation were beacons or daymarks sited near harbours or ports rather than on headlands or reefs, to help ships reach their destinations safely. The earliest lighthouses were in the Mediterranean and the oldest such structure of which written records survive was that on the island of Pharos, off Alexandra on Egypt's north coast. The Pharos lighthouse, which stood 466ft tall, was built between 283BC and 247BC and lasted until 1326.

The exact site and date of the first navigational lights to be shown from a part of the modern Welsh coastline are not known, although a Roman date has been suggested for possible lighthouse towers at both Flint and Holyhead. However, without firm evidence of any Roman building, it is probable that a medieval lighthouse at St Ann's Head was the oldest such structure in Wales. The next oldest was that at The Skerries off the north-west tip of Anglesey, followed by Flatholm in the Bristol Channel.

The development of lighthouses around the coasts of the British Isles mirrored the development of trade routes. The earliest British lights were situated on the south and south-east coast of England in order to assist vessels trading with France and north European ports. By the seventeenth century, the emphasis had changed, with lights along the east coast

▲ The lighthouse built in 1829 on Caldey Island is still operational, although the attached cottages are now leased as holiday homes.

established to help colliers carrying coal from ports in the north-east to London.

The changes in port usage are reflected in the evolving pattern of lighthouse construction. The expansion of trade through Bristol, passing South Wales, was also significant and led to the building of the light on Flatholm. While Bristol declined, the great coal ports of South Wales expanded, and eventually the impressive natural harbour of Milford Haven became a major port in the area, along with smaller ones at Swansea, Cardiff, Newport and Barry, all requiring their own aids to navigation.

Colonial trade involving west coast ports expanded during the eighteenth and nineteenth centuries, and came to be dominated by Liverpool, although London remained the largest port. The port's expansion, which created the need for lighthouses, was considerable; between 1772 and 1805 inward shipping, largely from America and the West Indies and including cargoes such as tobacco and sugar, increased from 77,000 to 331,000 tons, while the ignominious slave trade also played a role in port expansion.

As Liverpool expanded, to manage and run the port's affairs, the Liverpool Harbour Authority was set up in 1762 which, with its successor the Mersey Docks and Harbour Board, was responsible for the establishment and maintenance of a number of significant lights on the approaches to the Mersey, many on the Welsh coast from Anglesey eastwards.

The dominance of the Liverpool trade alongside the Welsh coast is illustrated by the evidence of the lighthouse dues collected from ships passing Smalls lighthouse in Pembrokeshire in 1831-32. From ships docking in Liverpool £11,206 was collected, while trade to Swansea, Neath, Bristol

Lighthouse History

▼ The Point of Ayr lighthouse overlooking the Dee estuary as modified in 1820. Now disused, the tower remains but the attached building has been demolished.

and Beaumaris was only worth £1,000 and £1,600 in dues for each port. Trade from Belfast, Dublin, Wexford, Cork, Glasgow, London and Hayle was worth between £100 and £1,000 in dues paid.

Trinity House

The organisation responsible for the operation and maintenance of the major aids to navigation today is the Corporation of Trinity House. The exact origins of Trinity House are obscure, but probably date back to the early thirteenth century when groups of tradesmen, such as seamen, masters of merchant vessels and pilots, formed guilds to protect their interests.

One of the earliest such organisations was the Deptford Trinity House, which was incorporated by Royal Charter after its members had petitioned Henry VIII to prohibit unqualified pilots on the Thames in 1513. Deptford was then a busy port and the main point of entry for the capital's trade, so pilotage duties were lucrative and Trinity House members wanted to retain their monopoly. Another similar organisation was the Trinity House at Newcastle-upon-Tyne, which was responsible for early aids to navigation on the Tyne at the time of its charter in 1536.

However, the Newcastle body's involvement in providing aids to navigation proved the exception rather than the rule as, despite erecting some towers in East Anglia, Trinity House was generally reluctant to build lighthouses. Instead it encouraged entrepreneurs to consider building them as profit-making undertakings. As a result, private lighthouse ownership became relatively widespread during the seventeenth century and the number of private lighthouses increased during the following centuries. Choosing the best position for a light, with sufficiently busy ports nearby

◀ Known as Cardiff Low Water Pier Head Light, this lighthouse was erected in 1870 and demolished in 1921 having been extinguished some years earlier. It was replaced by a light mounted on a pole.

from where revenue could be collected, was crucial for the light to yield a good return.

Although a proliferation of unnecessary lights was prevented, private light owners gained a reputation for greed and lights were built around the coast on a somewhat haphazard basis. As a result, large areas of the coastline remained unlit, and by the nineteenth century, with the level of trade increasing as Britain's industry expanded, the situation was clearly unacceptable. Trinity House had to accept the new demands, with the leases expiring on many privately-owned lighthouses forcing the Corporation to take over. In 1807, Trinity House assumed responsibility for the Eddystone light off Plymouth, and the next three decades saw considerable changes to lighthouse organisation in England and Wales.

These changes were formalised in 1836 with an Act of Parliament giving Trinity House of Deptford Strond complete authority over lighthouses and making it the body to which others, including the regional Trinity House organisations, had to apply for sanction of the position and character of lights. Although by this time the majority of English lights were under the jurisdiction of Trinity House, the 1836 Act centralised lighthouse management.

The 1836 Act also gave the Corporation the power to use a compulsory purchase order on all privately-owned lights. Although only ten lighthouses were still in private ownership, the compensation paid to owners cost the Corporation a staggering £1,182,546. The most notorious of all the patents was that dated 13 July 1714, giving William Trench permission to

▼ South Bishop is noteworthy for having the oldest unaltered lantern still in working order in Wales.

Lighthouse History

▲ A postcard from the early twentieth century showing a lighthouse at Alexandra Dock, Newport. Now demolished, this light was probably erected in 1875 when the dock was built but little more is known about this light.

build a lighthouse on the Skerries and to collect a compulsory levy from passing shipping for upkeep of the light. Skerries became the most profitable lighthouse around England and Wales and its owner in the nineteenth century, Morgan Jones II, refused to accept any offer until the matter was settled in court.

Between 1836 and 1841, he was offered £260,000, then £350,000 and finally £399,500 by Trinity House, but rejected each. However, he died in 1841 before the final negotiations were completed. A jury eventually awarded £444,984 in compensation in July 1841, thus demonstrating the considerable profits that were to be made from lighthouse ownership. Even after Trinity House took over The Skerries and halved its levy, the light still made a huge profit.

By the mid-nineteenth century more ships traded along the west coast and around Wales than anywhere else, and consequently the dues paid to the owners of The Skerries lighthouse and Smalls lighthouse were greater than those paid to any other in the UK. In 1852 £23,000 was paid for the use of Smalls light, about £18,000 for The Skerries, while other lighthouses in the British Isles raised about £5,000 or less in annual revenue. By 1822 the standard lighthouse due collected at British ports was one farthing per ton.

Once all the private lighthouses had been taken over, Trinity House gradually assumed control of lighthouse maintenance and construction during the nineteenth century. During the great period of lighthouse construction between 1870 and 1900, Victorian engineers and designers constructed and modernised at least fifty stations and built new rock towers. Lighthouses were also established at the major ports, and the major harbours of Holyhead and Fishguard,

8

developed in the nineteenth and early twentieth centuries respectively, both had significant lighthouses built to help guide ships in and out of port.

Harbour lights

Much of the literature about lighthouses focusses on the major lights, which are often impressive structures in spectacular locations. However, no less important are the many smaller lights found at most ports and harbours. They have developed in response to specific local circumstances, so their design, construction and purpose differ markedly and the variety of such lights around England and Wales is considerable.

Many harbour authorities are responsible for their own aids to navigation, and this has led to a variety of lights and beacons being erected. Some ports, where vessels need to follow channels, have leading or range lights which, when aligned, mark a safe passage. Others have long piers or breakwaters, the limits of which need marking, and on these some of the finest light towers have been constructed, such as that at Fishguard.

In areas like the north-east of England, where trade between ports was competitive, new harbours were built with grand lighthouses to mark their entrances, such as at Tynemouth and Whitby. In other areas, such as Wales where the main trade was in raw materials, more modest lights were erected at places such as Burry Port and Barry Dock. The growth of passenger vessels saw ports such as Fishguard and Holyhead vie for trade and build new harbours with lighthouses.

▲ The light on the east bank of the river Usk is typical of the smaller lights that help guide ships into a specific port.

▲ The small light marking the entrance to the port of Swansea.

◀ The lighthouse at the end of Holyhead Breakwater when it was manned. Originally operated by Trinity House, it is now under the auspices of the port authority Stena Line.

9

▲ Situated on the cliff edge, Nash Point high light was operated in conjunction with a low light until the 1920s to mark the Nash Sands, and is one of the most impressive towers on the Welsh coast operated by Trinity House.

▶ The lighthouse on the Admiralty Pier at Holyhead dates from 1821 and was designed by John Rennie.

Lightkeepers

Throughout the history of lighthouses, the lightkeeper has played an essential role in maintaining the light and keeping the lighthouse in working order. However, during the latter half of the twentieth century, the era of manned lighthouses came to an end as automation took over. Before automation, however, every light had to be manned.

The idealised view of lighthouse keepers conjures up a somewhat romantic image of men living in a tower with only the sea for company. While this was accurate for remote rock stations, such as Smalls, where keepers were confined to fairly cramped quarters for weeks at a time, the reality for most keepers was a little different. The lights on the mainland had a senior keeper who would be supported by two assistant keepers, usually with families. With automation, the lights are controlled from a central location with a locally-based attendant who is responsible for the general maintenance of the station.

The lighthouses of Wales

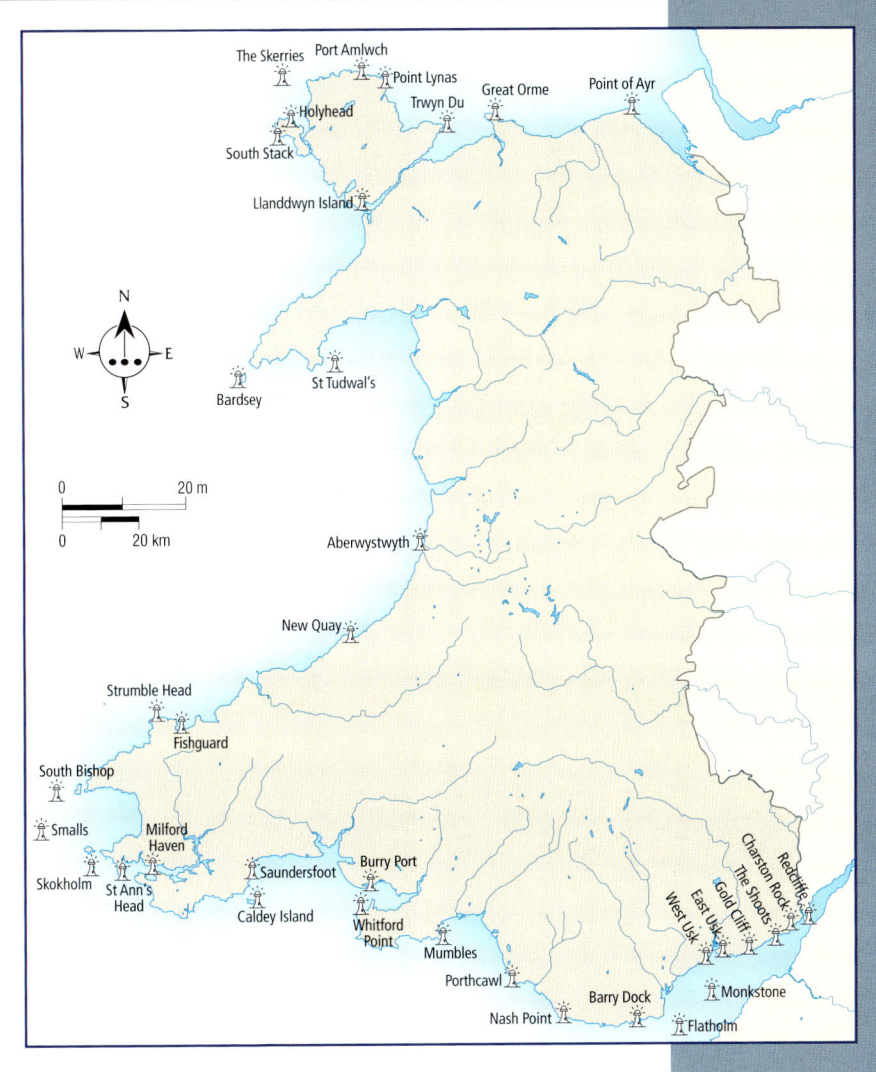

The lighthouse entries start on the south coast with the lights in the Bristol Channel on the Welsh side, and go west and then north to Anglesey, then east to the Dee estuary, ending at Point of Ayr. The photographs show the lighthouses as they are today, and a number of historic images have also been included. The information about visiting the lighthouses should be used only as a starting point, and it is advisable to consult road maps and Ordnance Survey maps if visiting any of the places.

11

Redcliffe

ESTABLISHED
1886

CURRENT TOWER
1910

OPERATOR
Gloucester Harbour Trustees

ACCESS
By walking down a long public footpath from Mathern Church across Caldicot Level

Situated on the shore about a mile north of Charston Rock, Redcliffe light was erected by the Great Western Railway Company in 1886, and in conjunction with the Charston Rock light formed a pair of leading lights through the Shoots, a narrow channel offshore. The fixed white light, powered by oil, was mounted on a wooden post.

The Gloucester Harbour Trustees, who took over responsibility for all aids to navigation previously owned and maintained by the Sharpness Lighthouse Trustees on 1 January 1891, commenced a programme of improvement and in 1910 they replaced the pole with a 33ft lattice steel tower. It was converted to acetylene gas with a flashing white light in 1926 and converted to electricity in 1965.

Following complaints that it was difficult to see, the white flashing light was changed to red for an experimental period in 1927, but was returned to white flashing and remained so until 1966 when it was changed to fixed blue. In 1982, when a back light was installed, the intensity of the light was increased by the installation of eight fluorescent tubes. A series of vertical white daymarks were also added to the mast.

The back light, situated 150 yards behind, consists of a 100ft abacus column with a bank of six blue fluorescent tubes. The Gloucester Harbour Trustees converted these and a number of other lights on the river to blue following complaints from local boat owners of background light pollution levels.

▼ This light was erected at Redcliffe in 1886 and is situated on the shore a mile north of Charston Rock.

Charston Rock

ESTABLISHED	1886
CURRENT TOWER	1886
OPERATOR	Gloucester Harbour Trustees
ACCESS	Best seen from the river, but it can also be viewed from the Black Rock picnic area east of Portskewett

As vessels pass upstream along the river Severn towards Gloucester, they have to manoeuvre through a narrow channel offshore from Portskewett called the Shoots. To mark this channel, a pair of leading lights was erected by the Great Western Railway Company. The front light, although correctly called Charston Rock, is sometimes referred to by the name of the adjacent Black Rock.

Built in 1886, the 23ft white-painted stone tower had a vertical black line. Maintained by Sharpness Lighthouse Trustees, the oil-burning light was operated in conjunction with Redcliffe to show a channel through the Shoots.

On 1 January 1891 the Gloucester Harbour Trustees took over responsibility for all the aids to navigation previously owned and maintained by the Sharpness Lighthouse Trustees, including Charston Rock and Redcliffe. The Charston light was converted to acetylene in 1926 and, in 1966, to battery power using the lantern and lens from Redcliffe. The light showed an all-round beam with reinforcement on the leading edge. In 1980 the lantern was removed and replaced by an all-round lens powered by batteries and solar power.

Over time, a number of complaints were made about the light's visibility, and between 1927 and 1928 it was changed to red flashing. However, since then it has shown white flashing with the intensity increased to today's values, which give a five-mile range with a leading edge range of eight miles.

▼ The light on Charston Rock, offshore from Portskewett, seen from Black Rock picnic area.

The Shoots

ESTABLISHED
1891

CURRENT TOWER
1986

OPERATOR
Gloucester Harbour Trustees

ACCESS
Easiest by boat, but distant views are possible from the west bank of the river Severn to each side of the Second Severn Crossing road bridge

The Gloucester Harbour Trustees, being aware of the need for good marking of the navigable channel, looked at the Shoots and, although the channel was marked by the leading lights at Charston Rock and Redcliffe, thet erected two pole beacons in 1891 known as the Upper and Lower Shoots Beacons. One beacon was on the western extremity of the English Stones, and the other on the edge of the high rock north of Sand Bay.

In 1892, the Upper beacon was removed and relocated on the edge of the rock just above the Lake. These beacons were significant as they were the first aids to be erected by the Trustees outside their area of jurisdiction. In 1949 a report suggested the lighting of these two beacons, as the lower beacon was two miles south of Charston Rock light and a light would greatly aid those entering the channel. However, although a request for loan monies was made in 1951 nothing was forthcoming, so the plan did not go ahead. In 1965 a further request to light the beacons resulted in the improvements to Charston Rock and Redcliffe described earlier.

The decision in 1986 to build a second Severn road crossing meant that the Shoots channel would be even more hazardous as vessels would need to alter course to avoid the new bridge's supports. As a result, four 53ft reinforced concrete beacons were erected in addition to lights on the bridge. The beacons were formed from pre-cast concrete rings with a concrete platform. The lights were powered by mains, wind or solar and from north to south are:

Lady Bench: a red column supporting a solar powered quick flashing red light. This is the front light, with Lady Bench Rear mounted on a steel gantry on one of the road bridge supports.

Old Man's Head: a yellow column with a black band supporting a solar-powered very quick-flashing white light, giving nine flashes every ten seconds.

Mixoms: a red column supporting a solar-powered flashing red light, giving three flashes every ten seconds.

Lower Shoots: a yellow column with a black band supporting a solar-powered quick-flashing white light, giving nine flashes every fifteen seconds.

▶ The Lady Bench light seen from the picnic area at Black Rock, with the Lower Shoots beacon beyond the road bridge, a supporting column of which can be seen far right.

▲ This yellow column, situated on the east side of the channel to the north of the motorway bridge, is known as Old Man's Head.

◄ The most northerly light in The Shoots Channel, situated on the west side of the channel, is known as Lady Bench.

15

Gold Cliff

ESTABLISHED
1924

OPERATOR
Newport Harbour Commissioners

ACCESS
Approached by taking road from Newport through village of Goldcliff then turning right to park; a short walk west along the embankment brings you to this small tower

This unique light is situated on a grassy bank just south of the village of Goldcliff to the south of Newport. Operated by the Newport Harbour Commissioners, it consists of a 9ft oblong sheet steel box with a pyramid roof. There is no lantern and the simple light is mounted on top in a circular lamp holder. Erected in 1924, the mains electricity-operated white light had a range of six miles when it was operational.

Some indication of its age can be gauged by the fact that it was powered by mains electricity, but it has been redundant for several years judging by the condition of the steel. The light originally marked the most southerly part of the headland to the east of the river Usk, where a channel passes close inshore of the Welsh Grounds. The erection of the beacon on Denny Island probably influenced the decision to disconnect this light.

▶ The deteriorating light at Gold Cliff stands near the cliff edge on the most southerly point of the headland to the east of the river Usk.

East Usk

Situated on the river bank east of the Usk, where the river joins the Bristol Channel, the East Usk lighthouse is operated by Newport Harbour Commissioners. It was erected in 1893 by the Commissioners and housed a second light at the mouth of the river to indicate the channel which, at that time, was close to the east shore. The light was operated in conjunction with the older light on the opposite bank at West Usk. The lighthouse on the east side of the river consists of a 36ft white prefabricated cylindrical steel tower mounted on six screw-pile legs.

The tower is topped by a gallery and a hooded lantern, which houses an electrically-powered flashing white light marking Sea Reach Channel with red and green sectors to either side. The light, visible for fifteen miles, is under the supervision of an attendant. The area around the tower is a nature reserve.

ESTABLISHED
1893

CURRENT TOWER
1893

OPERATOR
Newport Harbour Commissioners

ACCESS
Take the road from Newport to Uskmouth Power Station, park in the nature reserve car park; then a walk through the levels of the reserve and the lighthouse can be easily seen

◄ Situated on a nature reserve to the east of the river Usk, this light is the only operational one of what was originally a pair marking the entrance to the river.

West Usk

ESTABLISHED
1820

CURRENT TOWER
1820

DISCONTINUED
1922

ACCESS
Now a bed and breakfast, reached via the B4239 from Newport towards St Brides, then turning left after two miles through a farm gate and following a winding track to the lighthouse

Ships entering the port of Newport encounter a dangerous tidal race off St Brides where the rivers Usk and Severn meet, and this tidal race is the second fastest in the world. To guide vessels in the area, a patent for the construction of a light was first sought in 1807. This original application came to nothing, but in 1820 it was renewed and Trinity House subsequently commissioned a lighthouse on what was then an island on the west bank of the river Usk.

Correctly called West Usk lighthouse, it is also known as St Brides. The lighthouse, the first designed by James Walker, was a slightly tapered 56ft circular brick tower with gallery and lantern. Two lights, visible for eleven miles, were displayed from the lantern, one white and one red, with another white light 14ft lower down on the tower.

Some time before the end of the nineteenth century, keepers' dwellings were added in the form of a two-storey oval building surrounding the tower. This unusual structure is something of an architectural gem, particularly given the fact that it was James Walker's first lighthouse.

Although the brick buildings and tower were rendered and painted white, the lantern, complete with its conical roof, was painted black. The light was discontinued in 1922 and the lantern removed. The lighthouse was then cropped at gallery level and a shallow pitched roof added, while the cast iron gallery railings were retained.

Because of its location, the whole structure was mounted on a circular bed of solid granite blocks with a cast iron handrail. The handrail was cut off just above ground level after the light was decommissioned. In 1995, the present owner purchased the deteriorating building and restored it. The pitched roof was removed from the tower and a replica lantern installed with a cone-shaped roof, not dissimilar to the original, apart from the structure being painted white.

▶▶ In its current much altered state, the West Usk lighthouse has a replacement flat roof and a replica lantern.

▶ (left) An old photograph showing the West Usk lighthouse in its operational days.

▶ (right) This bell currently hangs at the door to the West Usk lighthouse, which is now a bed and breakfast establishment.

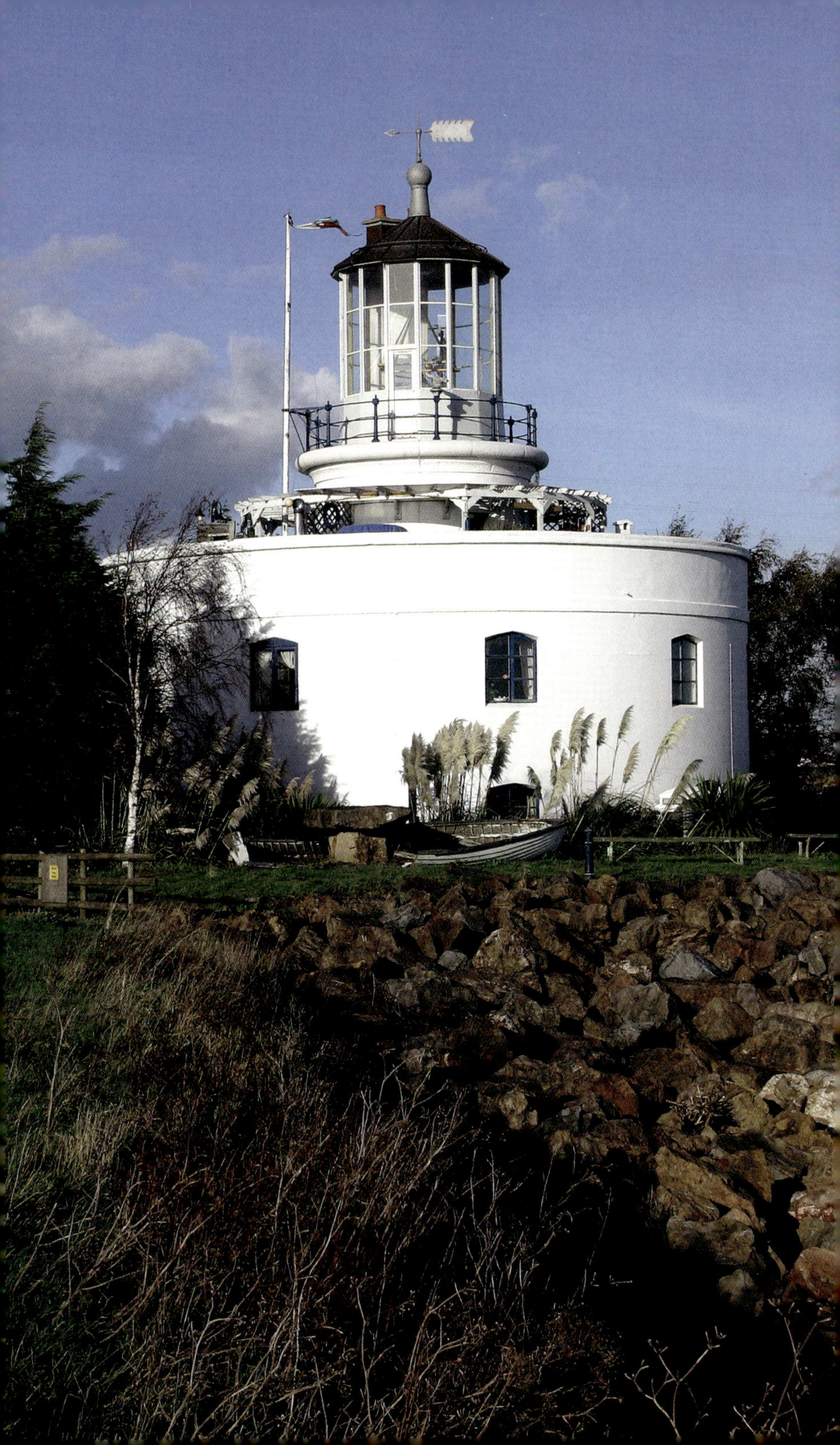

Monkstone

ESTABLISHED
1839

CURRENT TOWER
1993

OPERATOR
Trinity House

ACCESS
Can only be reached by boat

▶▶ Monkstone lighthouse at high water.

▼ The Monkstone lighthouse at low tide, with its unique fibreglass extension standing on a rock visible at low tide.

The Upper Bristol Channel is subjected to the second largest tidal range in the world. This makes it a difficult channel to navigate even and it is usual for vessels visiting ports such as Avonmouth, Sharpness and Gloucester to take on a pilot before entering the channel. The first navigational aid is the lighthouse on Flatholm Island.

Three miles upriver from Flatholm is Monkstone rock, a submerged reef which only breaks the surface at low spring tides. Located near to Flatholm Island, about three miles east-north-east of Lavernock Point and five miles south of Cardiff, it is one of many hazardous obstacles to shipping in the area. Other hazards include sandbanks, which are passable with care only at high tide, but are exposed at low water.

The lighthouse on Monkstone therefore not only marks the rock but also forms a reference point for the other hazards. The original 45ft granite tower, built in 1839, was an unlit beacon. However, in 1925 it was strengthened and fitted with a circular cast iron tower complete with a gallery, an iron lantern and an automatic acetylene light. The stone tower was reinforced with both horizontal and vertical iron bands which, along with the new tower and lantern, were painted red.

In 1993 it had a unique update when the iron tower and lantern were replaced by a red prefabricated 30ft cylindrical fibreglass unit. Mounted on top in polycarbonate lamp holders are main and auxiliary twenty-watt halogen lights powered by solar panels mounted in a vertical formation on the circumference of the fibreglass tower. This increased the height of the lighthouse to 75ft and improved the range of the flashing white light, which gives one flash every five seconds, to thirteen miles.

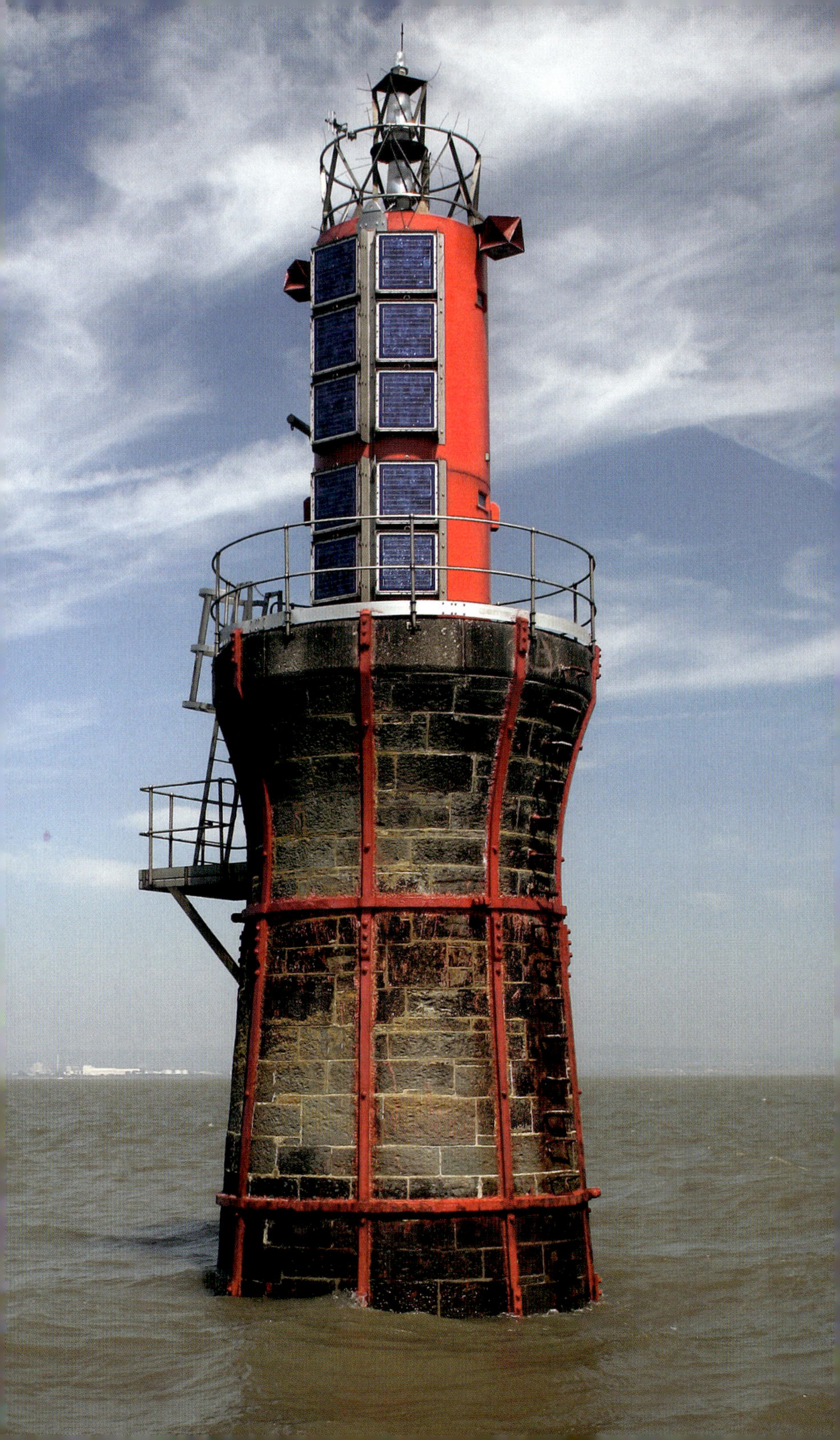

Flatholm

ESTABLISHED
1737

CURRENT TOWER
1820

AUTOMATED
1988

OPERATOR
Trinity House

ACCESS
Visiting the island, an historical and nature reserve, is possible via boat trips from Barry Dock

▶▶ The impressive lighthouse at Flatholm dates from the eighteenth century.

▼ The island of Flatholm, dominated by the lighthouse, is the most southerly point of Wales.

The area of water known as the Mouth of the Severn lies partly in England and partly in Wales, with the ports of Avonmouth and Bristol on the English shore and Cardiff, Newport and Chepstow on the Welsh side. There are a number of aids to navigation on both shores, but for the purpose of this volume only those on the Welsh side will be described.

As ships travel upstream, the first hazard is the island of Flatholm, the most southerly point of Wales, which lies approximately three miles south-east of Lavernock Point in the centre of the shipping channels where the Bristol Channel meets the Severn Estuary. It is perhaps surprising therefore that considerable wrangling took place before a light was displayed there. As early as 1733, John Elbridge, a member of the Society of Merchant Venturers of Bristol, petitioned for a light but to no avail.

In 1735, William Crispe informed Trinity House, he had taken a lease on the island and wished to build a light in their name but at his expense. He did of course wish to recoup his costs from ship dues. This again was rejected, but, after sixty soldiers were drowned in a wreck near Flatholm in late 1736, a further proposal by William Crispe was accepted and a 70ft stone tower was built on the summit.

Its coal light was first displayed on 1 December 1737. The elevation of the coal burner was such that it was the greatest in Wales, with only Flamborough Head in England exceeding it. Unfortunately for Crispe and his partner, they went bankrupt and handed the lease to Caleb Dickensen. In 1790 a severe lightning storm damaged the lighthouse and for a time the light had to be displayed from ground level.

Following complaints about the inadequacy of the light, Trinity House took over the lease in 1819. By 1820 they had increased the height of the white stone tower to 90ft and installed a lantern and an oil-fired Argand lamp with reflectors which

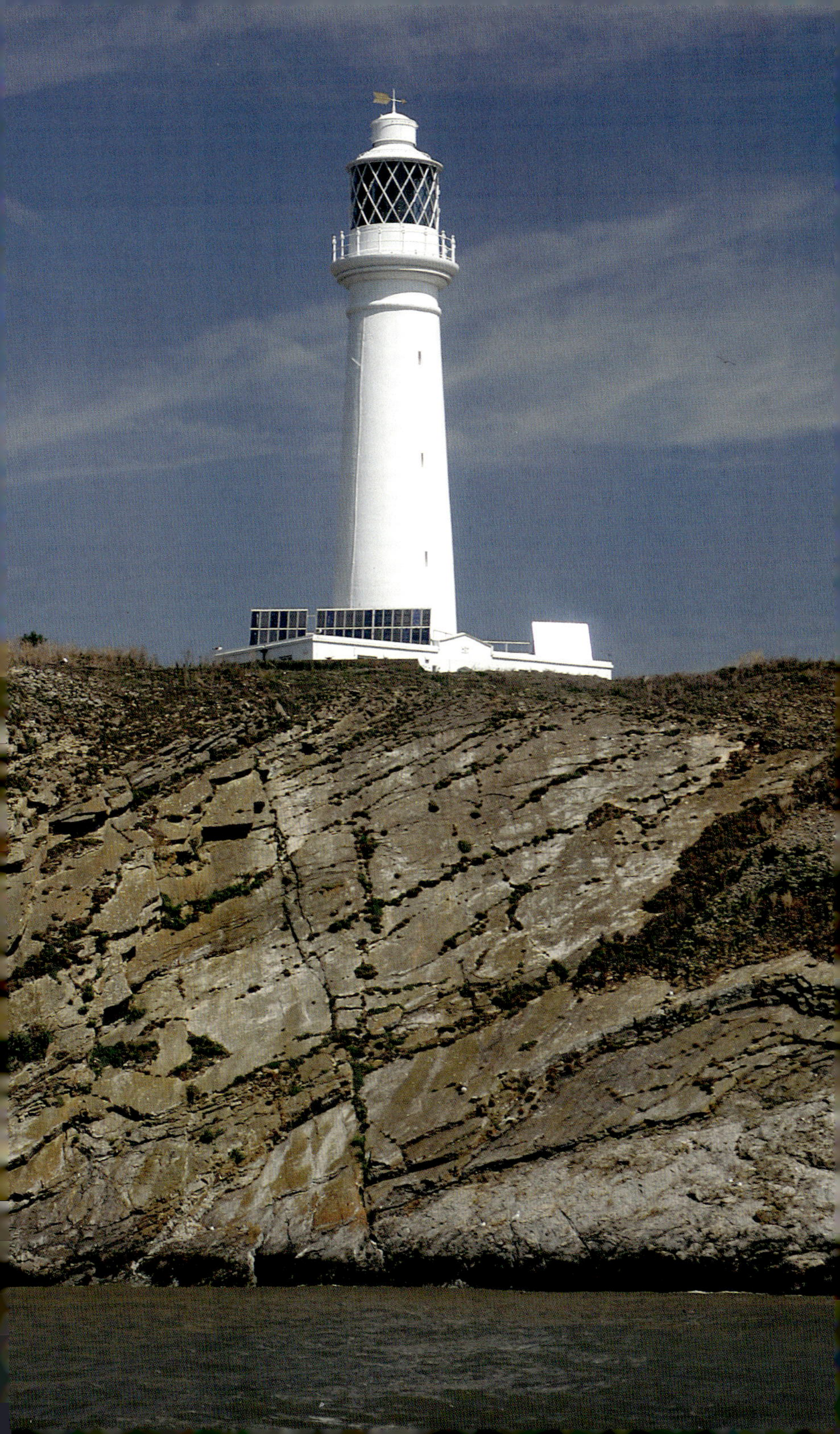

Flatholm

▶ Line drawings showing the successive adaptation of the lighthouse at Flatholm. The original eighteenth century structure has survived, with the walls almost 7ft thick at the base. The rebuilding of 1867 increased the height of the tower to almost 100ft.

1737   1820   1867

displayed a fixed white light. In 1825, the height of the light was increased by a further 5ft and a fountain oil lamp installed.

Further alterations were made in 1866 at which time a new iron gallery was fitted to the top of the stone tower and a larger lantern with a more powerful optic was installed. This increased the height of the lighthouse to 99ft. The light characteristic was altered to occulting in 1881. A Douglas multi-wick burner was installed in 1904 to improve matters, and in 1923 this was superseded by a Hood paraffin burner.

Equipment rooms were attached to the tower and the keepers' families were housed in cottages next to the lighthouse. In 1929 the lighthouse was redesignated a rock station and the families were withdrawn. The keepers left in 1988 when the station was automated, and in 1997, the lighthouse was converted to solar power. The flashing white light is visible for fifteen miles, with a red sector visible for twelve.

Barry Dock

In the nineteenth century the South Wales coal trade had expanded to such an extent, and the Taff Vale railway and Cardiff docks were so congested that they virtually ground to a halt. As a result, in the 1880s a new port was opened at Barry Dock.

As part of this development, a stone breakwater was built out from Barry Island, and in 1890 a 30ft white circular iron tower with gallery and lantern, complete with cupola roof and weather vane, was built on the end by Chance Brothers to a standard design. Painted white with a red lantern roof, it shows an electric quick-flashing white light visible for ten miles.

ESTABLISHED
1890

CURRENT TOWER
1890

OPERATOR
Associated British Ports

ACCESS
Breakwater closed to the public, but local anglers fish from the end; access to the dock is via a long flight of steps from the main road above

◀ The small lighthouse on the end of the Barry Dock West Breakwater is fenced off by palisade fencing topped with razor wire to prevent vandalism.

25

Nash Point

ESTABLISHED
1832

CURRENT TOWER
1832

AUTOMATED
1998

OPERATOR
Trinity House

ACCESS
Near St Donat's, the light is reached via the B4237 through Monknash, then along a toll road; the keepers' dwellings are holiday cottages

▶▶ Nash Point Low Light and the adjacent keepers' cottages have been converted into holiday homes

▼ The Low Light when in service, with the High Light under construction.

The entry to the Bristol Channel is impeded by a series of sandbanks known as Nash Sands, where the channel begins to narrow at the headlands between Porthcawl and Barry and making navigation for shipping more hazardous. In February 1830 an application to build an aid to navigation to mark the area was made by Thomas Protheroe, of Newport, together with a number of other owners from the Bristol area and, as a result, they established a pair of range lights at Nash Point about three miles east of St Donats in 1832. Designed by James Walker, they were built by Joseph Nelson, who died a year after their completion.

The High Light, situated to the east, is a 122ft cylindrical stone tower complete with gallery and lantern. Initially it was painted with broad black and white horizontal bands, but it was repainted white when the Low Light was disconnected. In 1851, manning levels at Nash were increased and the attached keepers' dwellings added.

In conjunction with the Low Light, it showed a fixed white light over the safe passage with a red light over the sands. When it became the sole light, the light configuration was amended to occulting white visible for sixteen miles with a red sector visible for ten miles. The lantern was glazed with rectangular panes but in 1867 it was replaced by a delicately glazed helical lantern as seen today.

The Low Light was situated about 300 yards to the west, and consisted of a white-painted 67ft conical tower complete with lantern and gallery similar to the high light. Unlike the High Light, the attached keepers' dwellings were erected in 1832 when the light was commissioned. Its light

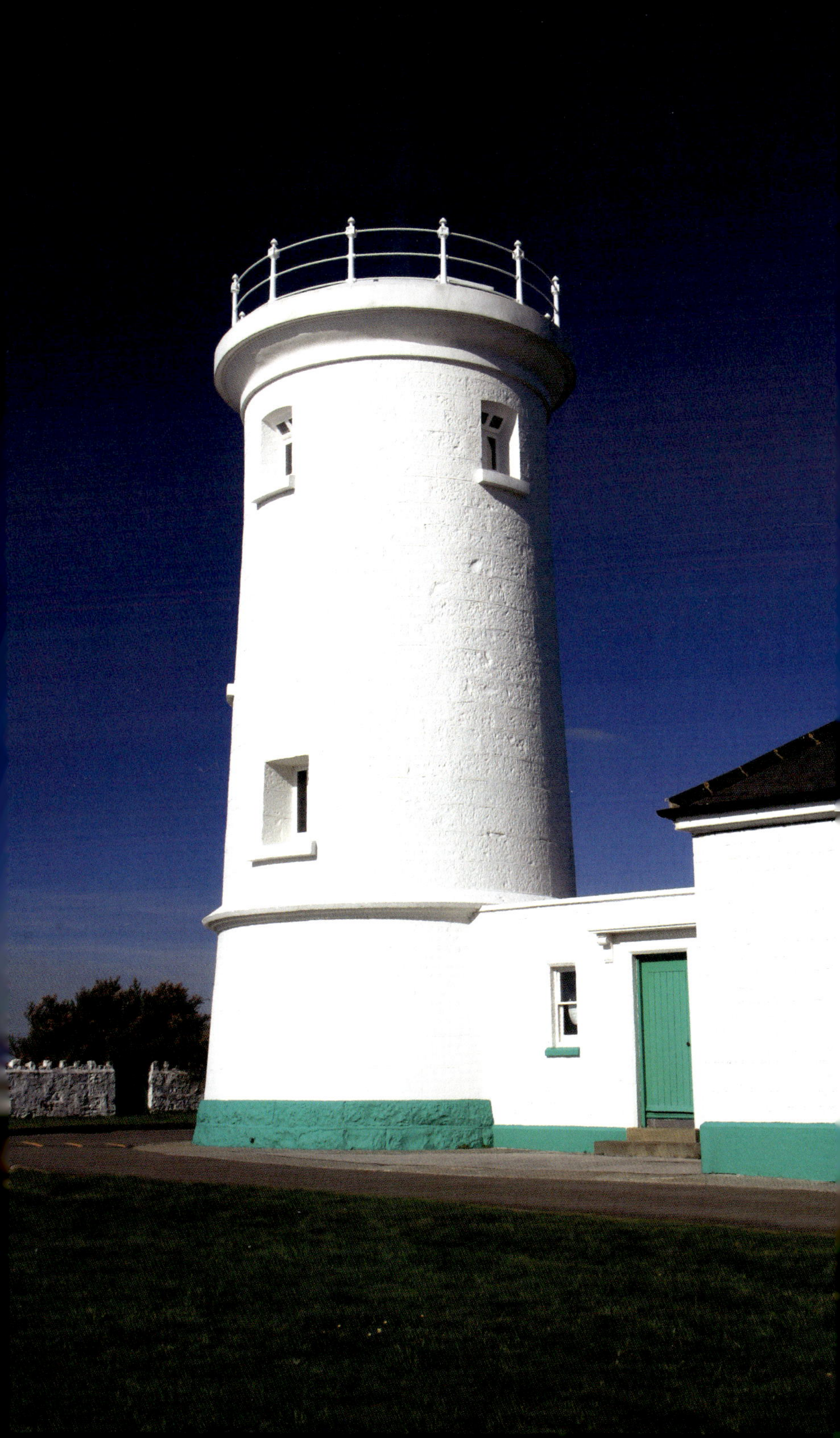

Nash Point

▶▶ Nash Point High Light was the last operational lighthouse in Wales to be automated, and regular tours of the lighthouse are carried out most weekends.

▼ The imposing fog horn, on the roof of the compressor house, is often activated during visitor tours. The building is situated between the two towers.

characteristics were identical to the High Light, as were the optics. It was discontinued in the 1920s when the High Light was reconfigured. By the 1970s, the lantern had been removed.

The original lights consisted of double rows of reflectors with thirteen Argand burners in the high light and twelve in the low light. When the high light was electrified in 1968 the Argand burners were replaced by a rotating optic. Today a 1,500-Watt lamp and a first order catadiotric fixed lens with two reinforcing panels gives a group flashing light twice every fifteen seconds with ranges of white, twenty-one and red sixteen miles.

Nash Point was the last South Wales lighthouse to be demanned with the light automated in 1998 and the keepers withdrawn two years later. For a while during the automation programme the station controlled Mumbles and Flatholm lighthouses as well as Breaksea Light Float.

The 1903-built Ruston Hornsby 20hp generator and fog signal compressor from the station were acquired by Leicester Industrial Museum in 1966. The modern foghorn is mounted on top of a white square flat-roofed engine room to the seaward side of the road, half way between the high and low lights and is sounded during the weekend visitor tours. In 1977, after the tuberous thistle was found on the site, the area inside the compound was designated a Site of Special Scientific Interest.

28

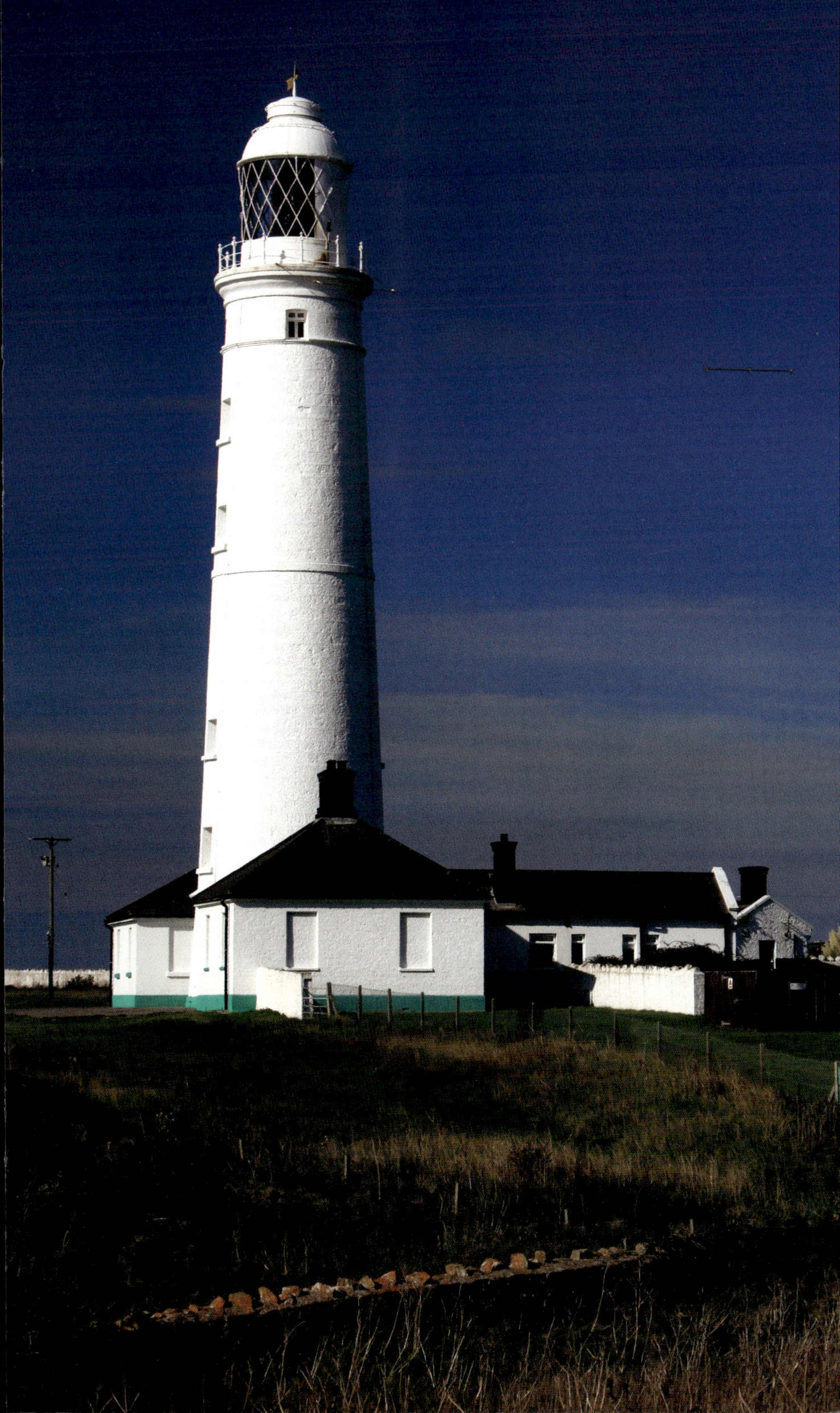

Porthcawl

ESTABLISHED
1860

CURRENT TOWER
1911

OPERATOR
Bridgend County Council

ACCESS
By walking along the breakwater, which in bad weather and strong winds can be very dangerous

▶▶ The small lighthouse at the end of Porthcawl breakwater.

▼ Heavy seas crash on the breakwater.

Although the harbour at Porthcawl was established in 1825 to service the metal trade, it was not until 1860 that a lighthouse, called Porthcawl Breakwater Light, was erected on the end of the stone breakwater. Although appearing ordinary at first glance, it is in fact one of only two surviving cast iron lighthouses in Wales. It consists of a 30ft hexagonal tapered tower without a gallery. Access to the light is via a cast iron doorway and an internal ladder.

When first commissioned, the light shone through a plain opening and the top had a pitched roof. It was painted to imitate a stone structure. The light was replaced in 1911 by the current arrangement; the top was removed and a replacement round-domed lantern with a Chance Brothers optic was crudely attached to the top of the tower.

The light, visible for six miles, is displayed through a glazed window and shows a fixed white light over the channel with red and green sectors to the sides. It was coal- and then gas-fired and, in 1974, it was converted to mains gas. It was eventually electrified in 1997, making it one of the last in Wales to be so converted. The tower is currently painted white with a broad black band at the base.

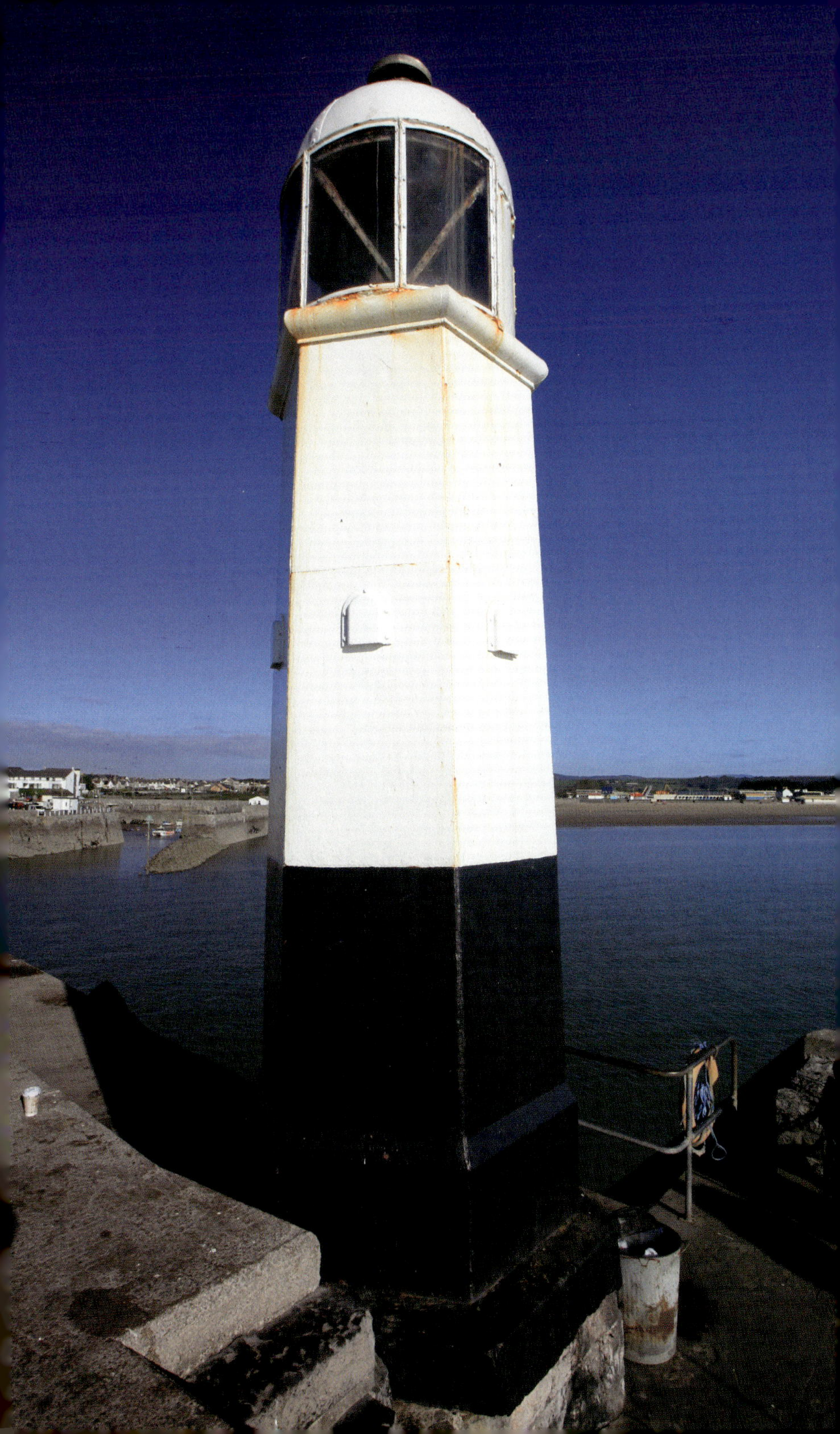

Swansea

ESTABLISHED
1792

CURRENT TOWER
1909 and 1971

OPERATOR
Trinity House

ACCESS
The lights are part of the dock complex which is difficult to access, although they can be seen from the outside of the marina

Although no lighthouses can be seen at Swansea today, a number of interesting lights have been built here. In 1792, when the west pier was to be built, a lamp was erected on a post at its proposed termination. In 1803, with the pier complete, a 20ft cast-iron octagonal tower was erected on the end. Designed by William Jernegan and cast at Neath Abbey, it stood on a stone plinth and had a small octagonal lantern. It was lit by candles in 1810, then by oil in 1845. Maintained by Swansea Harbour Commissioners, it was moved to the end of the pier when the pier was extended in 1878.

In 1909 the pier was again extended and the light replaced by a cast iron lantern with a domed top mounted on a wooden platform supported by a wooden trellis. In 1971, the east pier was reconstructed in reinforced concrete and a light, called Swansea East Pier, consisting of a concrete post with a simple light, was erected on the end. Showing a flashing red light, it is visible for nine miles.

In the early nineteenth century a 20ft white tower was built on the end of the inner east pier. In 1909 it was replaced when the pier was extended and a light, which still exists, was erected on the end of this structure. This consists of a 23ft wooden framework supporting a simple lantern showing a fixed green light, which is visible for seven miles. These lights are within the dock complex and are difficult to approach.

The first-order Fresnel lens, which was installed at Mumbles Head lighthouse, was given to the Swansea Transport and Industrial Museum in 1987. It is not on display but kept in storage at the museum. Between 2002 and 2005 the museum was rebuilt as the National Waterfront Museum.

▶ On display as a floating exhibit at the National Waterfront Museum is the old Helwick Lightship No.91, 104ft in length and built in 1937 by Philip & Son, Dartmouth. It has a hexagonal tower complete with lantern and gallery.

Mumbles

To guide ships past the Mixon Sands and Cherry Stone Rock, where hundreds of ships have been lost, Swansea Harbour Trustees were given a licence to erect a lighthouse on the outer of the two outcrops at Mumbles Head in the late eighteenth century. Work started in 1792 but in October that year the partly-constructed lighthouse collapsed.

Plans for a new light by William Jernegan, a local architect who had also been responsible for the Swansea light, were drawn up and in 1794 Trinity House gave the harbour trustees a ninety-nine-year lease on the lighthouse, which was completed later that year. In addition to the tower, a pair of two-storey keepers' houses was built. Two coal-fired lights were proposed, one above the other, to be distinguishable from the two lights at St Ann's Head and the single light at Flatholm. Thus came about the peculiar shape of the 56ft white stone octagonal tower, which is stepped halfway up, with a gallery at each stage.

Keeping two coal fires lit was expensive and so in 1799 a single oil light, with Argand lamps and reflectors in a cast iron lantern above the higher of the two galleries, was fitted. By the Act of 1836, the light was taken over by Trinity House which had further improvements carried out in 1860, when a dioptric light was fitted. The lens was configured in such a way that there appeared to be two beams of light, which partly simulated the original configuration.

In 1905 the characteristic was converted to an occulting light, and to produce the flashing light a hand crank was used to wind a series of weights. These were attached to a lever mechanism

ESTABLISHED
1794

CURRENT TOWER
1794

AUTOMATED
1934

OPERATOR
Trinity House

ACCESS
At low water, it is possible to walk from the beach by the pier across to the island, but the rocky terrain is not easily crossed; best viewed from the pier or the car park on the headland with vantage points along the adjacent coastline

▼ Mumbles lighthouse is surrounded by the remains of the Palmerston's fort.

Mumbles

▶▶ The Mumbles lighthouse is accessible at low tide but, as can be seen from this photograph, it is only possible to reach it with great care and no little effort.

that raised and lowered a metal cylinder around the light, but within the Fresnel lens, thus making the light appear to flash. The periods of dark and light could be adjusted to give different light characteristics.

Further changes were made in 1934, when, on the retirement of the last keeper, the station was modernised and the optic replaced. In 1969 an overhead electricity line was erected from the mainland and the light converted to electrical operation. By 1977 the original cast iron lantern had deteriorated and was removed. It was superseded in 1987 when the lantern and light from Lightvessel No.25 was transferred to Mumbles. The original first-order Fresnel lens was donated to the Swansea Transport and Industrial Museum for display.

In 1995 the station was converted to solar power and the main and emergency lights replaced by a pair of biformed Tideland M300 lanterns powered by quartz halogen lamps, one housed in the lantern room and another above. The group flashing white light is visible for sixteen miles. At the same time, fog detector equipment was installed; the fog signal, with a range of two miles, gives three blasts every sixty seconds. Control of the lighthouse, which was the last coal-fired tower to be built in Britain, was the responsibility of the British Transport Docks Board until Trinity House took over in 1975.

Between 1859 and 1861, one of Palmerston's forts was built around the tower but it was never used for its original purpose. It was, however, used to accommodate a small battery of soldiers during the Second World War before being decommissioned in 1957. Today, solar panels for the light are fixed to the top of its remains. Also on the island are the ruins of gun emplacements, while little remains of the original keepers' dwellings which were built onto the rock to the landward side of the lighthouse tower.

▶ This historic photograph shows the now demolished keepers' dwellings at Mumbles lighthouse. The original cast iron lantern was also in place at this time.

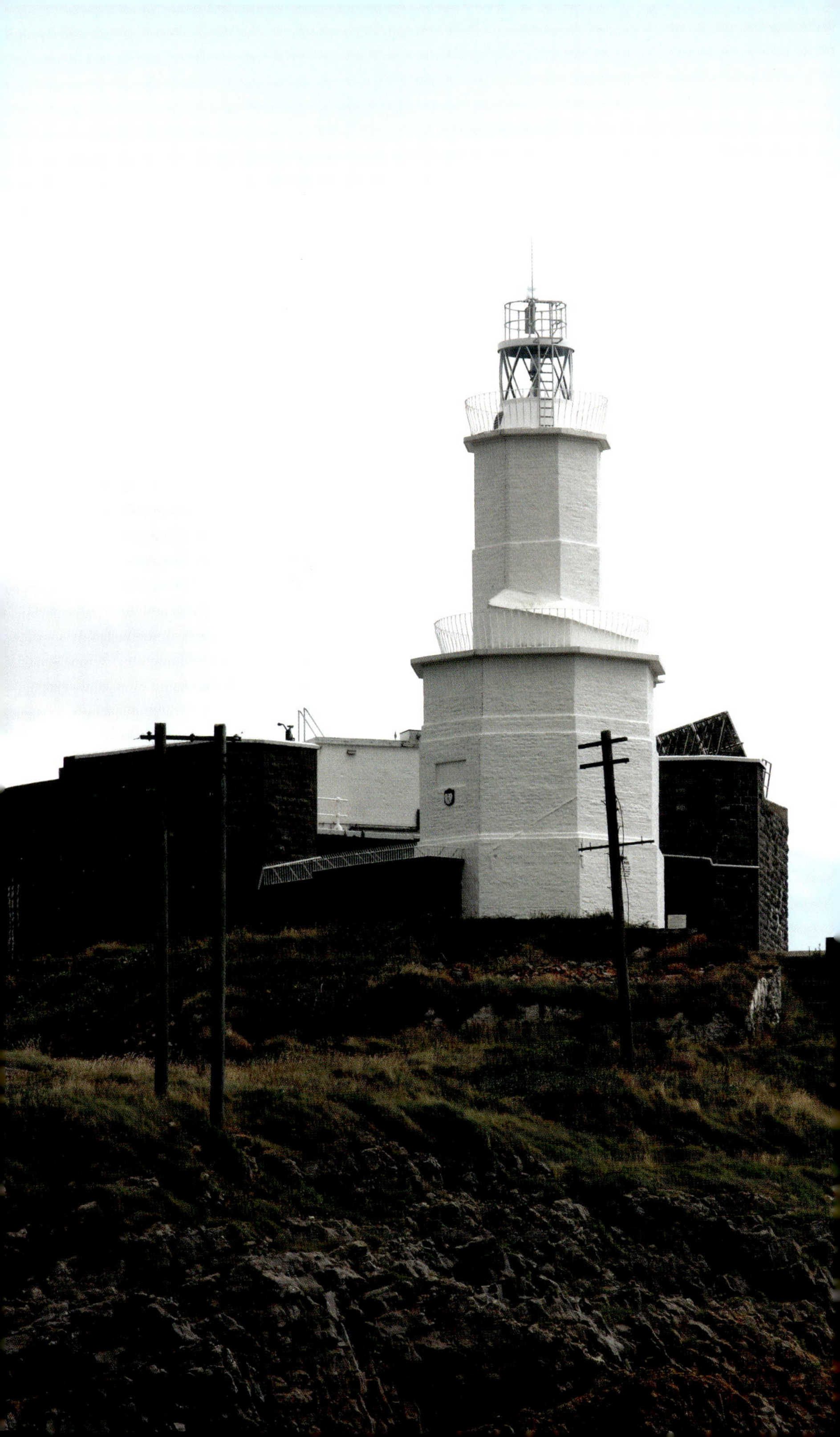

Whitford Point

ESTABLISHED
1854

CURRENT TOWER
1866

AUTOMATED
1919

DISCONTINUED
1939

OPERATOR
Llanelli Harbour Trust

ACCESS
With great care, the lighthouse can be visited at low tide by walking across Whitford Burrows, an area protected by the National Trust

In the nineteenth century, Llanelli was an important port and many ships entering the Loughor Estuary were lost off Whitford Point and its extensive sandbanks. As a consequence, Captain Luckraft, the Llanelli harbour master, designed a wooden lighthouse to be positioned about half a mile north of Whitford Point. Sometimes known as Chwittfford but more correctly as Whitford Point, it was erected in 1854 but so severely damaged by storms the following year that it had to be abandoned. After being repaired in 1857, it was later struck by the vessel Stark and extensively damaged.

By 1864 the lighthouse was such a problem that the local commissioners agreed to plans by John Bowen, a local engineer, for a new lighthouse 300 yards to the south. Built by Bennet & Co,
it was first lit in November 1866 and consisted of a 44ft ornate tapered cast iron tower with a gallery and lantern. Three Argand lamps and reflectors were fitted: one towards the Lynch Pool or south channel, one towards Burry Port, and one towards Llanelli. Its flashing white light was converted to automatic gas operation by the Llanelli Harbour Trust in 1919, after which it was visible for seven miles.

In 1921 the Trust built a new lighthouse to the south at Burry Holms, and the Whitford Point Light was extinguished in 1926. The Burry Holms light was itself discontinued in 1939.

During its operational life, the lighthouse's cast iron panels kept loosening. Bands were placed around the tower from 1880 onwards and by 1885 it was reported that 150 had been fastened round the cracking plates. The foundation on soft sand also gave concern, and concrete and stones were placed around the base in 1886. Despite these problems and seventy years of disuse, this, the only offshore cast iron lighthouse in Britain, still exists, having been a listed monument since 1979.

In 2000 the Llanelli Coastal Millennium Park attempted to save it from crumbling into the sea by offering it for sale at £1 on the proviso that the new owner repaired it. It was thought an agreement had been reached but this fell through and the lighthouse is still available to anyone willing to part with at least £100,000.

▶▶ The historic cast iron lighthouse at Whitford Point at high tide is surrounded by water. However, it can be approached at low tide by a long walk across Whitford Burrows and then with care across the beach.

▶ The lighthouse at Whitford Point is fully exposed at low tide.

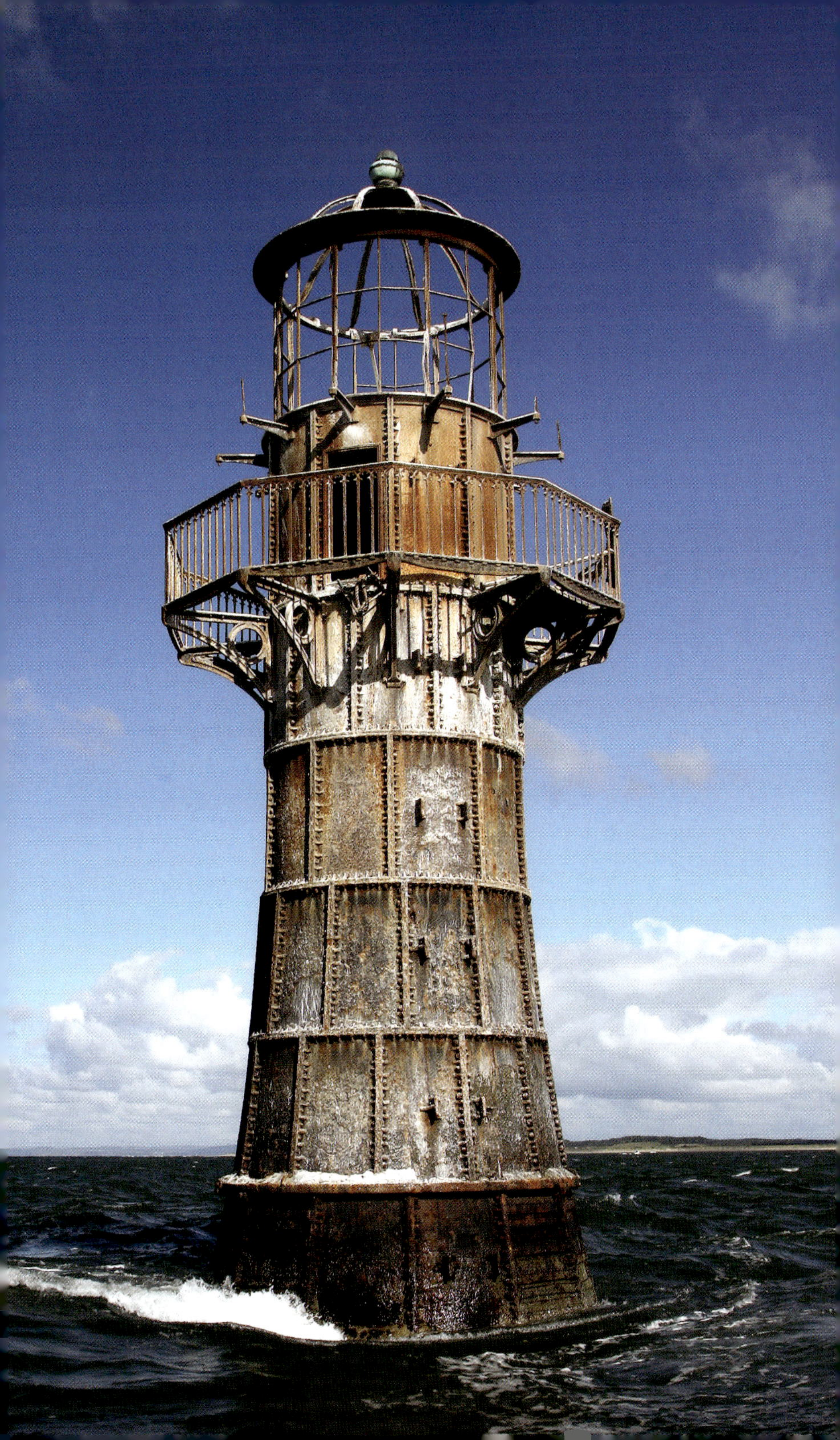

Burry Port

ESTABLISHED
1842

RESTORED
1996

OPERATOR
Carmarthen County Council

ACCESS
On west side of outer harbour by West Dock, reached via the breakwater

▼ Situated on the Western Breakwater at Burry Port, this lighthouse was fully restored in 1996 by Llanelli Borough Training.

The harbour at Burry Port was built between 1830 and 1836 to replace that at Pembrey, 400 yards to the west. In its heyday, Burry Port was the main coal-exporting port for the valleys, but now the dock houses the only marina in Carmarthenshire, for which extensive dredging was carried out in 2005.

In 1842, Trinity House gave permission for the Burry Port Harbour Authority and Navigation Commissioners to erect and maintain a lighthouse on the end of the west breakwater of the outer harbour. As this was a harbour light, the annual cost of its upkeep, which amounted to £32 in 1844, was not met by dues on shipping.

Sometimes known as Burry Inlet but more correctly Burry Port, the light consisted of a 24ft white-painted stone tower with a black gallery and red lantern. In 1995–6 the tower was restored by Llanelli Borough Training with the support of the nearby Burry Port Yacht Club, and a light, donated by Trinity House, was installed.

The restored light was formally opened on 9 February 1996 by the Mayor of Llanelli, Councillor David T. James. The current white flashing light is visible for fifteen miles. The light is now a significant landmark for the users of the nearby marina.

The neighbouring port of Pembrey Old Harbour also had a small lighthouse at one time to guide shipping into that port, but neither the light nor the port remain in existence.

Saundersfoot

The small picturesque harbour at Saundersfoot was built in the 1840s to export coal and lime from the surrounding area. In 1848 the Saundersfoot Harbour Commissioners erected an 11ft circular rubblestone lighthouse, with a door on its north side, on the end of the south harbour wall. Initially lit by candles, the light was housed in a peculiar lantern made up of iron glazing bars with an arched stone top bolted to the top of the tower.

An interesting feature was the use of a tide gauge, which consisted of a float in the harbour connected by wire to a red glass which obscured the light when there was insufficient water to enter. The light was converted to oil in 1861, as candles were considered inadequate.

The light was discontinued in 1947 following the closure of the local mines, but was relit in 1954. The old lantern was removed, the top of the lighthouse was rebuilt in rubblestone and a polycarbonate holder showing a flashing red light visible for seven miles was displayed.

ESTABLISHED
1848

CURRENT TOWER
1954

OPERATOR
Saundersfoot Harbour Commissioners

ACCESS
The pier is open to the public

◀ The small light on Saundersfoot South Pier was discontinued in 1947 but rebuilt and re-commissioned in 1954 when the port was revived as a yachting harbour used predominantly by pleasure craft. With the light holder added to the roof, the height of the structure increased to 17ft.

Caldey Island

ESTABLISHED
1829

CURRENT TOWER
1829

AUTOMATED
1927

OPERATOR
Trinity House

ACCESS
Trip boats from Tenby Harbour take about twenty minutes to reach the island and run from Easter to October, Mondays to Saturdays; the island is closed on Sundays

▶▶ The lighthouse on Caldey, which marks shoals and sands, is on the island's southern shore at the highest point.

▼ The lighthouse and its associated buildings from the landward side.

Although the lighthouse on Caldey Island is in a prominent situation on the highest point, it is the monastery that attracts most visitors. Monks first came to Caldey in the sixth century and, in the twelfth century, Benedictines from nearby St Dogmaels set up a priory on the island and remained until the Dissolution of 1536. In 1906 pioneering Anglican Benedictines purchased Caldey and built the present abbey, but their stay was relatively short, as financial difficulties forced them to sell in 1925; the present monks are of the Cistercian order.

The lighthouse, sometimes called by its Welsh name Ynys Byr, operates in conjunction with Lundy North and guides ships past St Gowan Shoals to the south-west and Helwick Sands to the south-east. Designed by Joseph Nelson and built by Trinity House in 1829 at a cost of £4,460, it consists of a 52ft circular white-painted tower with lantern and gallery. The original light consisted of twenty Argand lamps and reflectors.

A single-storey service building at its base is attached to a pair of two-storey keepers' dwellings. The light, which stands 64ft above high water, was initially oil-powered, but was automated and converted to acetylene in 1927 at which point the keepers were withdrawn and the cottages sold. The lantern itself was installed around the middle of the nineteenth century.

Caldey was the last Trinity House light to be operated by acetylene gas. A part-time keeper was employed to maintain the light until 1997 when the lighthouse was modernised and the light source changed to mains electricity. The new light is a 500 Watt halogen lamp with a second order 700mm catadioptric optic giving a flashing white light visible for thirteen miles. The light has two flashing red sectors which are visible for nine miles.

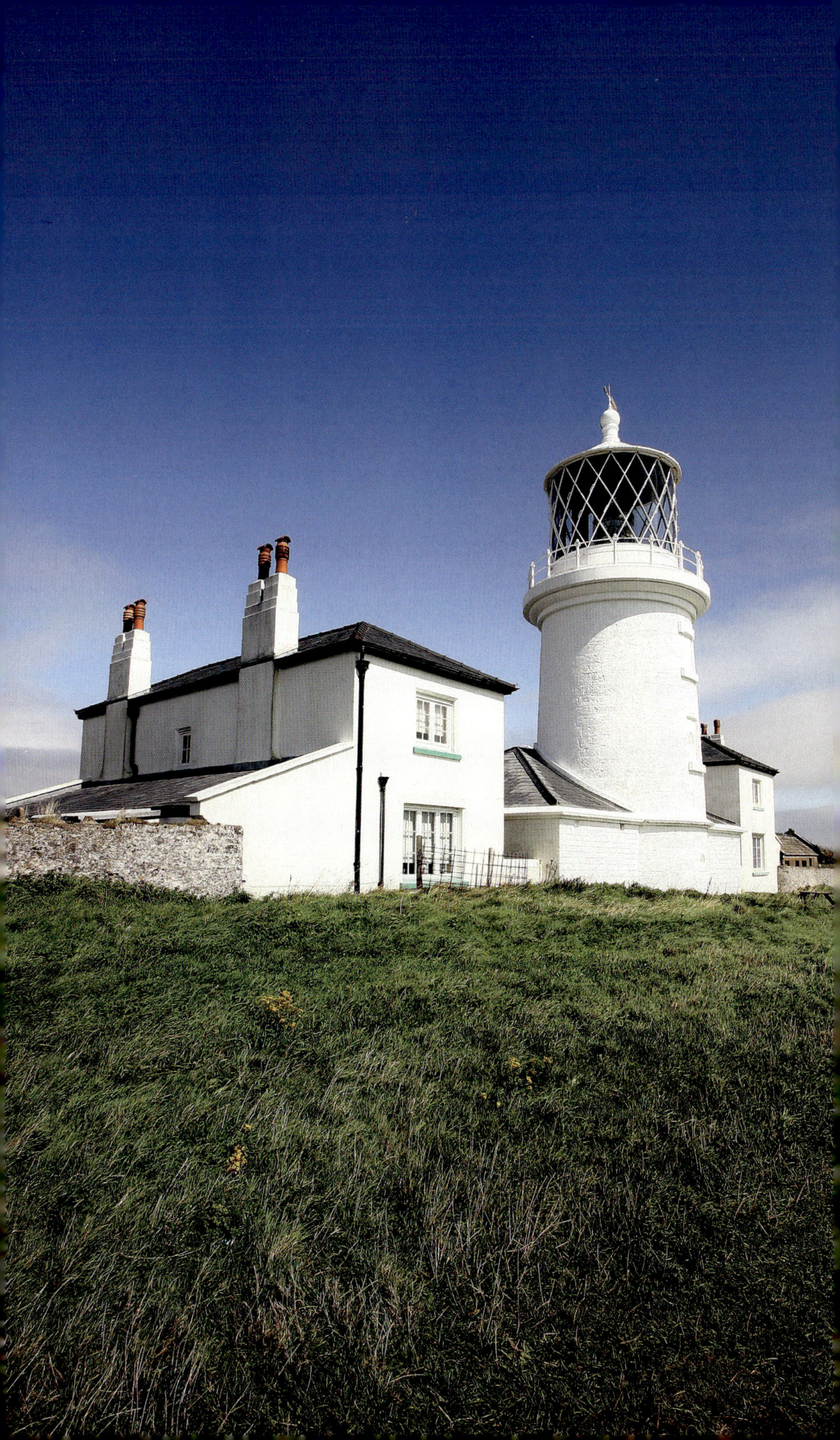

Milford Haven

ESTABLISHED
1870

CURRENT TOWER
1870 and 1970

OPERATOR
Milford Haven Conservancy Board

ACCESS
West Blockhouse and Watwick are approached via Dale then the road to St Ann's Head; turn left into Maryborough Farm road, then right to both locations; East and West Castle Head are approached via the Pembrokeshire Coast Path from St Ishmael's; turn left into Sandy Haven onto a single track road past Skerryford, then a gated path to both lights; other lights are best viewed from the Haven as they are in industrial areas

▶▶ The beacons at West Blockhouse Point at the entrance to Milford Haven, situated about a mile north-east of St Ann's Head.

▶ The range lights at West Blockhouse Point with (just visible on the cliff edge below the fort) the red beacon erected by Trinity House in 1957.

Vessels entering Milford Haven pass St Ann's Head lighthouse and then turn into the haven itself. To mark the West Channel a pair of leading lights designed by James Douglass was erected in 1870 by Trinity House on the north shore at West Great Castle Hill Head, four miles west of Milford Haven town. These lights were eventually handed over to Milford Haven Conservancy Board who operate them today.

The Front Range is a 17ft high square stone tower without a lantern situated on the cliff edge. There are dwellings at the rear. Painted white, the tower has a vertical black stripe and the buildings are trimmed with a black cornice. Of the two lights, one is shown through a narrow window and the other is a sector light on the roof. One is fixed red, white or green dependant on direction, with the other a flashing white light. Since 1970, when the lights in the area were modified, these lights have been sealed beam units visible for fourteen miles mounted on the roof alongside a radar antenna.

The Rear Range, 170 yards behind the Front Range on the ramparts of the old Iron Age fort, was a 42ft square tower of similar design without a lantern. The flashing white light, visible for sixteen miles, was shown through a narrow window, but was discontinued in 1970 when new aids to navigation were erected in the area. One of the improvements was the erection of a new light at East Little Castle Head. This new Rear Range replaced the old West Great Castle Head Rear Range light, and works in conjunction with the Front Range to mark the safe channel between St Ann's Head and the Mid Channel Rock.

The light was designed by Posford Pavy and is three-quarters of a mile from the original one. It is a curved circular 85ft white tower with a board containing a vertical black band and two lines of solar panels near the top. The sealed beam light units, which are mounted on a gallery on top of the tower, give an occulting white light visible for fifteen miles. So as not to obscure the new Rear Range, the height of the old Rear Range tower was reduced to 21ft.

Further improvements by Posford Pavy involved the

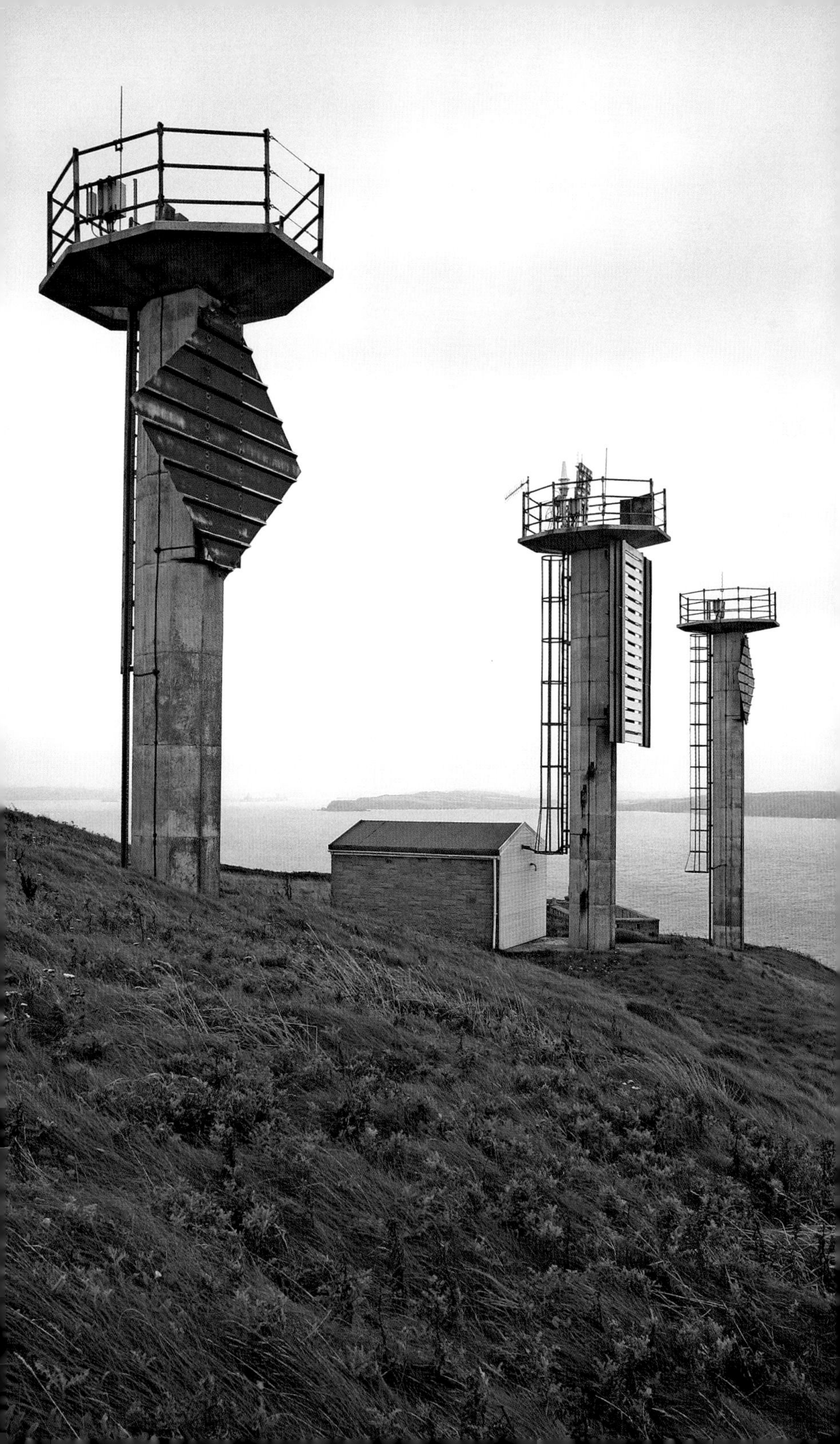

Milford Haven

erection of four reinforced concrete towers on the east side of St Ann's Head, three at West Blockhouse Point and one at Watwick Point. The West Block House structures consist of three octagonal reinforced-concrete towers 30ft, 37ft and 46ft in height, topped by octagonal concrete platforms supporting sealed beam lights.

The two outer columns carry black square daymarks and their flashing white lights operate as a pair of leading lights. The centre light has an octagonal black and white daymark and its flashing white light, visible for thirteen miles, operates as a Front Range to the Watwick Point light marking Haven Approach.

Situated about half a mile to the north at Watwick Point is the Rear Range which consists of a curved circular pinkish white tower similar to East Castle Head, but taller at 160ft. A large board contains a vertical black and white daymark near the top. The mains-powered sealed beam light units mounted on a gallery on top of the tower give a flashing white light which is visible for fifteen miles.

In 1957 Trinity House erected a beacon on the steep cliffs below West Blockhouse Fort. This consists of a round red metal lantern mounted on a concrete base located on the sheer rock face and reached by a steep flight of steps from the fort. The light was obtained second-hand from Rame Head lighthouse.

The whole of the Haven is extensively marked with aids to navigation, most mounted on the oil jetties. Two sets of leading lights are of note. On the south shore at Popton Point, opposite Milford Haven, are two Front Range lights mounted on steel lattice towers on the jetty, one outboard with a white diamond daymark and the other inboard with a white circular daymark. These operate with a Rear Range at Bullwell to mark the extremities of the channel to the south of Stack Rock. The Bullwell light is on a lattice tower carrying an arrowhead black and white daymark on the headland.

Further up the Haven, on the north side at Newton Noyes, is a similar formation of two Front and a common Rear Range to mark the Milford Shelf between the oil terminals. In the grounds of the oil depot on steel lattice towers, the inboard Front Range has a diamond black and white daymark and the Outboard Front Range and Rear Range both have a black and white daymark. All show fixed red lights. In the channel south of St Ann's Head is a rocky outcrop which is marked by a 40ft circular steel pole light called Mid Channel Rock.

▶▶ This graceful structure at Little Castle Head is of similar design to, but at 85ft somewhat shorter than, the 160ft tower at Watwick Point.

▼ The lights on the building at Great Castle Head now form a Front Range with Little Castle Head.

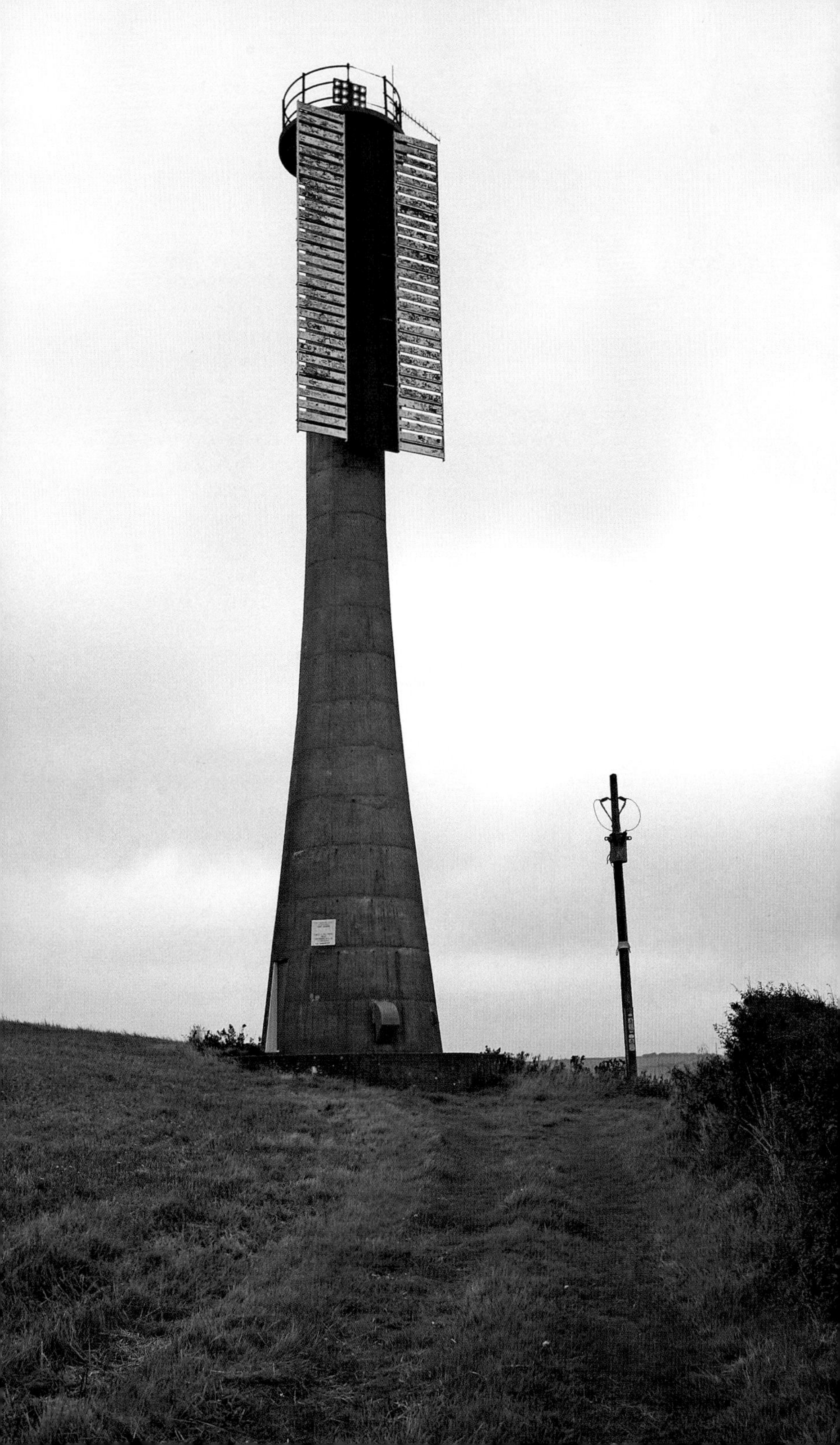

St Ann's Head

ESTABLISHED
1714
CURRENT TOWER
1841
AUTOMATED
1998
OPERATOR
Trinity House
ACCESS
On Pembrokeshire Coast National Park; it can also be reached by road from Dale village; the light station is now used for vacation accommodation; there are historical exhibits in the tower, but only paying guests have access to the observation room

▶▶ The original high light had its lantern removed and an observation gallery was added. The bulk of the building is now painted black and the accommodation is available as holiday rentals.

▶ The original high light, seen when in operaton, was discontinued in 1910 but remains standing.

St Ann's Head is the oldest lighthouse on the Welsh coast and stands on the western side of the entrance to Milford Haven, one of Britain's finest deep water harbours and used by tankers. The approach to the port can be hazardous, with dangerous reefs, situated almost mid-channel and in two groups, having to be negotiated. One of the greatest dangers, seven miles south-east of St Ann's Head, is the Crow Rock and Toes off Linney Head, a reef which has claimed many vessels. In addition to providing guidance for vessels using the Haven, the lighthouse is an important mark for passing coastal traffic, warning of the offshore dangers.

The first attempts to provide a light for the area were made in 1662, when Trinity House approved in principle a coal-fired light at St Ann's Head, supported by voluntary payment of dues, to guide Milford-bound shipping. However, the owners extracted dues illegally from shipowners and the light, then the only one on the west coast, was ordered to be extinguished by Parliament in 1668, a somewhat extreme measure given the lack of any other lights on the coast. Drawings suggest that this tower formed the western tower of a destroyed chapel, which is said to have commemorated the landing of Henry Tudor in the Haven in 1485 to claim the English throne.

Forty years passed before another light was established, although the local merchants petitioned many times for lights to be provided throughout the period. However, not until 15 March 1713 was a patent granted to Trinity House to build a lighthouse at St Ann's Head. Following its policy of the time, Trinity House leased the patent to the owner of the land, Joseph Allen, for ninety-nine years at an annual rent of £10. Allen agreed to build two lighthouses and keep them in good repair. To fund the lights, he was permitted to collect dues from the shipmasters at Milford Haven amounting to one penny per ton of cargo on British vessels and two pence on foreign vessels.

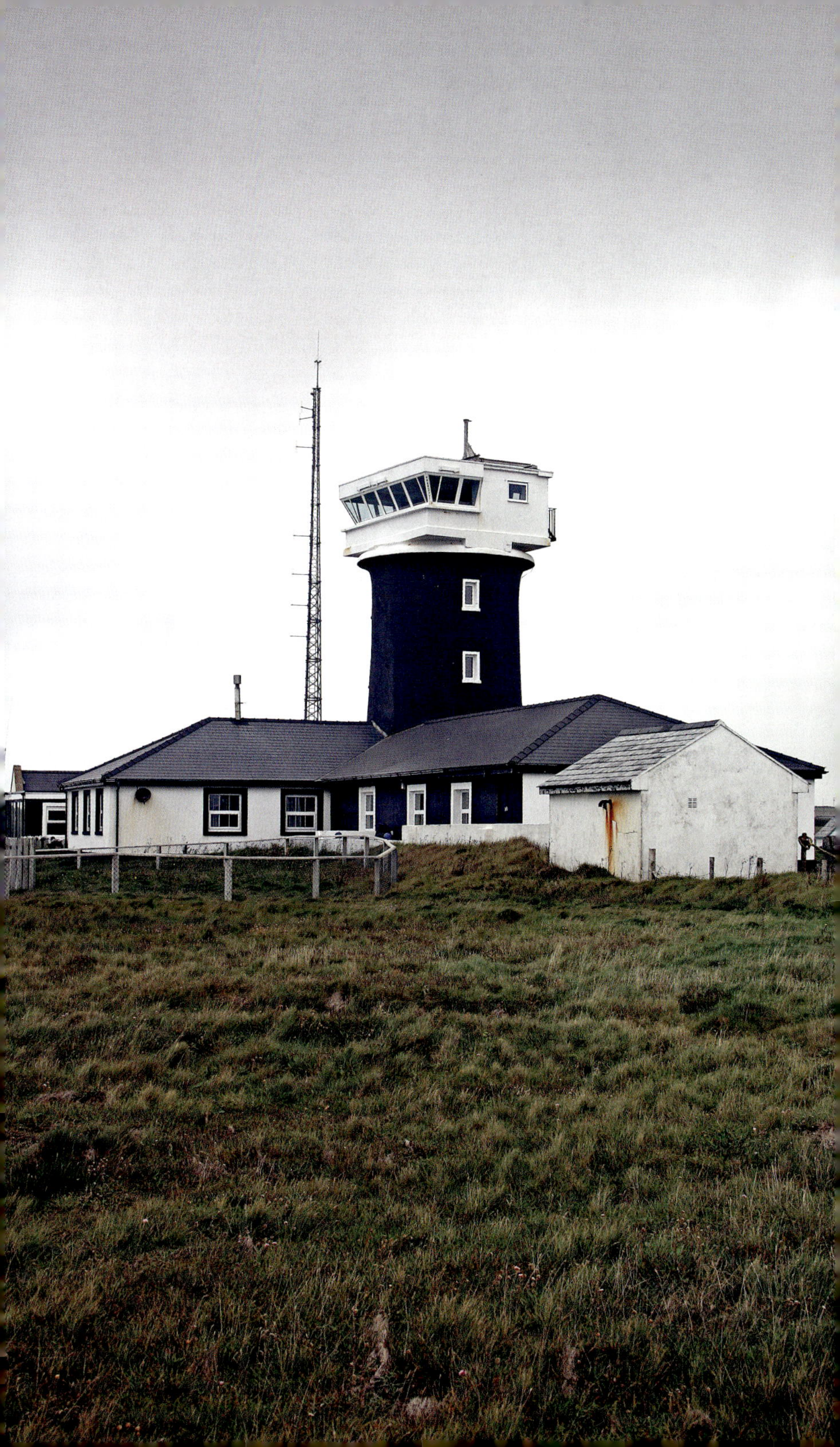

St Ann's Head

Allen established two towers near the old disused lighthouse, and coal fires were lit on them for the first time on 24 June 1714, before the lease was actually signed, highlighting the urgency of the matter. The use of two lights was to distinguish St Ann's from the single light at St Agnes in the Isles of Scilly. The High Light was a 75ft white-painted tapered masonry tower with a single-storey keepers' building attached, and the light was visible for twenty miles. In 1800 Trinity House installed reflected Argand lamps in lanterns, which cost £600 and was paid for out of the light dues. The Brethren also managed the lights at a charge of £140 per annum.

The front or lower light was rebuilt in 1841, when cliff erosion endangered the old tower. The new 42ft octagonal masonry tower with lantern and gallery, attached to a two-storey keepers' house, was situated 30ft from the cliff edge and this serves as the present lighthouse. When the rear light was discontinued in 1910, a Matthews burner was installed in the front light, and in 1958 the station was converted to mains electricity with generators for stand-by. The lantern in the discontinued light was removed early in the Second World War and the room was converted into an observation room.

The automation of the lighthouse was completed on 17 June 1998 when the keepers were withdrawn. The white and red light flashes every five seconds, with the white light having a range of eighteen nautical miles and the red seventeen. An area control station between 1983 and 1998, St Ann's was manned by four keepers and supported helicopter operations to Smalls, Skokholm and South Bishop after automation. Although unmanned, the lighthouse remains an operating base for Trinity House's maintenance teams.

▶▶ The lighthouse at St Ann's Head has been automatic since 1998.

▼ The lighthouse guards the entrance to Milford Haven. The adjacent keepers' buildings, pictured on the left, are not occupied.

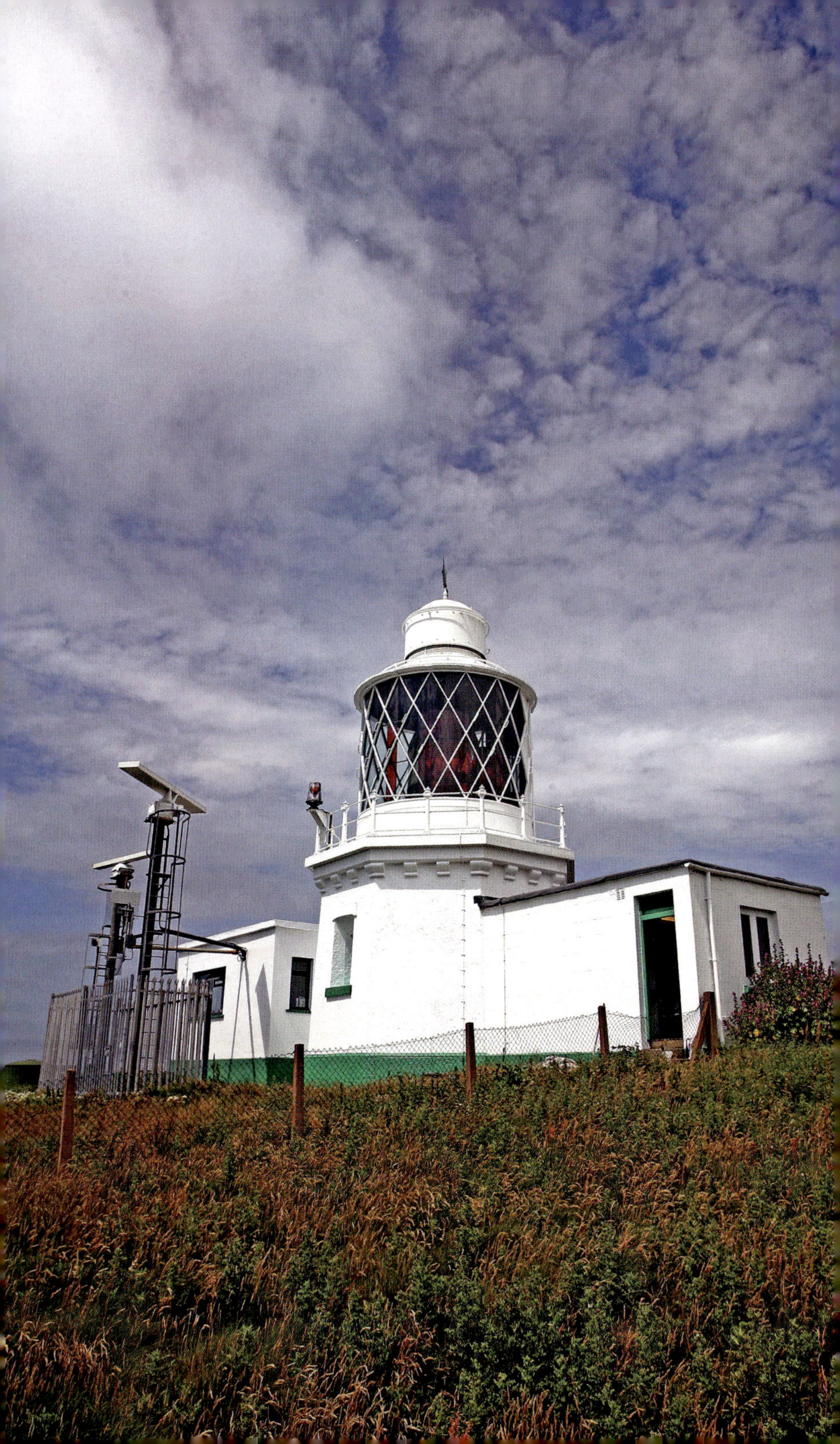

Skokholm

ESTABLISHED
1916

CURRENT TOWER
1916

AUTOMATED
1983

OPERATOR
Trinity House

ACCESS
Accommodation available at the observatory; island only reached by boat

The small island of Skokholm, which is just over a mile long and half a mile wide, lies off the Pembrokeshire coast. The island's high cliffs rise sheer from the sea to well over 100ft in places and it is a renowned seabird sanctuary. The lighthouse, situated on its south-west point, makes up the landward corner of a triangle of lights with South Bishop and Smalls, guiding ships clear of a treacherous coastline into Milford Haven or up the Bristol Channel.

The station was built during the First World War to the design of Sir Thomas Matthews and was first lit in 1916. The lighthouse buildings are unique in being the last built by Trinity House using traditional building materials. The white-painted brick hexagonal masonry tower, 58ft in height, complete with gallery and lantern, is unusual in that it is built into the two-storey keepers' buildings in the centre of the front elevation with a slight vertical projection in the front wall above a square front porch.

Before the lighthouse could be built, a jetty had to be constructed on the island so that building materials could be landed. Subsequently, the jetty was used for landing stores and supplies, which were taken the mile to the lighthouse on two small trucks running on a narrow gauge railway. The trucks were originally pulled by a donkey, which was subsequently replaced by a tractor. When the station was manned, relief was by tender from Holyhead, but now it is reached by helicopter.

Although records show it was first lit in 1916, a plaque inside the building says that it was officially opened in 1915. In the early 1970s a new electrically-powered Chance fourth order catadioptric rotating optic was installed and the lighthouse was automated in 1983. The light, visible for twenty miles, flashes every ten seconds, white or red, and is solar powered. The fog signal engine room is situated on the seaward side of the building.

▶▶ Skokholm lighthouse from the air. The buildings are constructed of stone rubble which is rendered and painted white. The solar panels on the roof of the service buildings can be clearly seen.

▶ The lighthouse is more than 175ft above high water and the tower itself is 58ft tall.

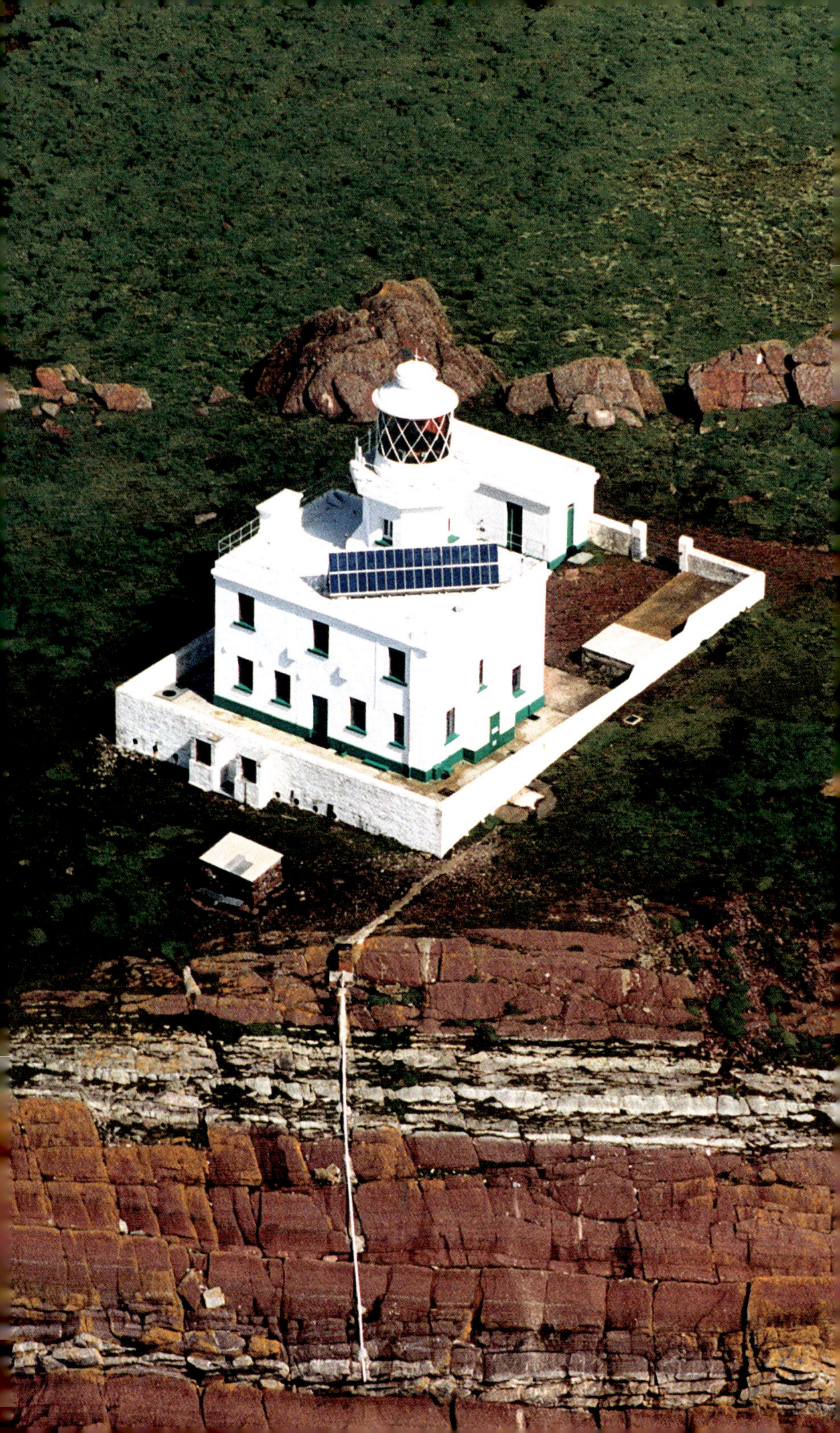

Smalls

ESTABLISHED
1776

CURRENT TOWER
1861

AUTOMATED
1987

OPERATOR
Trinity House

ACCESS
Can only be seen by boat or helicopter

Smalls is one of Trinity House's more remote offshore lighthouses and has an unusual and intriguing history. The small rock on which the lighthouse stands, situated about twenty-one miles west of St David's Head, is one of two tiny clusters of rocks lying close together in the Irish Sea, the highest of which projects only 12ft above the highest tides.

For more than two centuries a lighthouse on Smalls has warned passing ships of the rocks' dangers, with the first lighthouse erected there in 1776. The plans for this lighthouse were made by Welshman John Phillips, an assistant dock manager at Liverpool. He advertised for a tower design and selected that proposed by Henry Whiteside, a musical instrument maker from Liverpool who, in 1772, designed a model for the Skerries tower.

Whiteside's design for Smalls consisted of an octagonal timber house or hut perched atop nine legs or pillars, five of wood and three of cast iron, spaced around a central timber post, allowing the seas to pass beneath. The structure was 66ft tall and 17ft in diameter. The keepers' accommodation was at the top, just below the lantern. Welsh miners were employed to dig the foundations and undertake much of the construction work,

▶▶ The present Smalls lighthouse was completed in 1861 and was painted with broad red and white bands to distinguish it from other similar towers. These lasted until June 1997 when they were sand blasted off.

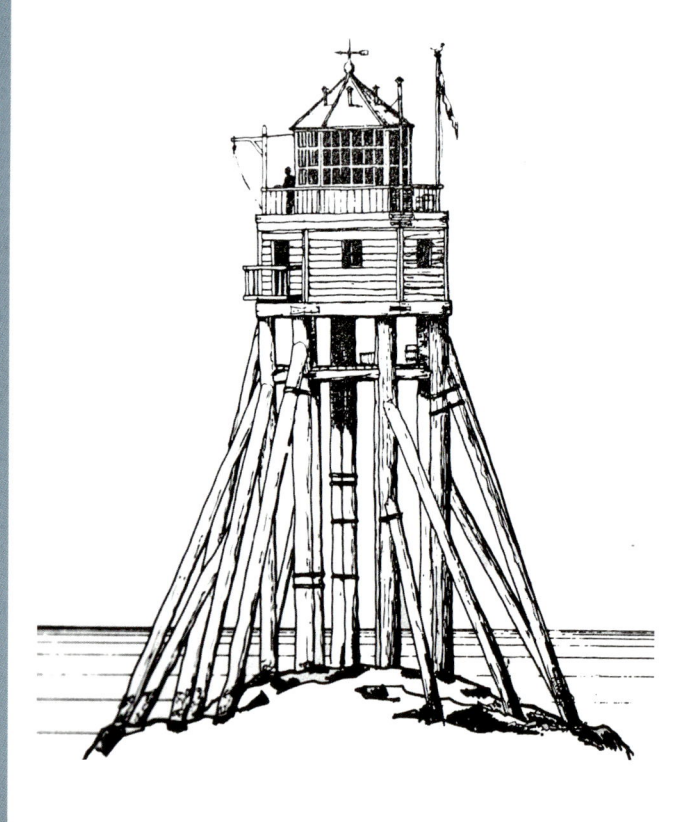

▶ An accurate drawing, by Douglas Hague, of Henry Whiteside's lighthouse of the eighteenth century after a number of extra oak struts had been added to strengthen the original nine.

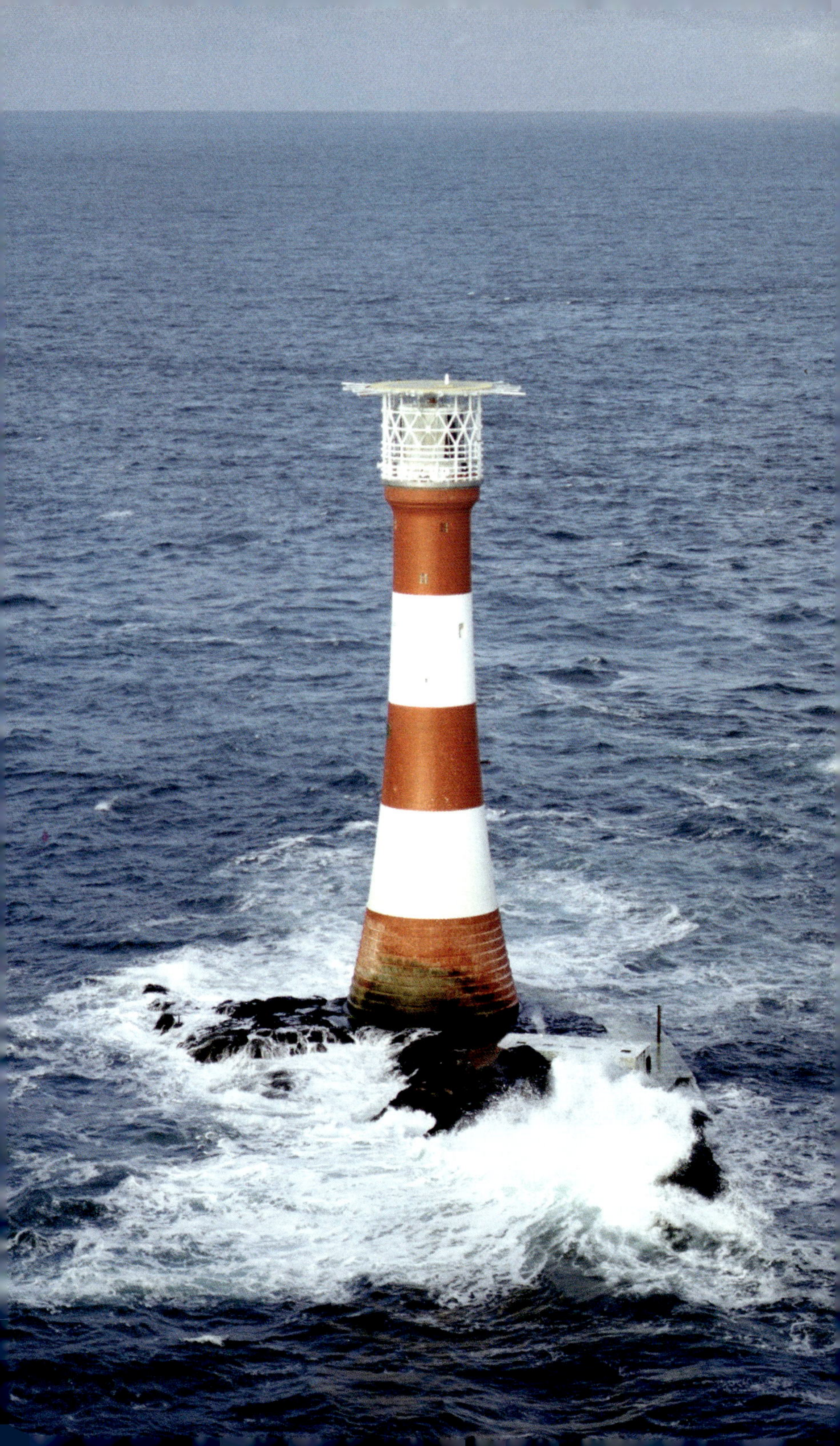

Smalls

although progress was slow because of bad weather during winter 1775–6. While postholes were being dug at the rock, the tower was built at Solva, a small harbour on the mainland. In spring 1776 the whole structure was taken to the rock for assembly.

By September 1776 the oil lamps were lit, but Whiteside's tower was not strong enough to cope with the conditions on the rock and it had to be abandoned in January 1778 after a series of storms. Repairs were too costly and difficult to carry out, particularly as Phillips had no funds, and so he withdrew the keepers and extinguished the light. He handed over his interest to a group of Liverpool merchants who persuaded Trinity House to take over the tower.

The Brethren obtained an Act of Parliament in 1778 which authorised the repair and maintenance of the light and the collection and levying of dues. Phillips was then granted a lease on 3 June 1778 for ninety-nine years at a rent of £5. The tower was reinforced and relit in September 1778 and remained

▶ The elegant nineteenth century circular stone lighthouse on the Smalls, with the solar panels mounted near the lantern added since automation in the 1986. The light remains one of the most important aids to navigation for shipping in the area.

54

Smalls

in operation until 1861, when it was replaced. It suffered considerable damage a number of times and as a result had to be strengthened. Trinity House eventually bought the lease in 1836 for £170,468.

The light is supposedly the scene of a tragic episode which occurred around 1800 and involved two lighthouse keepers, Howell and Griffith. Apparently, Howell died unexpectedly one night and Griffith put the body in a coffin which he made from the interior woodwork and lashed to the lantern rail outside. When the usual relief boat arrived, having been prevented by storms from getting close to the rock for several months, Griffith had been driven mad. After this, three keepers were always appointed to lighthouse teams.

The present lighthouse, 141ft tall, was built under the supervision of Trinity House's then Chief Engineer, James Douglass, to a Walker design based on Smeaton's Eddystone tower. The tower took just two years to build, a considerable feat, and was completed in 1861. It was painted red and white, but in June 1997 the stripes were no longer considered necessary and so the tower was grit blasted back to natural granite.

Various improvements were made during the 1960s and a concrete helipad was built over the station's water and oil tanks. This was replaced in 1978 by a helipad above the lantern, and automation came in 1987. The white light, which flashes three times every fifteen seconds, is visible for twenty-five miles.

▲ The lighthouse on Smalls seen on a rough day, with waves washing the rocks. An elevated helipad was constructed above the lantern in 1978 and the lantern itself was painted red during 1997.

South Bishop

ESTABLISHED	1839
CURRENT TOWER	1839
AUTOMATED	1983
OPERATOR	Trinity House
ACCESS	Can only be viewed by boat

▶▶ South Bishop lighthouse stands on the route of migrating birds which, attracted by the light's rays, flew into the lantern's glass panels. Many were killed and so Trinity House, in conjunction with the Royal Society for the Protection of Birds, built special bird perches on the lantern for use during the migration season and the mortality rate has been much reduced.

▶ South Bishop seen from the sea. Before helicopters, keepers had to climb steps cut into the sheer rock face to reach the lighthouse.

The rocky outcrop of South Bishop, also known as Emsger, is situated in St George's Channel, almost five miles south-west of St David's Head. The lighthouse operates mainly as a waymark for vessels navigating offshore and marks the northern entrance to St Bride's Bay. It also acts as a guide for vessels navigating around the Bishops and Clerks group of rocks, of which South Bishop is the largest and most southerly.

The lighthouse dates from the 1830s. An unsuccessful application for a light at South Bishop was first made to Trinity House in 1831 on behalf of shipping interests trading to Cardigan. Another application was made in 1834 on behalf of those using Bristol and St George's Channel, but a further five years passed before a light was constructed. Designed by James Walker and erected by Trinity House, the 36ft white-painted brick tower was completed and first lit in 1839.

The lighthouse tower has a lantern and gallery and is attached by a short corridor to a pair of two-storey pitched-roofed keepers' houses, which were intended for two families. However, due to the dangers of what is an extreme environment, it is doubtful if anyone other than the keepers lived on the rock, which is so exposed that the seas sometimes flood the courtyard and break lower windows. In 1971 a helipad was constructed on the island, but the pad was very exposed and often flooded in high tides and heavy seas, and so landing was not always practicable. Before helicopter, the keepers and their supplies were landed by tender.

The light was converted to electric operation in 1959, and automated and demanned in 1983. Since then, it has been converted to solar power with the solar panels situated between the lighthouse and the helipad. The current light, powered by a 70 Watt Mbi lamp with a fourth order catadioptric lens, flashes white every five seconds and has a range of nineteen miles. The fog signal is in an adjacent building and gives three blasts every forty-five seconds.

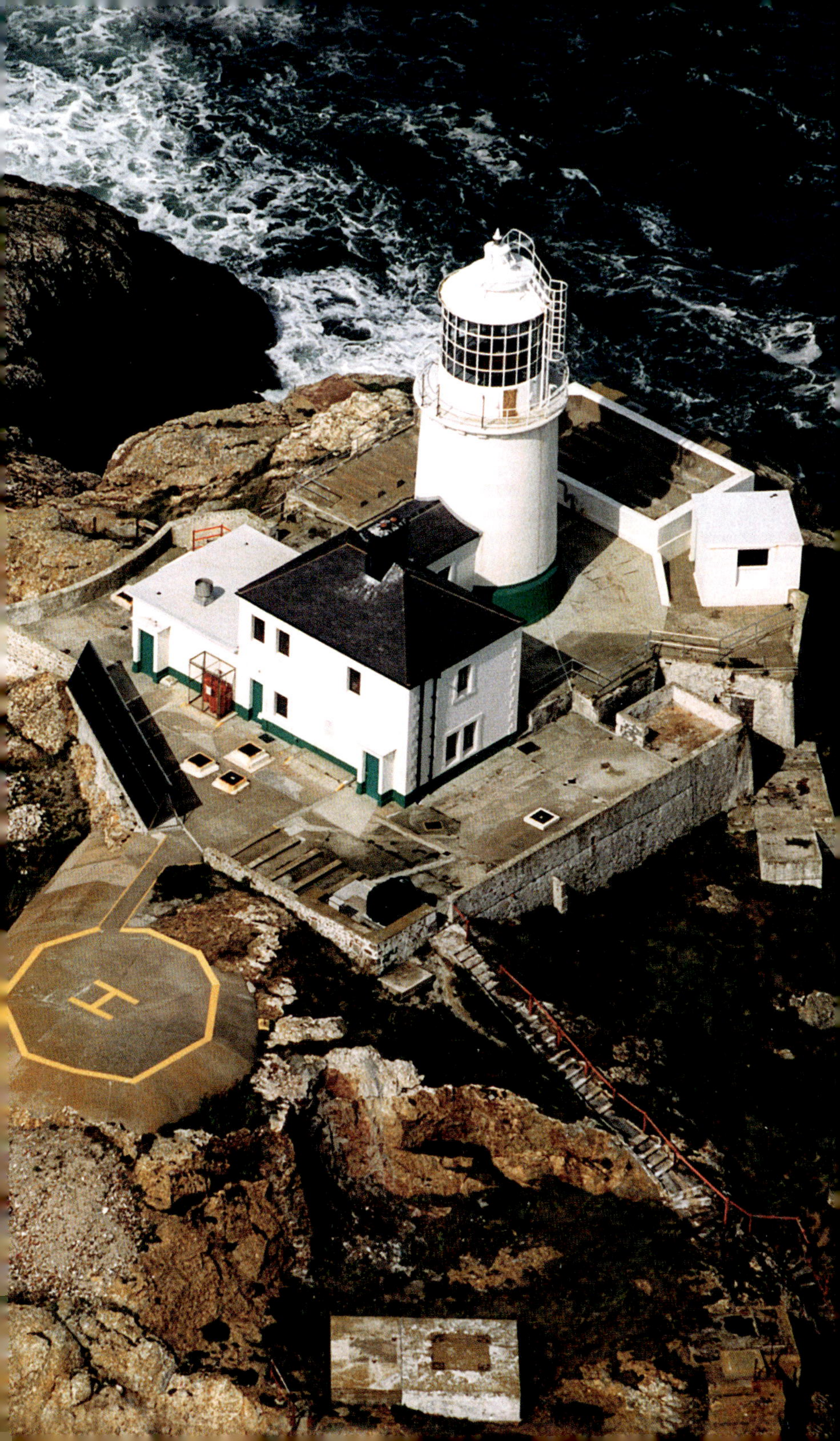

Strumble Head

ESTABLISHED
1908

CURRENT TOWER
1908

AUTOMATED
1980

OPERATOR
Trinity House

ACCESS
The island itself is not open, but an approach to the footbridge can be made from the Pembrokeshire Coast Path; it is possible to approach by car from Goodwick, near Fishguard, and the headland is signed along the minor roads

▶▶ Strumble Head lighthouse is siuated on a small island.

▼ The light covers the shipping channel out of Fishguard.

With the completion in 1905 of the new north breakwater at Fishguard, Trinity House looked at the aids to navigation required to safeguard shipping entering and leaving Cardigan Bay, particularly as steamers to Ireland were on the increase after the harbour opened in 1906 and Rosslare Harbour was developed on the Irish side of the Channel. They chose to build a lighthouse on the rocky outcrop called Ynys Meicl, or St Michael's Island, situated off the headland of Strumble Head. Completed in 1908, the light was designed to work in conjunction with South Bishop five miles off St David's Head in St George's Channel.

A narrow footbridge was built to connect the island to the mainland but even then the rocky outcrop made the building of the lighthouse as difficult as it would have been for a true offshore station. In order to get equipment across the gap and to the top of the outcrop, the builders constructed a jackstay cable between two winches, one on the headland and one adjacent to the lighthouse. This method is no longer used and all of the associated equipment has been dismantled and removed. Heavy items are now brought to the station by helicopter. Another unusual feature is that one handrail on the bridge doubled as a pipe carrying oil into the tower's basement.

The lighthouse consists of a 56ft white circular stone tower complete with gallery and lantern. A pair of white stone flat-roofed keepers' dwellings is attached to the tower on the seaward side. To one side is a white single-storey flat-roofed service building built in 1967 to house a foghorn which replaced an earlier explosive fog signal.

58

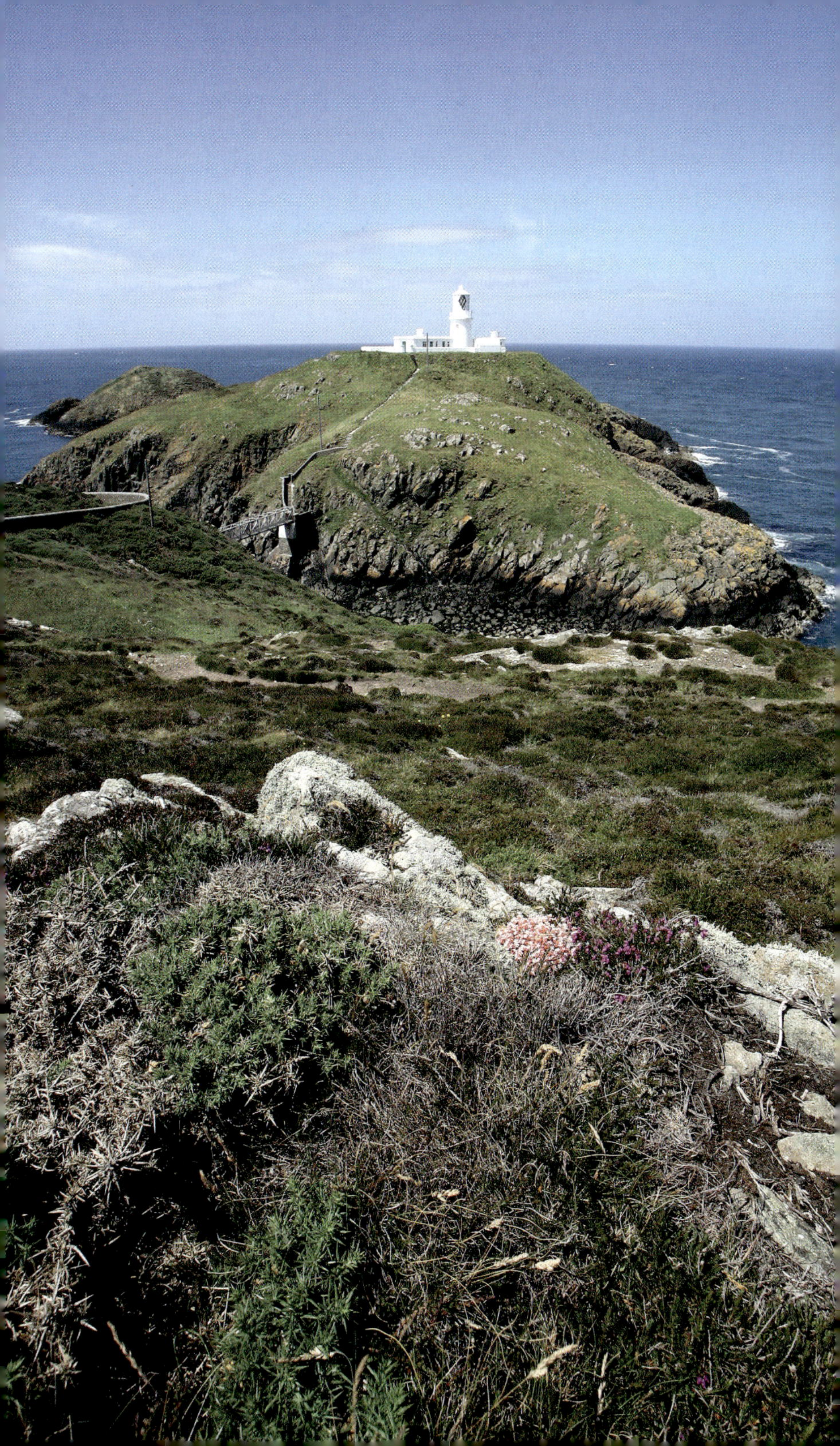

Strumble Head

▶▶ Close-up view of Strumble Head lighthouse tower which is 56ft tall and 148ft above high water. The first order catadioptric optic has a range of twenty-six miles and is the original one dating from 1908.

The charges for this signal were kept in a wood-lined white stone service building which can still be seen. It was originally classified as a rock station.

The original light source was paraffin, with a large mechanically-driven revolving lens system weighing four and a half tons and supported on a bed of mercury, showing a white flashing light. A massive clockwork mechanism rotated it, driven by a quarter-ton weight which, suspended on a cable, dropped gradually down a cylinder running from top to bottom through the tower. The drive had to be rewound every twelve hours.

The light was converted to electricity in 1965, and the first order catadioptric unit produces a flashing white light visible for twenty-six miles. The light was fully automated in 1980 and is now controlled from the Control Centre at Harwich.

▶ The lighthouse and its associated buildings are maintained by an attendant who visits occasionally to make sure everything is in working order.

▶ The small island on which the lighthouse is situated is connected to the mainland by a bridge. The red handrail, to the right, carried oil at one time.

60

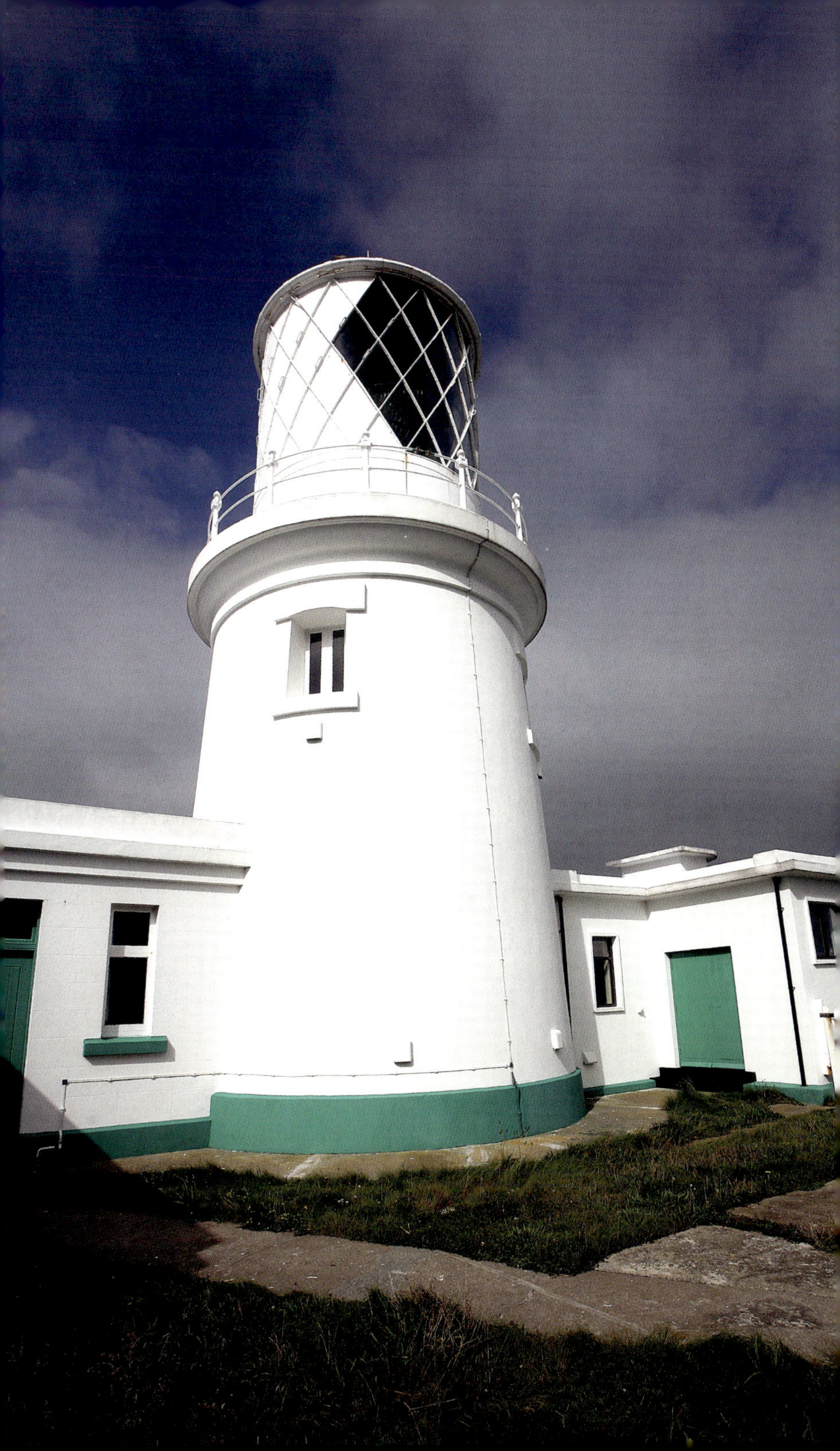

Fishguard

ESTABLISHED
1913

CURRENT TOWER
1913

OPERATOR
Stena Line

ACCESS
North breakwater is only accessible from ferry port by agreement with Stena Line; access to the east breakwater is on the roundabout at Parrog adjacent to ferry terminal entrance; the range lights are a climb from the ferry terminal, and the fog signal at Pen Anglas Point is found by a detour from the coast path

▶▶ The lighthouse, which is operated by Stena Line, is situated at the end of the breakwater and was completed in about 1913 when the breakwater itself was finished.

▶ (Left) The lights above the harbour are fixed green range lights visible for five miles.

▶ (Right) The light on the east breakwater has solar panels mounted on each side of the light.

In the early years of the twentieth century a plan was formulated to construct a harbour at Fishguard which would rival those at Southampton and Liverpool and accommodate ocean-going liners. In 1905, the Great Western Railway constructed not only a railway terminal at Goodwick, just to the west of Fishguard, but also an 800-yard-long stone breakwater out from Pen Cw, or the Cow and Calf, to enclose a huge area of water to the north-west of the old harbour at Lower Fishguard.

A year later, on 30 August 1906, the first ferry to Rosslare set sail from the harbour and in 1909 the liner Mauritania stopped on her voyage from Liverpool to New York. She was unable to dock due to lack of water depth but passengers were ferried off by boat and a carnival procession took place in the town. Although the ferry trade continued, that was the last the port saw of the big liners.

When the northern breakwater was built, a substantial lighthouse was constructed on the end. It consisted of an octagonal 46ft stone tower with a double gallery and single lantern. The tower was reduced in width at each gallery. The area below the lower gallery remains its natural stone colour but the area above and the domed lantern are painted white. For such a fine lighthouse, surprisingly little is known about its history and today its flashing green light, visible for thirteen miles, is powered by electricity with solar panels nearby. The lighthouse also carries a fog bell.

The east breakwater itself was built about 1913 and it is likely that the light on the end is of the same date. This light consists of a 36ft open lattice steel tower which supports a small solar-powered red flashing light visible for ten miles. On the hillside above the ferry terminal is a pair of white triangular range marks, each of which has a small fixed green range. These range lights originally marked an Admiralty mooring buoy to the north-east of the northern breakwater light, but this was removed in about 1990. An electric-powered compressed air foghorn is sited approximately a mile to the north-west at Pen Anglas Point.

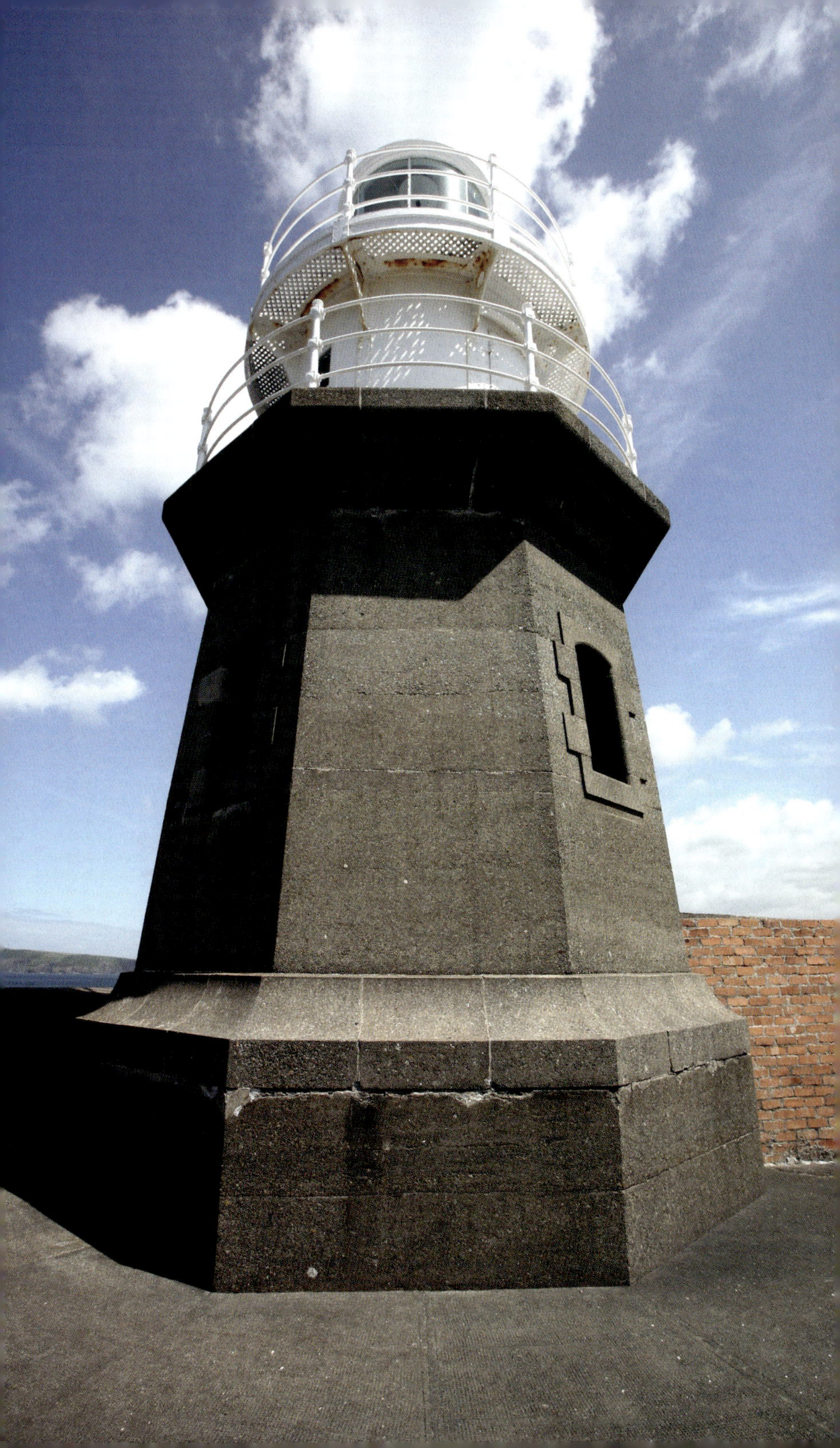

New Quay

ESTABLISHED
1839

CURRENT TOWER
Not in existence

OPERATOR
Harbour Trustees

ACCESS
The site is open to public and is on the end of the pier

▶ The navigation light at the end of the old pier.

▼ The tower which supported a small directional navigation light but is now demolished.

In the eighteenth and nineteenth centuries New Quay was a bustling fishing port. In order to improve the anchorage, several proposals were put to the harbour authorities for a larger pier or breakwater. In 1820 the engineer John Rennie proposed a breakwater and pier to enclose a large area of sea, but his scheme proved too expensive. Instead, a smaller breakwater, completed in 1835, was commissioned from Daniel Beynon.

In 1839, a 30ft tapered circular tower, operated by the Harbour Trustees and made of rough stone, was erected on the end. The white-painted tower did not have a lantern as such and the fixed white light visible for six miles was displayed through a window in the red domed top. In 1859 a violent storm swept away the end of the pier as well as its lighthouse. They were rebuilt and the light continued to shine until 28 February 1937, when it was again washed away.

With trade in decline and the harbour silting up, it was decided not to rebuild the light, known locally as the Pepper Pot. It has since been replaced by a polycarbonate navigation light on a wooden post, which carries a plaque as a memorial to those lost in the two World Wars. In 2006 the possibility of restoring the Pepper Pot was discussed. The pier is open to the public.

Aberystwyth

Aberystwyth harbour is fed by the rivers Ystwyth and Rheidol, the steepest river in Britain. In its heyday it was one of the busiest ports in Wales, with ships sailing regularly from there to Liverpool carrying grain, cheese, salmon, wine, whisky, and fruit. Today, however, its main activity is pleasure craft and in 1995 a new £9 million marina, named Y Lanfa, was opened for business and significantly remodelled the harbour by providing permanent berths for over 100 vessels.

To help guide these vessels into the tidal entrance, a small polycarbonate lamp holder showing a green light on top of a 30ft tower was built. The tower, situated near the end of the south breakwater, is painted white with two green bands and is formed from nine precast concrete rings.

ESTABLISHED
1990s

CURRENT TOWER
1990s

OPERATOR
Associated British Ports

ACCESS
On end of south breakwater which is open to public

◀ The green and white tower on the south breakwater at the entrance to Aberystwyth harbour.

St Tudwal's

ESTABLISHED
1877

CURRENT TOWER
1877

AUTOMATED
1995

OPERATOR
Trinity House

ACCESS
Landings are not allowed on the island so the light can only be seen from the sea

▶▶ Only the light tower at St Tudwal's remains in Trinity House ownership.

▼ Close-up of the tower showing the solar panels.

St Tudwal's lighthouse is situated on St Tudwal's Island West, one of two small islands in Tremadoc Bay on the southern side of the Lleyn Peninsula. According to tradition, the island is named after the saint who lived there in the sixth century, and the remains of a priory known to have existed in the eleventh century are to be found on the east of the island. The light was established to assist the schooners that carried general cargo and slate from the quarries of North Wales at a time when such trade was commonplace. It was needed because Bardsey light to the west was obscured from some directions to ships traversing the west side of Tremadoc Bay.

The site for the lighthouse was purchased by Trinity House in 1876 for £111. A 36ft cylindrical masonry tower, with lantern, gallery and adjacent single-storey keepers' dwellings, was completed the following year to the design of James Nicholas Douglass. The occulting white light was significant in that it was controlled by the first occulting optic apparatus manufactured by Chance Bros. The light is also notable for its conversion to acetylene operation in 1922 and its subsequent operation by means of a sun valve.

This mechanism, invented by the Swedish lighthouse engineer Gustaf Dalen, consisted of an arrangement of reflective gold-plated copper bars supporting a suspended black rod. When lit by the sun during hours of daylight, the black rod absorbed the direct heat which reflected from the other bars and expanded downwards, thereby cutting off the supply of gas. This innovation enabled the light to become unmanned and in 1935 the keepers' dwellings were sold. As with other Trinity House lighthouses, St Tudwal's is maintained by an attendant.

In 1995 the lighthouse was modernised, electrified and converted to solar-powered operation after which the light was powered by a 100-Watt halogen lamp and a second order 700Mm fixed optic with a red sector. The light displays one white flash with a range of fourteen miles and one red flash which has a range of ten miles every fifteen seconds.

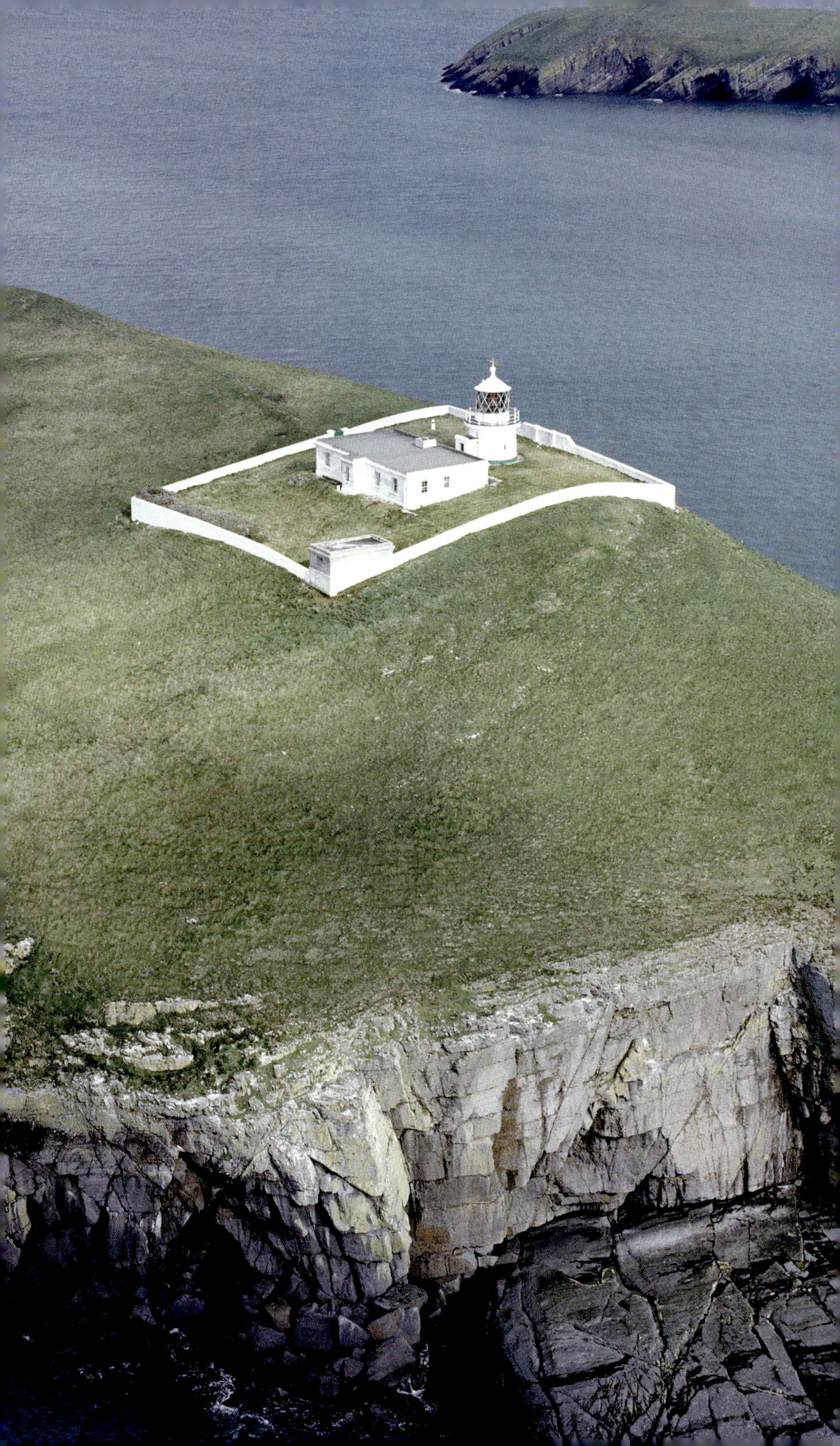

Bardsey

ESTABLISHED
1821

CURRENT TOWER
1821

AUTOMATED
1987

OPERATOR
Trinity House

ACCESS
Bardsey is accessible by passenger ferry from Porth Meudwy; the light at Pen Diban can be reached by walking from the ferry landing site

▶▶ The distinctive square tower and fog signal on Bardsey Island.

▼ The dwellings are no longer occupied and an attendant maintains the site.

The small island of Bardsey, separated from the mainland by Bardsey Sound, was a place of ancient pilgrimage known as 'the island of 20,000 saints', with a journey there regarded as the equivalent of one to Rome. However, the Welsh name for the island, Ynys Enlli, means 'island of the tides'. As it is situated at the end of the Lleyn Peninsula, opposing currents can create boiling seas in the Sound with the often dangerous combination of wind over tide making navigation hazardous.

The two-mile-long island, home to colonies of sea birds and grey seals and part of a national nature reserve, is surrounded by outcrops of sharp rocks. The lighthouse, on the southerly tip where the land is flat, guides vessels through St George's Channel and the Irish Sea. The 99ft tower and single-storey keepers' houses were erected by Trinity House under the supervision of Joseph Nelson in 1821. The tower cost £5,470 12s 6d, with a further £2,950 16s 7d for the lantern which, in 1910, was raised to increase its range. Following this change, the Cardigan Bay lightvessel to the south was removed. The lighthouse tower, unusual in being square, is striped in red and white bands. The white light has a range of twenty-six miles.

In 1965 the lighthouse was electrified; in 1987 it was converted to automatic operation, and until 1995 was monitored from the Trinity House Area Control Station at Holyhead, but it is now monitored from Harwich. A locally-based part-time attendant carries out routine maintenance.

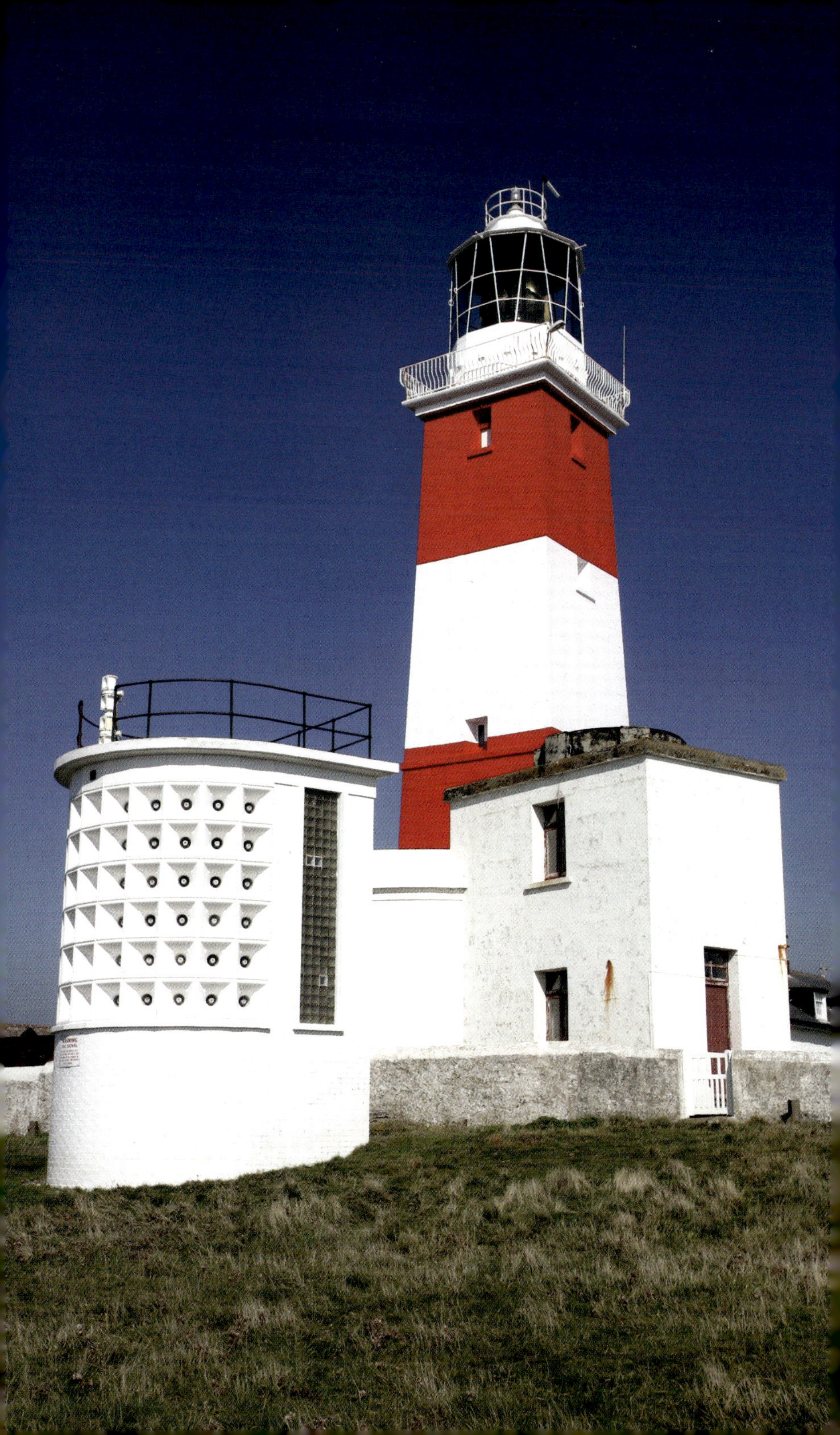

Llanddwyn Island

ESTABLISHED
1845

CURRENT LIGHT ESTABLISHED
1975

AUTOMATED
1987

OPERATOR
Trinity House

ACCESS
Within the Llanddwyn Island National Nature Reserve; the nearby pilot house contains a small display of local history

▶▶ The 1845 tower on Llanddwyn Island displayed a light until 1975.

▼ The small tower which supports a small directional navigation light.

Llanddwyn Island is more of a peninsula than an island, except at the highest tides. It is situated on the south shore of Anglesey, about three miles west of the southern entrance to Menai Strait. The earlier history of the light on the southern tip of the island is uncertain but by 1823 two towers existed, presumably day marks.

The first accurate information is that in 1845 alterations were made to one tower, known as Twr Mawr, costing £250 7s 6d, and a light was first exhibited from there on 1 January 1846.

The white-painted circular 36ft tower has a conical slate roof with living quarters within the tower, similar to some local windmills. It was unique in that it displayed a light from a lamp room attached to the tower at ground level, with the tower itself used solely for accommodation.

The optic, which dates from 1861, consisted of a silver-plated reflector and Fresnel lens, and was originally lit by six Argand lamps with reflectors. The light, which was visible for seven miles, was made redundant in 1975 when it was transferred to a nearby tower. The lower half of the tower was painted red in 2004 for the film Half Light.

On the extreme seaward perimeter of the island, south-east of the 1845 light, is a white-painted conical tower, known as Twr Bach, which was built between 1800 and 1818 of rubble stone and has a domed top. A solar-powered electrical navigation light, operated by Trinity House, was placed on the top in 1975 to replace the light on Twr Mawr. The flashing light shows white or red depending on the direction, visible for seven miles and five miles respectively.

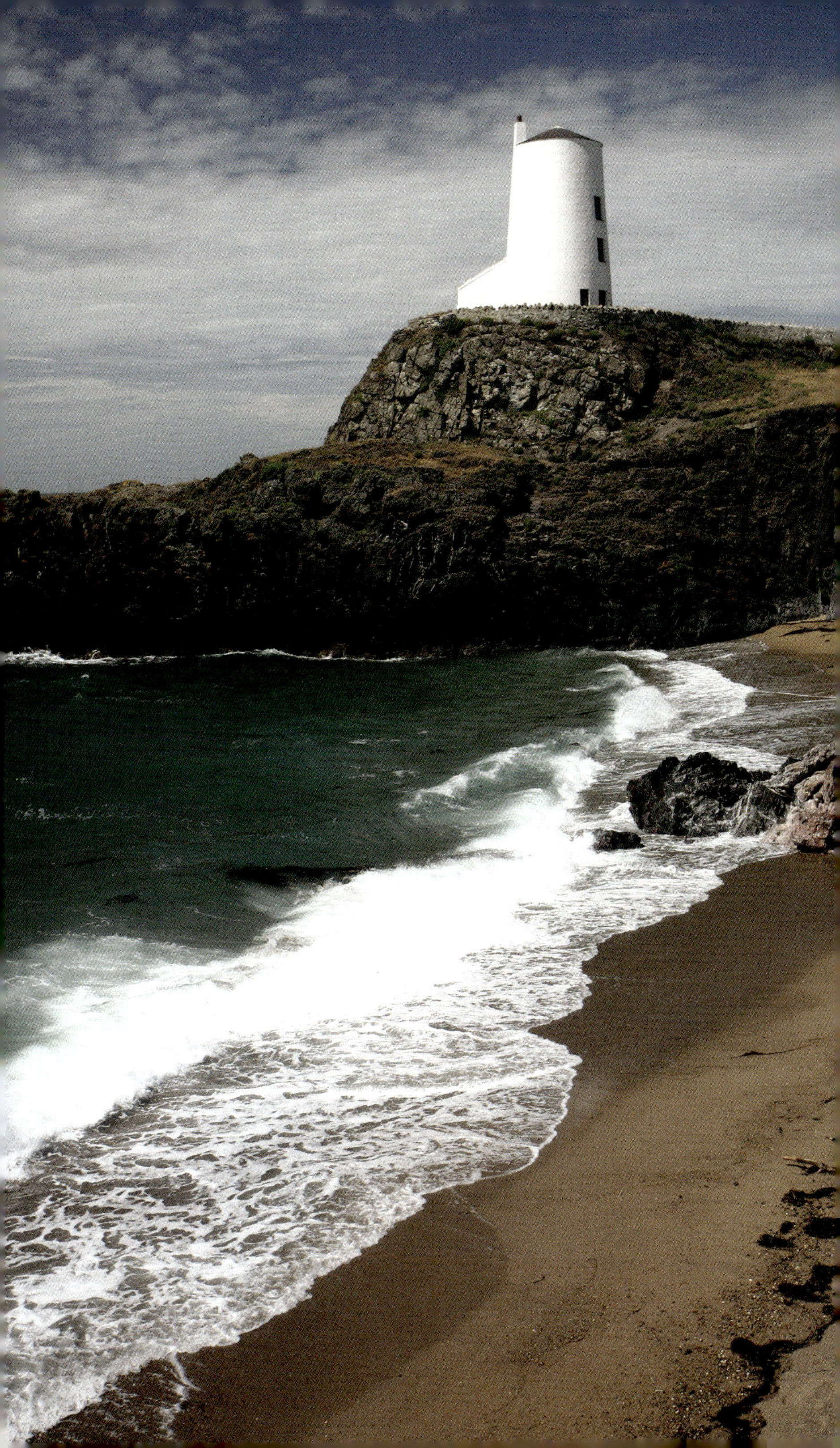

South Stack

ESTABLISHED
1809

CURRENT TOWER
1809

AUTOMATED
1984

OPERATOR
Trinity House

ACCESS
Situated on the north-west coast of Anglesey, the lighthouse has a visitor centre at the top of the steps and the tower is open for guided tours daily April to September

▶▶ Looking down on South Stack lighthouse, a scene which has inspired visitors, artists and photographers. The lamp is 212ft above high water.

▶ An unusual old postcard of South Stack showing the lower lantern which no longer exists. There is now just a space inside the round wall.

The tiny islet of South Stack Rock is separated from Holy Island, on the north-west coast of Anglesey, by 100ft of chaotic seas, and forms a significant danger to shipping entering or leaving Holyhead harbour. A lighthouse to mark the rock was first proposed in 1665, when a petition for a patent to erect a light was presented to Charles II. However, this was not granted and the idea lay dormant until the shipping lanes off Anglesey, on the approach to the port of Liverpool, became busier.

Almost 150 years later, in August 1808, the foundation stone was laid and on 9 February 1809, the lighthouse, built at a cost of £11,828, first showed a light. The station was designed by the engineer Daniel Alexander and built by Joseph Nelson. The 92ft white-painted stone tower, with single-storey keepers' quarters and a service building attached, was originally fitted with Argand oil lamps and reflectors and a revolving Argand lamp was installed in 1818.

Around 1840 a railway was constructed and this enabled a lantern, which displayed a subsidiary light, to be lowered down the cliff to sea level when fog obscured the main light. In the mid-1870s the main lantern and its associated lighting apparatus were replaced by a new lantern, and in 1909 an early form of incandescent light was installed. In 1927 this was replaced by a more modern type of incandescent mantle burner.

The station was electrified in 1938 and automated on 12 September 1984, when the keepers were withdrawn. The current first order catadioptric optic flashes white every ten seconds and the light has a range of twenty nautical miles.

The site has an unusual inverted fog bell, which weighs two and a half tons, and an ingenious arrangement whereby, when fog or low cloud obscured the light, a small clockwork-operated lantern, 10ft square and mounted on wheels, was lowered down a quarry-like railed

72

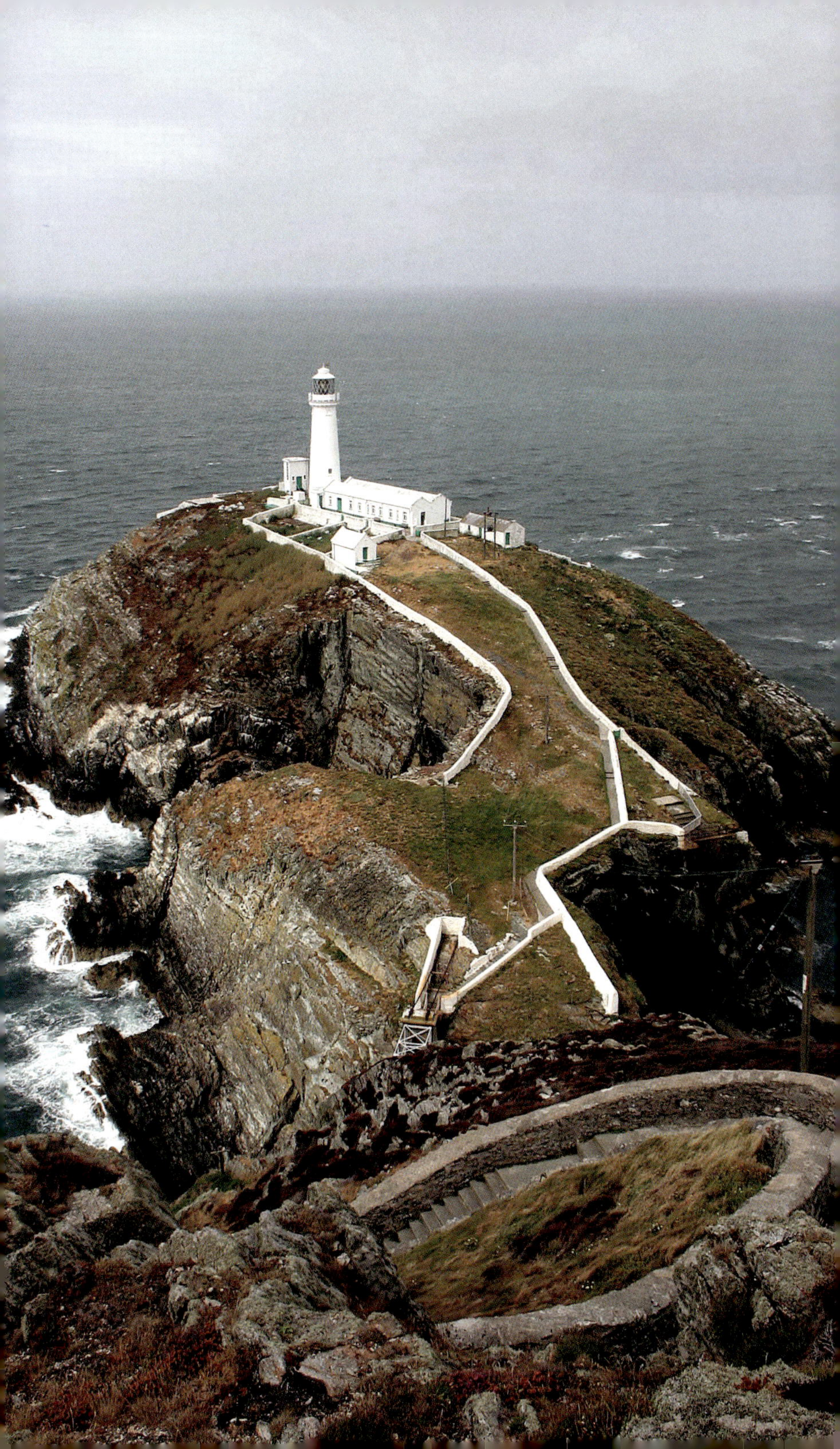

South Stack

▶ An aerial view of South Stack shows the path down to the island, the keepers' accommodation and the fog horn.

▶▶ South Stack lighthouse and fog horn from the sea. The horn gives a one second blast every thirty seconds and has a range of three nautical miles.

▼ South Stack lighthouse seen from the adjacent cliffs.

incline to within 50ft of sea level. The builder and engineer of this unusual object was Hugh Evans. Only the bed of the incline survives. A compressed-air horn was later fitted on the site and this in turn has been replaced by an electronic fog signal.

Various methods of crossing the chasm between the mainland and the rock have been employed, starting with a hempen cable along which a sliding basket, carrying a person or stores, was drawn. This was replaced in 1828 by an iron suspension bridge, and then in 1964 by an aluminium bridge.

The present footbridge, completed in mid-1997, was funded largely by the Welsh Development Agency allowing the island and lighthouse to be reopened to visitors after thirteen years. The station is a Trinity House Visitor Centre, the only one in Wales, offering public access to the tower. The former Trinity House Fog Signal Station at North Stack was also sold off.

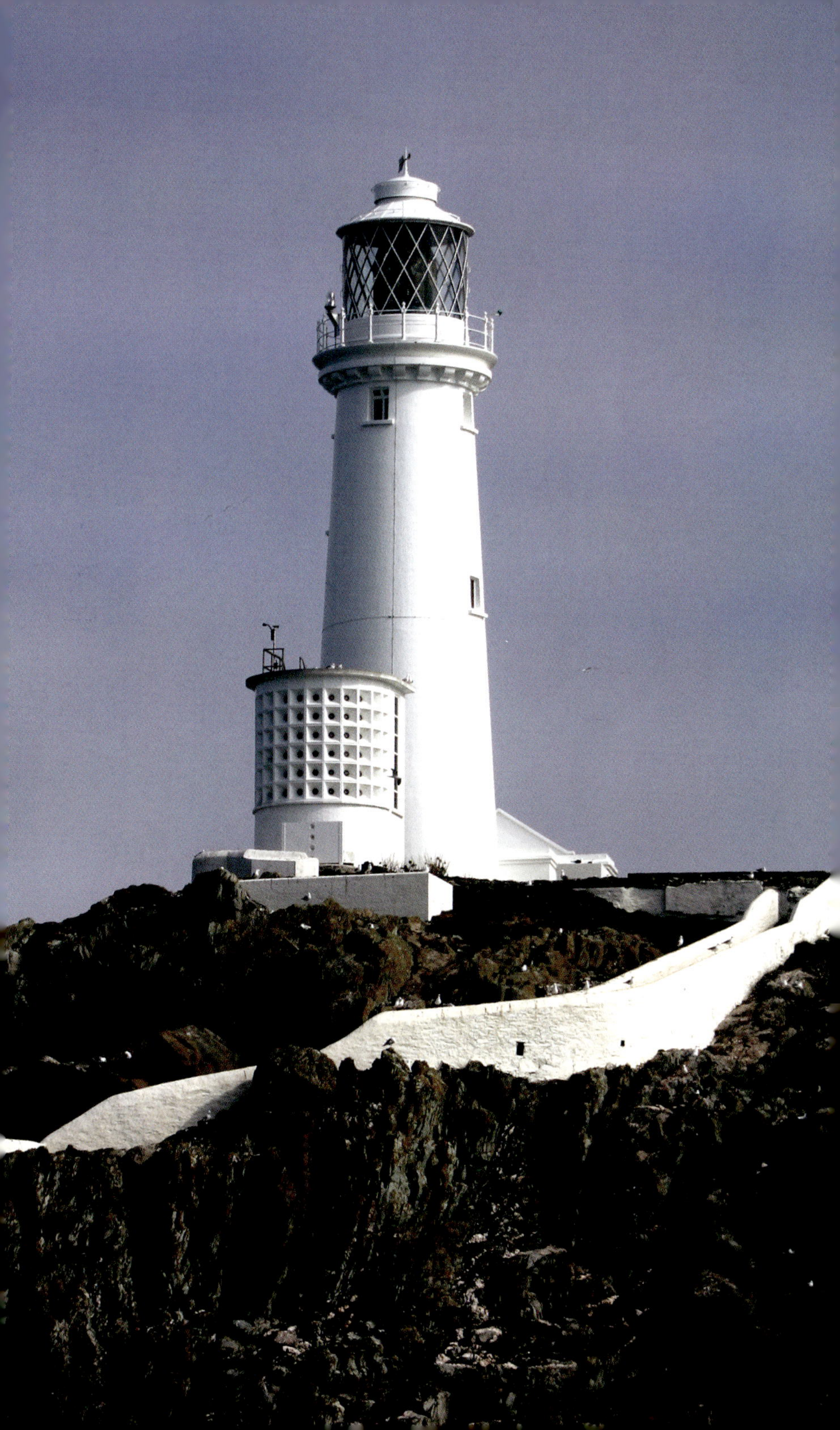

Holyhead Admiralty Pier

ESTABLISHED
1821

CURRENT TOWER
1821

OPERATOR
Stena Line

ACCESS
The pier is in port operator Stena Line's area of activity and access is restricted, but the light can be seen from the fish dock pier or from one of the ferries

▶ The lighthouse on Admiralty Pier seen from Irish Ferries fast craft Jonathan Swift.

▼ Admiralty Pier is in the old part of Holyhead harbour, with the tower significant because of the lantern's age.

Until the early 1800s, vessels at Holyhead moored in the creek beyond Salt Island and although a lighthouse was built to guide them, little is known about it. By 1821 work had commenced on what is now the inner harbour, while the Admiralty or Mail Pier was built out from Salt Island to provide berthing for the cross-Channel ships from Ireland. In the same year, John Rennie (1761-1821) had an earlier lighthouse, by Daniel, replaced by the one that stands today on the end of the pier. He also designed a similar lighthouse on the pier at Howth, the mail terminal for Dublin, and oversaw its construction.

The Holyhead light consisted of a 48ft tapered stone tower with a gallery and lantern. The iron railings around the gallery were ornate and the lantern, with a copper domed roof, was made up of four tiers of lightly-glazed panels. A wooden jetty was built around the lighthouse in 1864 on which a railway station was built.

When the outer harbour was completed in 1873, this light, often referred to as Holyhead Mail Pier Light or Salt Island Light, was subsidiary to the new breakwater light and was reduced to a signal light. Originally showing a white light visible for a mile, it later showed a red light.

At one time, two signal lights mounted on a pole were displayed above the lantern and these showed a white light when the inner harbour was open and a red light when it was closed. These lights have been removed, and the lantern light now shows lights in the configuration once shown on the pole. Around the tower the pier is now a workshop area for the port, while the tower itself is historically significant because of its designer.

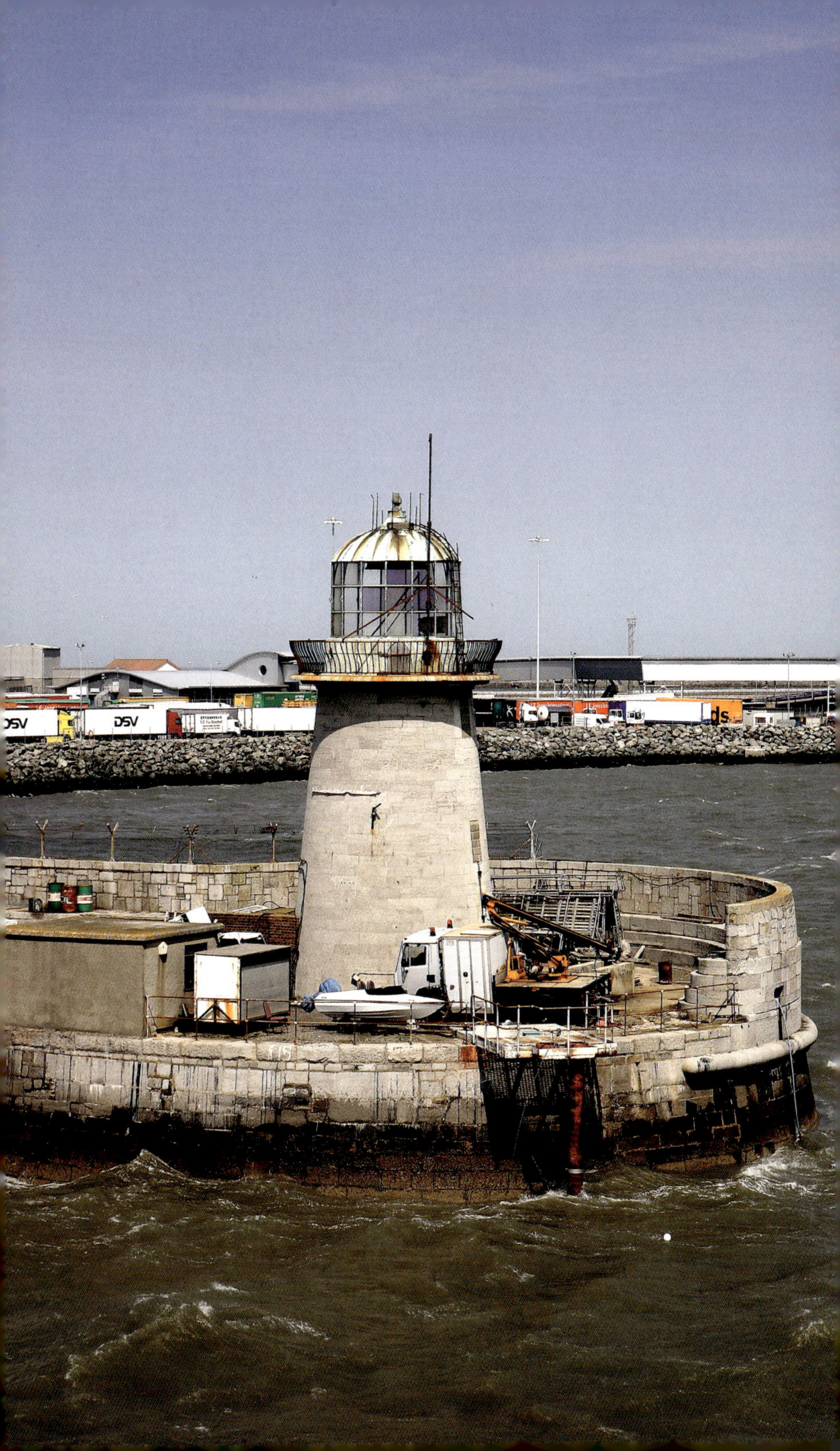
DSV
DSV

Holyhead Breakwater

ESTABLISHED
1873

CURRENT TOWER
1873

AUTOMATED
1961

OPERATOR
Stena Line

ACCESS
The breakwater is accessible in good weather

▶▶ The lighthouse at the end of Holyhead Breakwater has a circular lantern with the domed apex surmounted by a weathervane.

▼ Holyhead Breakwater is the longest such structure in the country.

Holyhead port, which now caters mostly for ferry traffic to Ireland, was developed in the nineteenth century. Building the huge breakwater, which, at 1.87 miles long, is the UK's longest such structure, took twenty-eight years. Work began in 1845 and lasted until 1873, with an average of 1,300 men employed on the project. About seven million tons of limestone from Anglesey's eastern coast around Moelfre were used. The breakwater was officially opened on 19 August 1873 by Albert Edward, Prince of Wales.

Situated at the north-western end of the town, the breakwater was topped by a promenade leading from Soldier's Point and culminating in an impressive lighthouse, which was probably designed by John Hawkshaw, the superintendent engineer who oversaw the harbour works from 1857 to 1873. The tower has a roll-moulded string-course projecting above the first floor level, and is unusual in being 22ft 3in square. Painted white with a single black horizontal band, it was completed in 1873 as work on the breakwater was coming to an end. A moulded cornice supports a walkway around the circular lantern.

The lighthouse was manned until November 1961 and was built square to make the living quarters more comfortable. One of the last keepers was David John Williams, who subsequently became a Trinity House speaker giving talks on the service. The tower is 63ft high and 70ft above the high water mark. The light has a range of fourteen miles and is the responsibility of the port authority, now Stena Line. Inside, much of the original living accommodation remains intact.

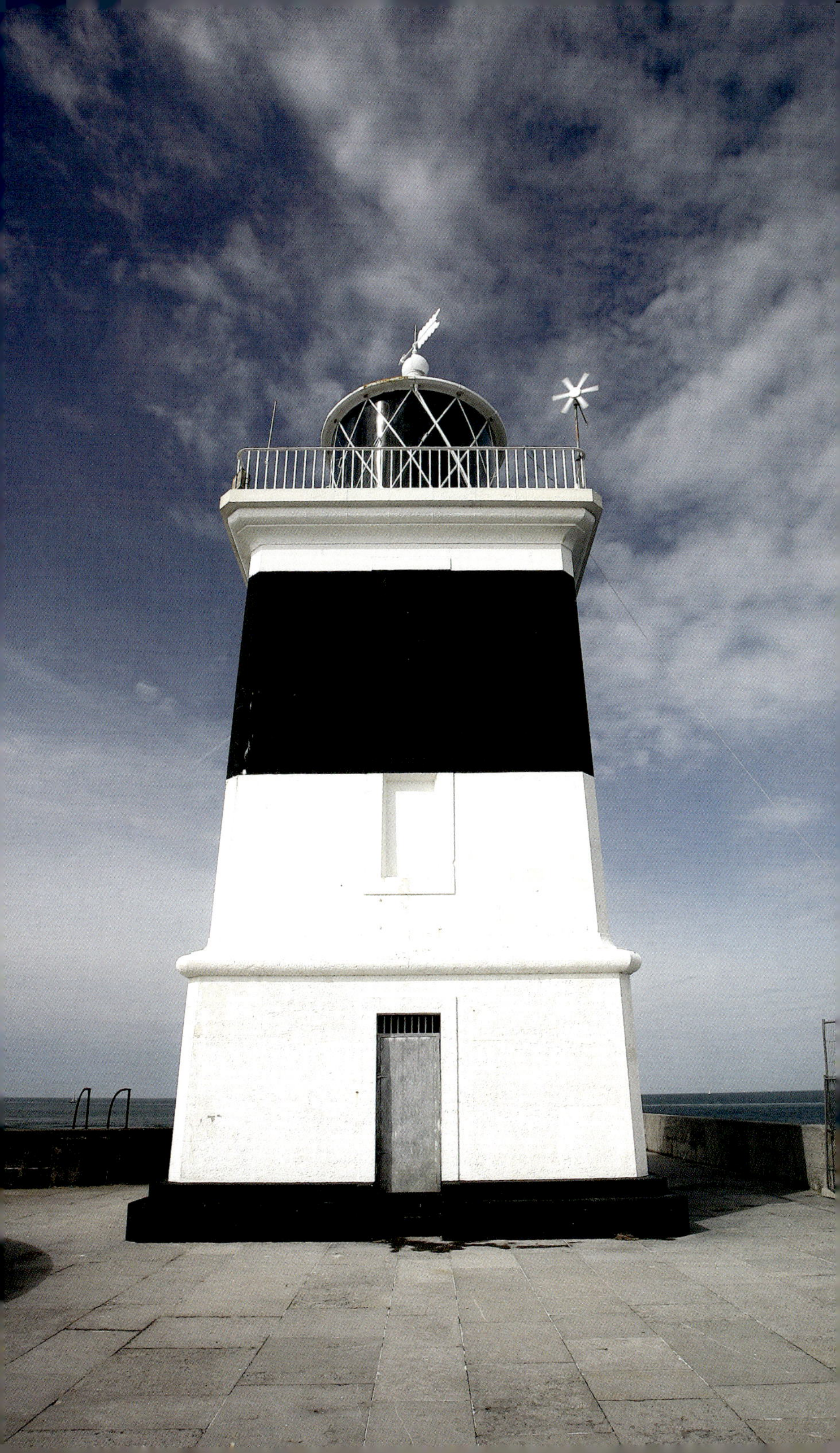

The Skerries

ESTABLISHED
1717
CURRENT TOWER
1759
AUTOMATED
1987
OPERATOR
Trinity House
ACCESS
Trips to the Skerries are available by charter boat out of Port Amlwch

▶▶ The historic Skerris lighthouse, with the 1903 red sector light tower visible in front of the main tower.

▼ An old postcard of Skerries lighthouse before the red sector marker was built.

The Skerries are a small group of rocky islets, seven miles off Holyhead, to the north-west of Anglesey, which have some of the oldest lighthouse buildings in existence. The keepers' dwellings are reputed to be the oldest such buildings surviving in the British Isles. The treacherous nature of the waters and the amount of passing vessels made this rocky outcrop a magnet for speculators who saw that profits could be made from a lighthouse.

In 1658 a proposal was made for a light by the first of these speculators who wanted to profit from ships' dues. This, and another in 1705, were refused, but in 1713 a sixty-year lease was agreed, and in 1717 the first light, erected on the highest point of the island, was completed by the builder William Trench. It was coal-fired and despite predictions, it was not a financial success; the owner died in 1725 in severe debt. To add to his woes he also lost his son off the rocks.

An Act of Parliament of 1730 enabled his son-in-law Sutton Morgan to increase the shipping dues and confirmed the patent on his heirs forever. In 1759 Trench's tower was rebuilt in limestone by Sutton Morgan's heirs at a cost of £3,000. The light, mounted on a slightly tapering 28ft tower, was displayed in a coal brazier. This tower was increased in height in 1804 by owner Morgan Jones, who had inherited it in 1778, and an iron balcony was added with railings enclosing the oil-burning lantern. The oil-burner was enclosed in a glazed lantern room and covered by a cupola.

In 1838 Trinity House began purchasing private lighthouses, but the owner of the Skerries refused to sell as his light had proved to be very profitable.

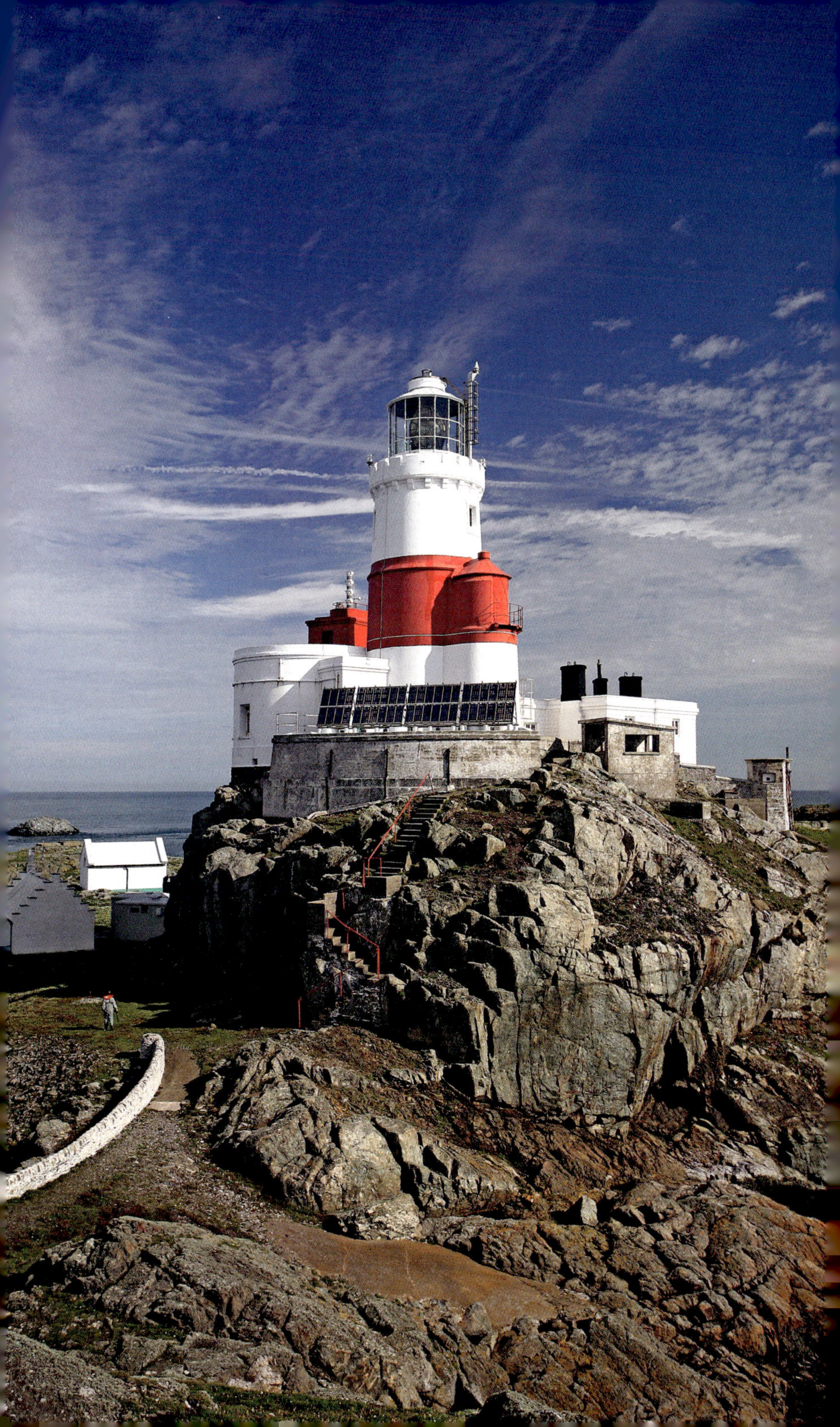

The Skerries

By 1840 it was the only private light left in the British Isles, but in 1841, after the death of the owner, the Corporation purchased it. Trinity House then had the station remodelled, and, in 1848, it was extensively altered by James Walker. A freestanding keepers' house was built, enclosed by a castellated-walled cobbled courtyard with private facilities, which still stand.

The tower was increased in diameter at its base with Walker's trademark design producing a reduction in its diameter halfway up. The balcony was rebuilt in castellated stone supported by brackets on corbels. A new cast iron lantern, almost 14ft in diameter with glazed square panes around a dioptric light with mirrors, was installed, topped by a finial. The light was then displayed from a height of 119ft above high water.

In 1903 a solid circular tower was added to the south-west of the tower to carry a sector light. Access to this tower is provided by an improvised landing in the main tower. The buildings for the fog signal, which gives two blasts every twenty seconds, are arranged concentrically around the main tower.

In 1927 the light was converted to electricity with the original generator later augmented by solar power. The 76ft tower, which stands atop the outcrop, is painted white with a broad red band, as is the adjoining engine room. The lighthouse was automated in 1987 and a helicopter pad was built nearby. Today the flashing white light, produced by a one kilowatt lamp and a first order catadioptric lens, gives two flashes every ten seconds and is visible for twenty-two miles.

▶▶ The solar panels can be seen to the front of the tower, with the stairway up from the landing stage.

▼ The treacherous Skerries rocks present a severe hazard to passing vessels.

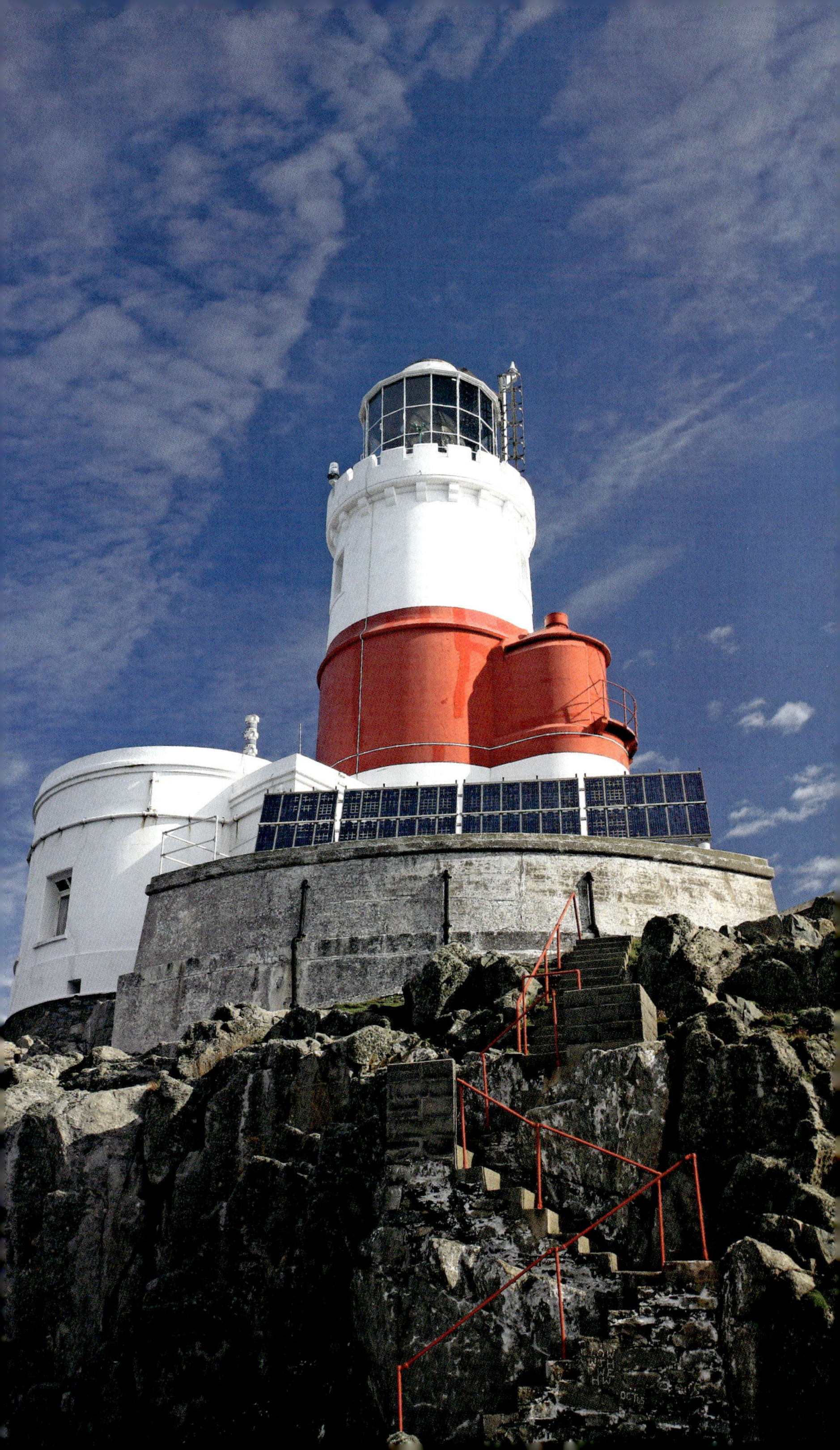

Port Amlwch

ESTABLISHED
1768

CURRENT TOWER
1853

DISCONTINUED
circa 1972

OPERATOR
Isle of Anglesey Council

ACCESS
At the end of the short pier in the harbour

▶▶ The 1853-built building on the end of the 1816-built pier was at one time a watchtower, and until about 1972 also served as a lighthouse.

▼ The 'old world' charm of the original dock remains despite the erection of a new concrete dock to seaward.

Port Amlwch with its small harbour was once one of the busiest ports in Wales. Its expansion began in 1768, when the Parys Mountain copper mine, at that time the largest in the world, was opened and the harbour was enclosed by two small piers. At the end of each pier a small stone octagonal tower was built, displaying a white light from the top.

With increasing trade, there was a need to give extra protection to the harbour, so in 1816 a new 150ft-long outer pier was constructed. On the end of the new outer pier a 16ft square stone tower, with a white light visible for four miles, was commissioned in the same year. The New Seaman's Guide of 1821 stated that there were 'small white houses displaying lights at night', which would suggest that the light on the original short pier was still operational.

The new lighthouse, also used as a watchtower, was altered in 1835, and in 1853 the tower which exists today was built on the western end. This tower is not instantly recognisable as it consists of a 15ft slightly tapered tower with a rendered-brick lantern room roofed in local slate. The light, which was displayed through a window only visible from the seaward side, had a range of six miles.

It would appear that by this time only one light was displayed at the port. It is not certain when this light was declared non-operational but it was probably when a new fixed navigation light mounted on a white metal column was placed on the new dock, about 100 yards to seaward, constructed in 1972 for the Liverpool Pilots when their pilot boats and workshops moved to Amlwch from Point Lynas. The new concrete dock facility has not impinged on the old dock, which retains much of its 'old world' charm. In the churchyard of nearby St Elaeths Church is a lighthouse memorial gravestone.

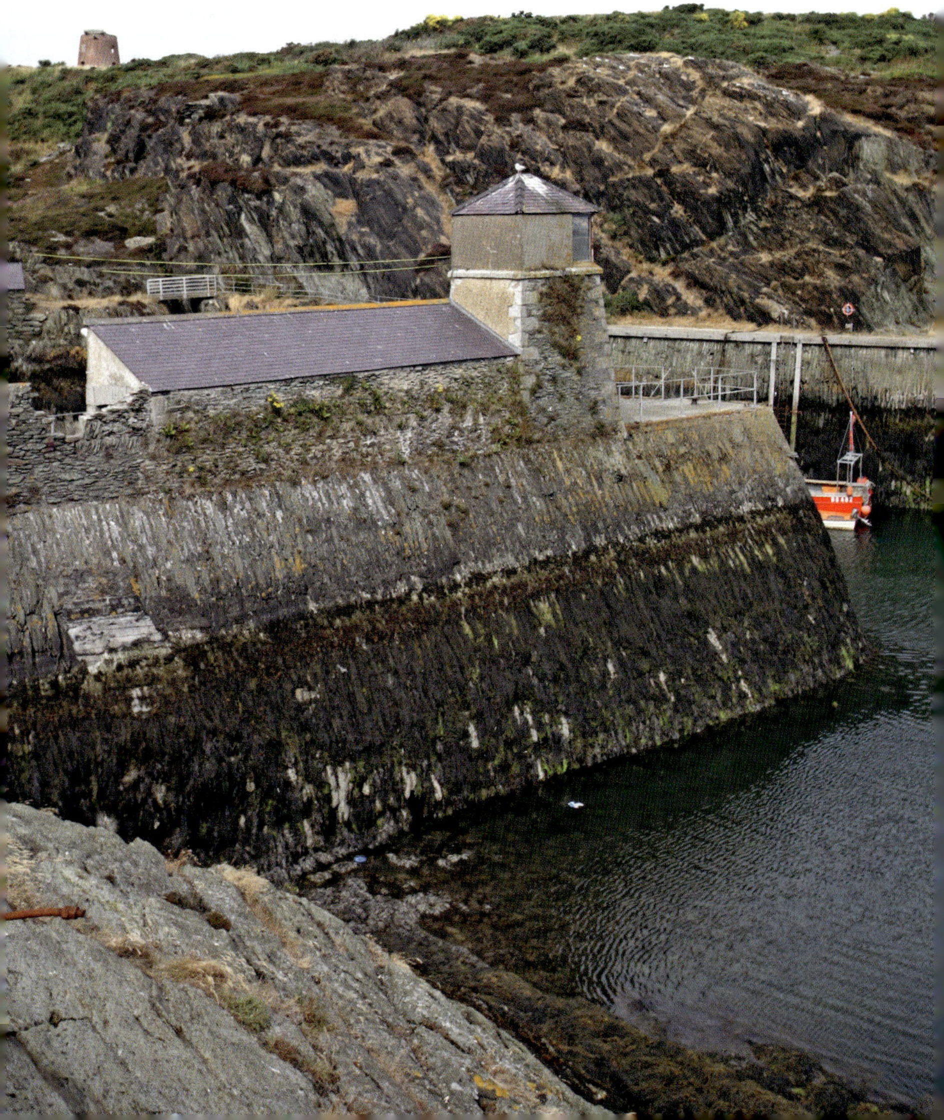

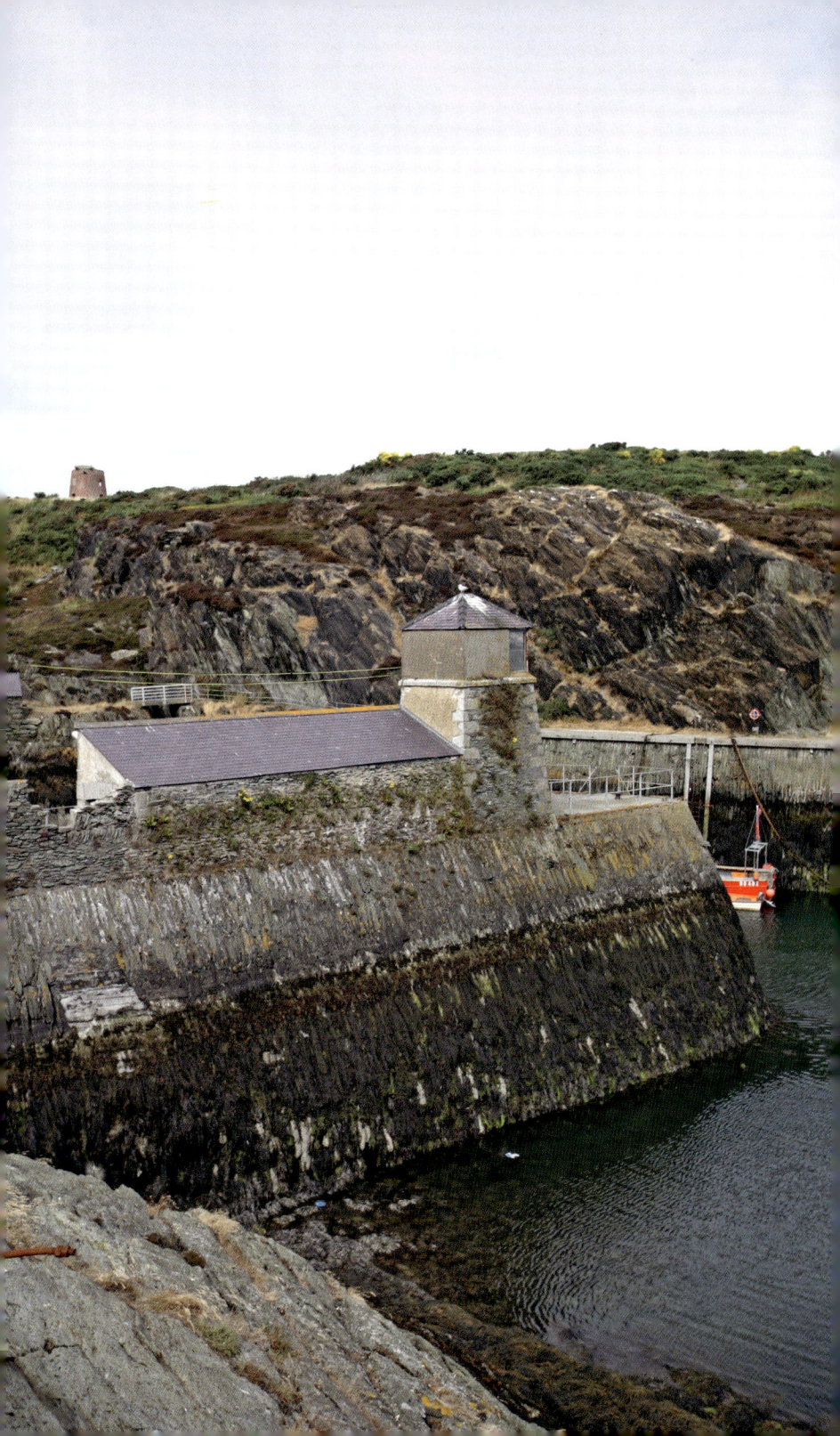

Point Lynas

ESTABLISHED
1779

CURRENT TOWER
1835

AUTOMATED
1989

OPERATOR
Trinity House

ACCESS
Access to the inside of the complex is restricted, but the lamp room can be seen from the coast path

▶▶ The castellated square tower fronted by a ground floor lantern is sited on ground almost 40m above sea level.

▼ The castellated building at Point Lynas was designed by Jess Hartley, engineer to the Mersey Docks and Harbour Board.

Point Lynas, on Anglesey's eastern coast, was an ideal site from where pilots could board ships into or out of Liverpool. In 1779 Liverpool Town Council set up a pilot station and leased a house on the point from which, in order to assist shipping, two lights were shown out of windows in a building on a site about 300m to the south of the present site. Two eleven-inch reflectors provided small lights which were displayed to the east and west.

In 1781, the first part of the current castellated complex was built, primarily to provide accommodation for the pilots. It was also clear that the lights were inadequate as they were often obscured by smoke from the nearby industries and, more importantly, did not provide a light to the north-east quarter.

Although Alan Stevenson suggested that a 70ft lighthouse should be built to overcome the difficulties, it was decided to abandon the original location and move to a site up the hill to the north. In 1835, a two-storey extension was built onto the north side of the pilot station, including a ground floor 12ft semi-circular lamp room. This lamp room was increased in size to 15ft in 1874 and completely refurbished in 1879.

The original argon-powered light, visible for sixteen miles, was converted to oil in 1901. In 1951 generators were installed and the lamp was converted to electricity. Mains electricity was connected in 1957 and the occulting light, visible for twenty miles, was uprated.

During the refurbishment of the site in 1879, the local signal station was moved into the complex and a set of signal lights was displayed from a 75ft pole. This site, operated by the Mersey Docks & Harbour Co, was taken over by Trinity House in 1973; the light was automated in 1989, and the pilots moved to Amlwch Pier.

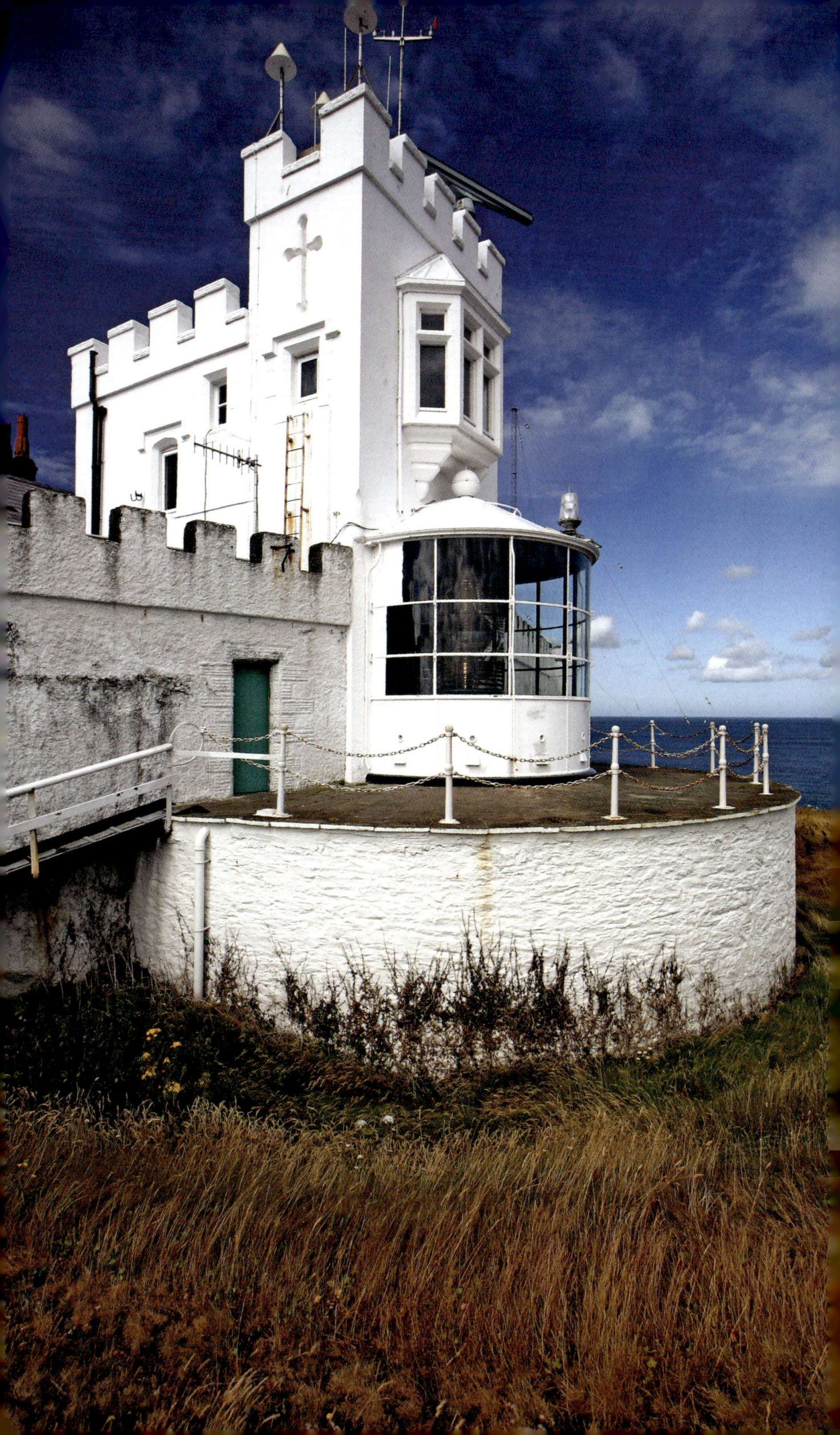

Trwyn Du

ESTABLISHED
1838

CURRENT TOWER
1838

AUTOMATED
1922

OPERATOR
Trinity House

ACCESS
Situated north of Beaumaris, Trwyn Du is reached via a toll road from Penmon; trip boats in summer run from Beaumaris to Puffin Island

▶▶ Trwyn Du lighthouse was built in 1838, and its stepped base made it the first wave washed light built by James Walker.

▼ A small reef between Puffin Island and Penmon, called Perch Rock, is also marked by this cone-shaped beacon with its top section painted red and complete with a small white lantern.

In the early nineteenth century, the eastern tip of Anglesey was a graveyard both for ships entering the Menai Strait from the north and for those in Red Wharf Bay awaiting fair weather before rounding the Skerries. On 17 August 1831 an incident took place which in all probability hastened the decision to provide an aid to navigation in this dangerous area.

The steamer Rothsay Castle, on her regular trip from Liverpool to the Menai Straits, left Liverpool at about 11am but because of the rough weather she made little headway. Despite requests from the passengers the captain refused to turn back. By midnight he had still not made land and an hour later she struck Dutchman Bank and, out of control, struck a sandbank off Penmon. Of the 150 passengers on board, 130 were lost.

As a result, Trinity House agreed to erect a lighthouse on a reef off the mainland between Trwyn Du or Black Head and Puffin Island. Commenced in 1837, it was a 96ft circular black and white stone tower stepped at the base with a single step halfway. Completed by James Walker at a cost of £11,589, the acetylene-powered light was first exhibited in 1838. The castellated gallery is painted black with the white lantern showing a flashing white light visible for twelve miles, topped by a conical roof complete with a weather vane.

The lighthouse, although not particularly spectacular, is noteworthy as the first wave washed lighthouse built by James Walker, and is thus the forerunner of his more famous lights at The Needles, Smalls and Wolf Rock. Some of the innovative features included a stepped base with vertical walls, as distinct from the graceful curves normally incorporated into such towers.

The lighthouse, sometimes known as Penmon or Black Rock, was originally manned by two keepers but it was converted to automated acetylene in 1922 and the keepers were withdrawn. It was converted to solar power in 1996 when a Tideland 1300 lantern with a first order catadioptric fixed lens and a thirty-five-Watt halogen lamp were installed with a range of twelve miles. Another feature of the renovations of 1996 was a unique mechanism to sound the fog signal, which comprises a 178 kilogram bell which is struck once every sixty seconds.

Although the lighthouse marks the reef offshore, the straight between Puffin Island and the mainland has a rocky outcrop called Perch Rock in the middle of the channel. This rock, a short distance to the east of the light, is marked by a beacon.

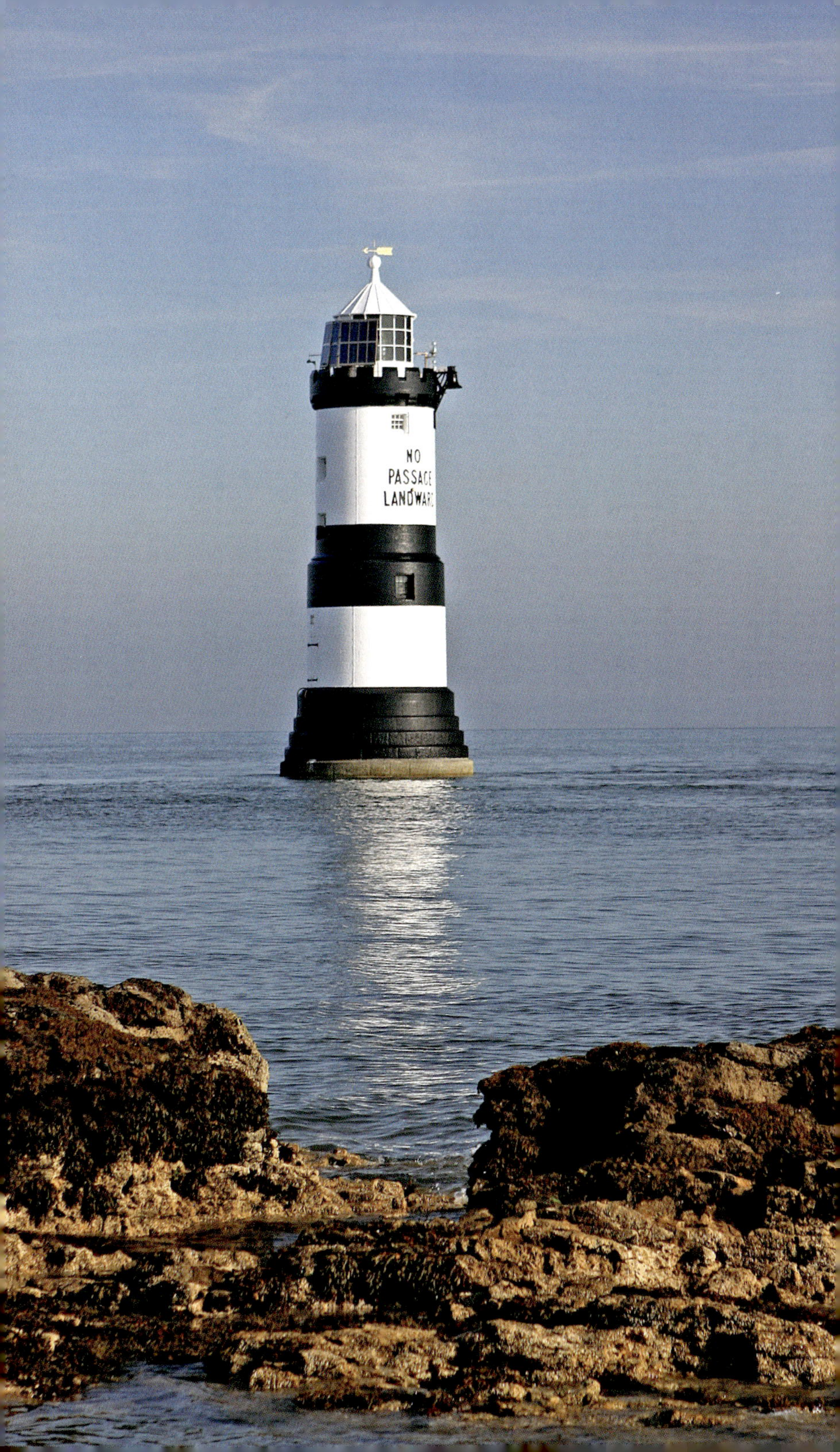
NO
PASSAGE
LANDWARD

Great Orme

ESTABLISHED
1862

CURRENT TOWER
1862

AUTOMATED
1973

DISCONTINUED
1985

ACCESS
The one-way anti-clockwise toll road gives a partial view of the lighthouse after about two miles; the lamp room is part of the bed and breakfast accommodation

▲ The plaque surmounting the central doorway on the south-eastern side records the building's origins.

▶▶ Despite its squat appearance, the Great Orme light was the highest in Wales.

▶ An old postcard showing the lighthouse being passed by a paddle steamer.

The lighthouse on Great Orme at Llandudno is perhaps noteworthy more for its internal than external appearance. Constructed in 1862 for the Mersey Docks and Harbour Company to the design of engineer-in-chief George Lister, who also worked on alterations to the Point Lynas light in 1871, it was cut into steep limestone cliffs on the most northerly point of Great Orme's Head, 325ft above sea level, to became the highest lighthouse in Wales.

The need for a lighthouse on the Great Orme was first recognised in 1861, and a letter recommending its establishment was approved by Trinity House. Constructed with dressed limestone, the building's 37ft high walls were topped with castellated edges and the two-storey accommodation had a flat roof. The light was displayed from a semi-circular lamp room attached to the seaward side of the building at ground level, similar to Point Lynas. An interesting internal feature was the extensive use of Canadian pine boarding inside the accommodation block which, at 20ft high, provided privacy between the main keeper's and second keeper's accommodation.

The flashing white light, visible for twenty-four miles and first shown on 1 December 1862, was created by paraffin wick burners. These were replaced in 1904 by vaporising petroleum mantle-burners, which were in turn superseded in 1923 by dissolved acetylene mantle-lamps. The station, electrified in 1965, passed into Trinity House's control in 1973 and a white rendering was applied. The light was extinguished on 22 March 1985 and control of the building reverted to the Mersey Docks and Harbour Company, which subsequently sold the property.

The Fresnel lens is now an exhibit at the Orme's Summit Visitor Centre, where it can be seen illuminated to give an idea of its intensity. Situated in the Great Orme Country Park, the lighthouse is now a bed and breakfast in which the old lamp room is used as the sitting room offering sea views. The bedrooms are named after the use the rooms were put to during the light's operational era.

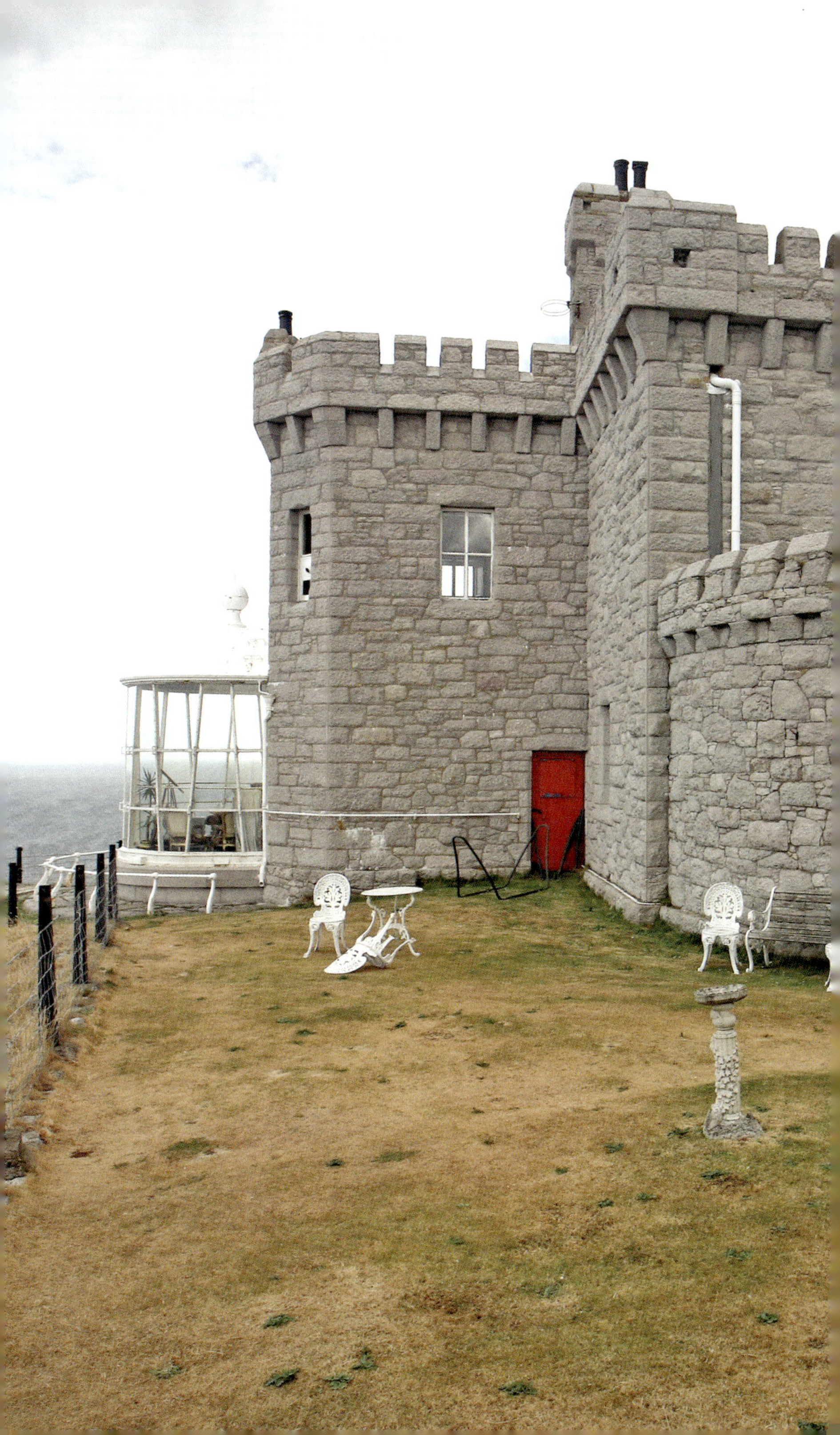

Point of Ayr

ESTABLISHED
1777

CURRENT TOWER
1777

DISCONTINUED
1883

OPERATOR
Flintshire County Council

ACCESS
Located within the Gronant and Talacre Site of Special Scientific Interest; access is on foot from the car park at Talacre, just off the A548 coast road

▶▶ The lighthouse at Point of Ayr, at the entrance to the river Dee, is now a historic attraction managed by Flintshire County Council.

In medieval times Chester was an important port dealing mainly with the French wine exporting region and Liverpool was still a small creek. The entry into the Dee was treacherous, so as early as the thirteenth century lights were displayed at Whitford Garn in Flintshire and Hilbre Island off Hoylake, for which the Earl of Chester paid an annual sum for thier upkeep. Although the Dee was canalised in 1733 to enable larger ships to navigate it, it was not until 1776, following the loss of the Dublin packets Nonpariel and Trevor, that proposals to improve the lighting arrangements were carried out.

Initially it was suggested that two lighthouses and a series of buoys be provided, but the cost was prohibitive. A wooden lighthouse built on the surrounding hillside was suggested, but it was eventually agreed that a lighthouse should built at Point of Ayr. Situated at Talacre to the east of Prestatyn, on the northernmost point of the west side of the Dee estuary, this lighthouse was one of a series which guarded Liverpool Bay.

Today, due to the change in the coastline, it is difficult to appreciate how lights at Hoylake, Bidston Hill and Leasowe interacted with Point of Ayr or Y Parlwr Du, Talacre. Locally it was known as the lake light to distinguish it from the two lights at Leasowe, which were referred to as the sea lights.

Designed by H. Turner, it was built at a cost of £349 8s 1d and the 52ft circular stone tower, complete with gallery and lantern, was supported on screw piles driven into the sand. The tower had three floors with a basement coal store. The lighthouse now lies between the high and low watermarks.

In 1819 Trinity House took over responsibility for the lighthouse and in 1820 had it refurbished, increasing the height to 58ft and installing a new lantern which exists today and is reputedly the oldest in Wales.

When operational the tower was painted in alternate red and white bands, with a red gallery and a white lantern with a red roof. One white light shining seaward towards Llandudno was displayed from the lantern, with a second facing down the Dee towards Dawpool in Cheshire at a height of 8ft. The lights were discontinued in 1844 when a new screw pile lighthouse designed by James Walker was built by Gordon & Co of Deptford.

This structure was made up of nine cast iron piles driven into the sand with one central and eight outer supports. There was a double-skinned corrugated iron accommodation block, on top of which was a gunmetal lantern. In 1883 this light was replaced by a lightship and nothing remains of the pile light.

The lighthouse is now well below the high tide mark and is only isolated at low tide. In 1996 the tower was restored and it is currently all white with a black gallery and a red lantern. The original small attached dwelling has been demolished.

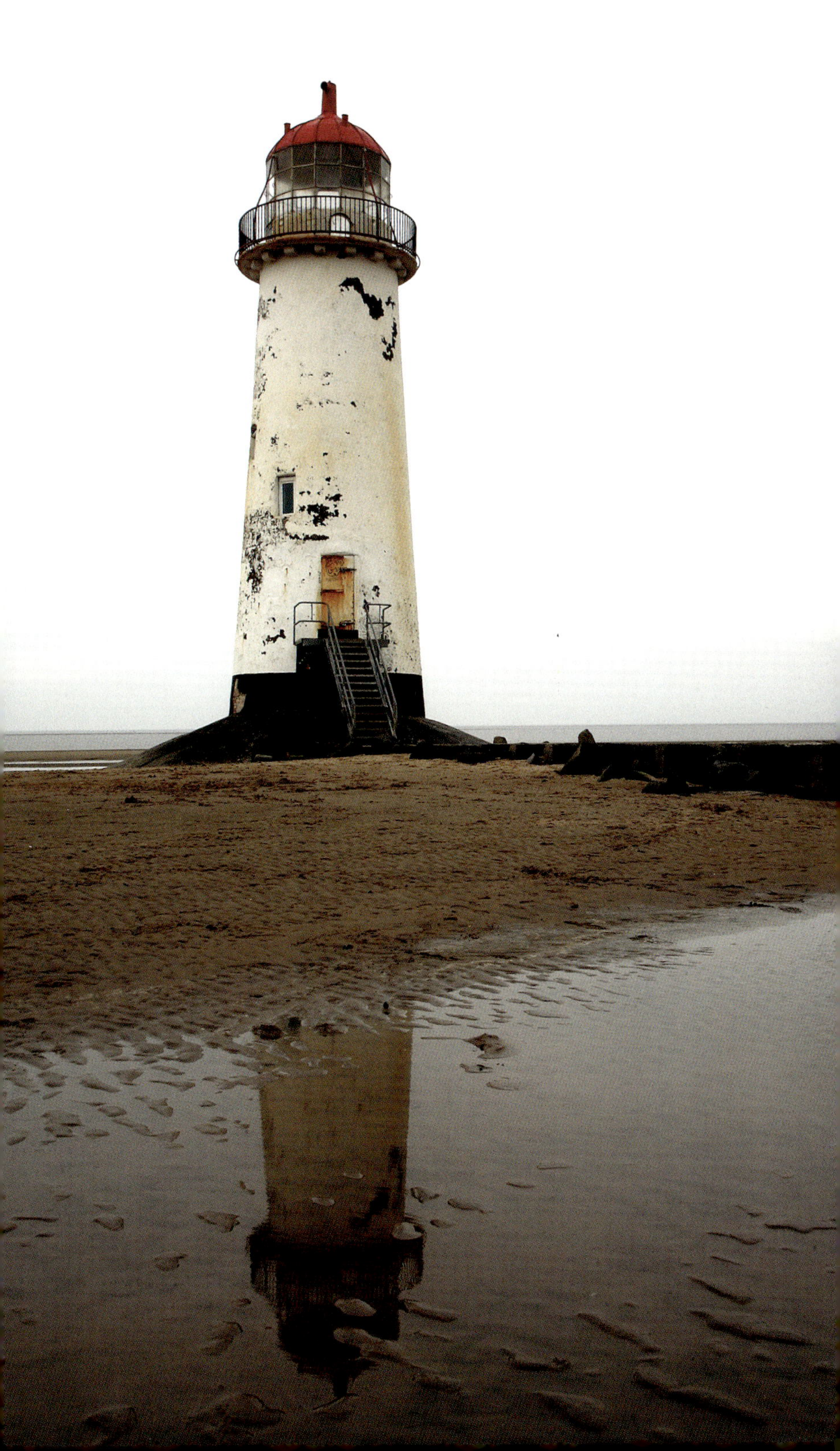

Glossary

▲ Burry Port.

▲ West Usk.

Acetylene A highly combustible gas which burns with an intensely bright flame.

Argand lamps A bright and relatively clean-burning lamp invented by Francois-Pierre Ami Argand in 1783.

Automated An unmanned light controlled externally; all the major UK lighthouses are automated with Trinity House controlling and monitoring its lights from the Corporation's Depot in Harwich.

Beacon A structure, usually land based, either lit or unlit, used to guide mariners.

Characteristic The identifying feature of a lighthouse is its characteristic; for example the light could be described as fixed, or flashing.

Daymark Light towers often also serve as daymarks, landmarks that are visible from the sea during daylight acting as aids to navigation.

Dioptric lens A development by Augustin Fresnel consisting of a bull's eye lens surrounded by a series of concentric glass prisms. Dioptric lenses were classified by their focal length.

Elevation The elevation refers to a light's height above sea level; the higher the elevation, the greater the range.

Flashing light A light where the period of light is less than the period of darkness.

Fog signals A sound signal used to warn mariners in times of fog or heavy weather.

Gallery A walkway beneath the lantern room to enable access for maintenance.

High light The taller or higher of a pair of lights.

Isophase light A light where the periods of light and dark are equal.

Keepers The persons responsible for maintaining and keeping the light at an aid to navigation, including the associated buildings.

Lanby The abbreviated term for Large Automatic Navigation Buoy, a modern floating unmanned aid to navigation often used in place of a ligthship.

Lanterns The glass-enclosed space at the top of a lighthouse housing the lens or optic; lanterns are often encircled by a narrow walkway called the gallery.

Lightship A vessel powered or unpowered designed to support a navigational aid.

Low light The shorter or lower of the two lights used to mark a channel or hazard.

Occulting Where the period a light exhibited is greater than its period of eclipse; this can be achieved in several ways.

Range lights Lights displayed in pairs which are used to mark a navigable channel.

Reflector A system which intensifies light by reflecting the light source into a beam, both to increase intensity and to enable the beam to be manipulated to produce differing light characteristics.

Training wall A bank or wall erected below water level in a river or harbour mouth to train the water flow.

Appendix

Bibliography

Bowen, J. P.: British Lighthouses (Longmans, London, 1947).

Hague, Douglas B.: Lighthouses of Wales: their architecture and archaeology (Royal Commission on the Ancient and Historical Monuments of Wales, 1994).

Hague, Douglas B. and Christie, Rosemary: Lighthouses: Their Architecture, History and Archaeology (Gomer Press, Dyfed, 1975).

Jackson, Derrick: Lighthouses of England and Wales (David & Charles, Devon, 1975).

Nicholson, Christopher: Rock Lighthouses of Britain (Patrick Stephens, Somerset, 1995).

Sutton-Jones, Kenneth: To Safely Guide Their Way: Lighthouses and Maritime Aids of the World (B&T Publications, Southampton, 1998).

Woodman, Richard and Wilson, Jane: The Lighthouses of Trinity House (Thomas Reed Publications, 2002).

Websites

www.lighthousedepot.com Comprehensive list of world lights with details, photos, locations and links.

www.trabas.de/enindex.html List of world lights including minor lights with photos.

www.unc.edu/~rowlett/ lighthouse/index.htm Comprehensive list of world lights with historic outline, photographs and links.

www.trinityhouse.co.uk Trinity House website with details of all their lighthouses.

www.michaelmillichamp. ukgateway.net Main focus is on England and Wales with details of operational and non-operational lights.

www.lighthousesrus.org Mainly an American lighthouse site, it has photos and details of British lights.

Acknowledgements

A number of people have assisted with the compilation of this book. The following helped in various ways and we are grateful to Vikki Gilson at Trinity House; Geoff Badland at Strumble Head; Brian Thomson of Holyhead lifeboat; Dave Herbert of Portishead lifeboat; Gareth Williams and his Stena Line colleagues at Fishguard port. The work of the late Douglas Hague has been utilised and his contribution to the history of Welsh lighthouses is acknowledged.

All photographs are by Nicholas Leach, except the following: Tony Denton pages 12, 13, 14, 15, 44; Trinity House 49, 51, 53, 57, 66; supplied by Michel Forand 7, 8; John Mobbs 5, 9 (lower), 10 (lower), 34, 64 (lower), 72, 90 (lower); Gerry Douglas-Sherwood, Association of Lighthouse Keepers 36, 46, 66; Mat Dickson 50, 54, 56; Porthcawl lifeboat station 30.

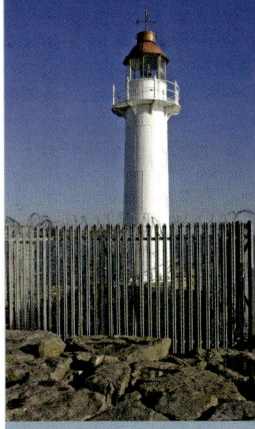

▲ Barry Dock.

▲ Admiralty Breakwater, Holyhead.

Index

Aberystwyth 65
Alexander, Daniel 72, 76
Amlwch 80, 84, 85
Anglesey 5, 6, 70, 78, 80, 84, 86, 88
Argand lamp 22, 26, 33, 40, 70, 72
Avonmouth 22
Bardsey 1, 66, 68
Barry Dock 11, 22, 25, 95
Beynon, Daniel 64
Bidston Hill 92
Black Head 88
Black Rock (Portskewett) 13, 14
Black Rock (Twyn Du) 88
Breaksea Light Float 26
Bristol Ch 5, 6, 17, 22, 26, 50, 56
Bullwell 44
Burry Inlet 38
Burry Port 11, 38, 94
Burry Port Harbour Auth 38
Caldey Island 9, 40
Cardiff 6, 20, 22, 25
Cardiff Low Water Pier Head 6, 7
Cardigan Bay 56, 58, 68
Chance Bros 25, 30, 50, 66
Charston Rock 13
Chepstow 22
Cherry Stone Rock 33
Chester 92
Cow and Calf 62
Crow Rock 46
Dalen, Gustaf 66
Dee Estuary 92
Denny Island 16
Douglas multi-wick burner 24
Douglas, James 42
Douglas, James Nicholas 66
Dublin 7, 76, 92
East Usk 17
Eddystone 8, 55
English Stones 14
Evans, Hugh 74
Fishguard 10, 62
Fishguard Breakwater 62
Flamborough Head 22
Flatholm 5, 6, 20, 22, 24, 26, 33
Flint 5
Fresnel lens 32, 34, 70, 90
Glasgow 7
Gloucester 13
Gloucester Harb Trustees 12, 14
Gold Cliff 16
Goodwick 62
Great Castle Head 42
Great Orme 90
Great Western Railway Co 12, 13, 62

Hague, Douglas 52, 55
Hawkshaw, John 78
Holyhead 5, 6, 10
Holyhead Admiralty Pier 10, 76, 95
Holyhead Breakwater 6, 78
Hood paraffin Burner 24
Howth 76
Hoylake 92
James, David T. 38
Jernegan, William 33
Jones, Morgan 8, 9, 80
Lady Bench 14
Lavernock Point 20, 22
Leasowe 92
Little Castle Head 42
Liverpool Bay 92
Liverpool Town Council 86
Llanddwyn Island 70
Llanelli 34, 36
Llanelli Harbour Trust 36
Lower Fishguard 62
Lower Shoots 14
Luckraft, Captain 34
Matthews burner 48
Matthews, Sir Thomas 50
Menai Straits 70, 88
Mersey Docks and Harb Co 90
Mid Channel Rock 44
Milford Haven 6, 42, 44, 46, 48, 50
Mixoms 14
Mixon Sands 33
Mumbles 26, 32, 33, 34
Nash Point 11, 26, 28
Needles 88
Nelson, Joseph 26, 40, 68, 72
New Quay 64
Newcastle-upon-Tyne 7
Newport 6, 17, 18, 22
Newport Harbour Commrs 16, 17
Newton Noyes 44
Old Man's Head 14
Pembrey 38
Pen Cw 62
Penmon 88
Perch Rock 88
Pharos lighthouse 5
Phillips, John 52, 54
Point of Ayr 8, 92
Point Lynas 84, 86, 90
Popton Point 44
Porthcawl 10, 30
Portstewett 13
Prestatyn 92
Protheroe, Thomas 26
Rame Head 44
Redcliffe 12

Rennie, John 64, 76
Rosslare 62
Rothsay Castle 88
Salt Island 76
Sand Bay 14
Saundersfoot 39
Severn, River 13, 14, 17, 22
Sharpness Lighthouse Trustees 12
Skerries, The 5, 8, 9, 80, 82
Smalls 6, 9, 52, 54, 55
Smeaton 55
Soldier's Point 78
Solva 64
South Bishop 56
South Stack 72, 74
Southampton 62
St Ann's Head 46, 48
St Brides 18
St David's Head 52, 56, 58
St George's Channel 56, 58, 68
St Michael's Island 58
St George's Channel 56
St Tudwal's 66
Strumble Head 58, 60
Swansea 6, 32, 33, 34
Swansea East Pier 32
Swansea Harb Commissioners 32
Swansea Transport and Industrial Museum 32, 34
Talacre 92
Tideland lamp 34, 88
Toes off Linney Head 46
Trench, William 8, 80
Trinity House 5, 6, 7, 8, 9, 11, 18, 20, 22, 26, 32, 34, 38, 40, 42, 44, 48, 52, 55, 56, 58, 64, 66, 68, 72, 78, 82, 86, 88, 90, 92
Trwyn Du 88
Twr Bach 70
Twr Mawr 70
Tynemouth 10
Upper Shoots 14
Usk, River 10, 17, 18
Walker, James 18, 26, 55, 80, 88, 92
Watwick 44
West Blockhouse Point 44
West Usk 17, 18, 94
Wexford 7
Whitby 11
Whiteside, Henry 52
Whitford Point 36
Wolf Rock 88
Y Lanfa 65
Y Parlwr Du 92
Ynys Byr 40
Ystwyth River 65

96